CW00865132

Art Fairy

Flower Sea

Floras Athena

outskirts
press

Art Fairy
Flower Sea
All Rights Reserved.
Copyright © 2019 Floras Athena
v1.0

This is a work of fiction. Names, characters, businesses, places, events, locales, and incidents are either the products of the author's imagination or used in a fictitious manner. Any resemblance to actual persons, living or dead, or actual events is purely coincidental.

The opinions expressed in this manuscript are solely the opinions of the author and do not represent the opinions or thoughts of the publisher. The author has represented and warranted full ownership and/or legal right to publish all the materials in this book.

This book may not be reproduced, transmitted, or stored in whole or in part by any means, including graphic, electronic, or mechanical without the express written consent of the publisher except in the case of brief quotations embodied in critical articles and reviews.

Outskirts Press, Inc.
http://www.outskirtspress.com

ISBN: 978-1-9772-1048-7

Cover Photo © 2019 Tianhe Lan. All rights reserved - used with permission.

Outskirts Press and the "OP" logo are trademarks belonging to Outskirts Press, Inc.

PRINTED IN THE UNITED STATES OF AMERICA

Chapter 1

MUSIC AND ART

The reason why no great is born,
it is we neglect the process of forming the great soul.

*I*t is because our education has neglected the growth of great so that our education has produced no great.

To Oris, dreaming to be a great musician and artist just as Mozart, Beethoven and Joe Hisaishi, he must understand the forming process of their souls and talents, he must pay the same or even more time and effort.

But in our education, it takes us a lot of valuable time and energy to force us to cram and practice exam every day.

From ancient time to the present, there are no worthy or great in all fields, like our children nowadays, waste a lot of precious time and energy to cram, do exam problem and practice exam.

From ancient time to the present, the great talents and greats in all fields have devoted most of their time and energy to the cultivating of talent and the accumulating of knowledge.

Cram and doing exam can neither train up excellent talent nor accumulate a great deal of knowledge.

So, we must get rid of most of the time we cram and do exam problem, and then spend more time and energy on what we love.

Cultivate talent and accumulate knowledge.

Only in this way can we stand out in the fields we love.

On the Rose Nebula, blue star of Lyra burst out the eternal pure white magnificent radiance of dream.

"Even if let me eat brilliant moon jellyfish everyday, I must be a kind and outstanding musician! Artist!"

From childhood, Oris White always had the blazing enthusiasm for art just flaming like shining silver blue star.

He rarely ran out like fool porcupine, and never played in home like idiot husky. The little horse was sleeping on the floor like springbok. Big ball and little car lay on the old couch side as a fawn by stream and quiet rabbit by mirror lake.

Only the swan red velvet flower-carved piano chair, it's the Sakura Tree Throne in sunshine where Oris was reluctant to leave.

In the kingdom of art, there was no hereditary forever!
Only struggle to enhance talent and create happiness
for the world,
then you can be the happiest little prince and little princess
of the whole world!

Before Mom's Ballerina Mermaid legs were broken, seeing her son glued to the piano all day long and became a butterfly fairy, Mom often threatened him couldn't eat the Christmas tree cake, and then could force her son to reluctantly part away from the piano.

Occasionally tired of playing the piano, staring at the oriole and mirror lake blue kingfisher outside the sakura curtain, Oris was singing the opera that his mother taught him just like a nightingale fairy. The gorgeous singing was flying with piano and violin's melodies in clouds and sunshine.

Benefited from the flaming interest, thanked to the hard cold effort, Oris White learned playing the piano and violin at four years old, composed at five, held his first solo concert at eight.

At nine years old, Oris could play luxuriant impromptu on the piano.

Oris loved music! Loved art!

He was eager to be a resplendent and great musician and artist just as Mozart, Beethoven and Joe Hisaishi!

There was a lot of people more than parrot fishes in Aegean Sea who have passion in art but doesn't know working hard. And There were numerous winners and dazzling awards in the world.

But like Mozart, Beethoven and Joe Hisaishi who actually made distinguished contributions to human beings and created happiness for the world, was the one in a million.

Oris was a passionate, hard working and suffering kid of summer sakura.

Except the love to music was like gorgeous colorful tulip sea, Oris also suffered from father's ice, bloody, hellish training and beating.

And humiliated by teachers every day, bullied by classmates every day, when he came home from school, Oris would be forced to play the piano by Dad with steak knife and mop stick.

If his playing was not perfect like sparkling moon, then Dad would gave his young son a sea of fists. Often being hungry for a whole day, but even a fairy cookie wasn't allowed to eat.

Only Oris's playing was perfect like flowering sakura tree, Dad just shook his whiskey bottle and nodded, then drunkenly said, "You big turtle dumbass! Grew up with drinking African crocodile urine and eating Swedish blue whale shit! Finally you are a little like a fucking muscian!"

Finally allowed Oris to drink fish urine and eat whale shit.

Oris's family was at the edge of extreme poverty as cliff of glacier volcano. Dad was a miserable, unemployed tenor, all his life was frustrated mediocrity, just smoking and drinking all the day.

When Dad was in drunken brawls, he gave vituperate and abuse to the young son. It's more terrifying than the croissant devil in Hellfire River.

Once, Dad got drunk, he put the husky and Oris on his shoulders and running crazily, even sober people couldn't catch up.

Then Oris was slammed into the rocky road, the rose wound on arms hadn't healed for two weeks. And the husky was so scared that the next day left away from home.

Oris's Mom, she was born in a poor family, but through the bloody tearful struggle, she became an excellent ballerina. But in a grand performance, the stage suddenly collapsed, the metal spotlight on the dome fell down, broke Mom's brilliant legs.

Dad had run all the hospital of country, drained all money, but it failed to reverse Mom's dark fate. Then Oris's family became poor as parrot pixies in Owl Carcass Mountain. Even if Oris wanted to eat a piece of Sicilian bread, Dad would be sad for two days.

Mom's body also withered as lotus in rainstorm, only lying in bed with tears burning eyes, all the day recalling the past with sakura in sunshine and butterfly memories.

In addition to singing tenor in the orchestra and theater, Dad also taught the violin and piano in private. But this musician lived so fucking bad! He Ran through the whole city theater, song and dance troupe to humble job, all of them kicked him out of the door without mercy.

Taught piano, be criticized by bear kid's parents who didn't understand any music at all. Be beaten and cursed crazily by a 5-year-old girl who was forced to play the piano by her parents, "Do you believe I can plug your mouth with husky shit!!! You red boar dick!!! Fuck your mother!!!"

These kind of kids' parents were rich and powerful African ostrich Titan Python bastard. So Dad didn't dare to fight back a dick, just said, "Do you believe I'll put a rhino shit in your mouth! You fucking little chimpanzee!!!"

Only humiliation! Finally only could get some miserable income enough to buy some Alps blueberry cake rolls.

Damn bad!!!

So, Dad branded the determination in his mind, even if the sacrifice was whole family's lives, Dad must cut through son's volcano meteor shower talent that under the Arctic glaciers!

Oris just turned four, Dad's heart was burning like magma and gave his son a hellfire river of music lesson, cruel teaching left with the unforgettable fire rose brand in Oris's soul.

The neighbors recalled those years, every morning they saw a weak deer kid standing in front of the piano, crying with star tears and fire rain, sobbing as a falling tree of windbell flower in summer rainstorm.

At that time, Oris was shorter than a Swedish fox dog, needed to climb a cherry chair to get the piano keyboard. If he hesitated for a little cherry, Dad would be ferocious with mop sticking hard at him, taking a steak fork to tie him crazily, then whipping him hard with a belt.

When allowed to rest, Oris would be stuffed a cracked galactic violin in his hand. At the same time, his head was filled with Aurora, snow, cold, ice music knowledge. A cat claws could count clearly the days that Oris wasn't beaten or locked up in the basement.

Dad still didn't allow Oris to sleep, often slapped his face when he slept in the dream of mirror lake, kicked him to the piano for more time in the hell training.

Shortly afterwards, Dad already had galactic confidence with son's piano ability, he cost a whole Dragon Forest of money and arranged a piano solo concert for his son in the biggest theater in city.

The announcement showed "Oris White, his only 6-year-old son".

Since Mozart played for the queen of Austria at the age of six, all fathers who aspired to forge prodigies didn't want their sons to be older than Mozart. Even Mozart's father also revised the date of his son's birth.

In fact, Oris was already eight years old.

If Dad wanted the history of music to repeat, he had been disappointed. Oris's concert didn't cause the attention and report like dazzling meteor rain all over the sky.

Dad wanted to take me as a prodigy to make a big fortune from me, but I seemed to be more foolish than curly wild boar. The piano keys of that day were very out of control, I even broke four strings at the first tune. As soon as came back, I was slapped ten pieces of fire shit by Dad.

"Fuck your mother! You let me lose so much money! Chop you up and throw you into the Nule to feed crocodiles! And It's not enough!!!"

The flame of blood rushed to ring my ears.

Not long before the show, Oris's parents borrowed money to squeeze their son into a noble school.

Thief of grade one, robber of grade two, beauties danced ballet in grade three, handsome boys in grade four were chasing girls, love letters from grade five were all over the sky, swans in grade six were pair with pair.

But Oris's family was so poor, he wore the ragged clothes that patches as scale, stood at the stately classroom, classmates saw the new small warbler boy with dishevelled hair, a dirty face and dull eyes, everyone thought his mother must be dead.

"Was your mother like a turtle egg eaten by Sri Lankan crocodile?"

Oris hit back a dragon dick right away, "Was your mother broken like an ostrich by boars in Madagascar?"

Then he was trampled and kicked by a lemon tree of lemurs, wild-cats and baboons. Since then, Oris had long been bullied by some dog boys such as blocking him in the toilet and abusing him crazily, forcing him to eat dry feces a few days after shitting, sometimes took the liquid poops, blackboard eraser and dirty cloth covered with chalk then stuffed in his cat mouth.

He dared not tell the teacher!

Neither mother nor father could protect him!

A husky who once abused him recalled, "I couldn't see about Oris's genius meteor rain would burst so striking star light in the future! Now he must feel, those classmates who had abused him are all the iceberg-husky dicks that fucked ten thousands Chihuahuas."

Oris especially loved improvisation, but his piano fantasy was always suppressed by Dad, Dad always made his heart pricked like mermaid scales.

"You dare to strum? Be careful! I'm fucking smacking your ears!!!"

Even on the violin, Oris's fingers couldn't help making the melody of butterfly dream.

But Dad's soul and spirit were polluted by dogma of school education, he was a tragedy without creative imagination. He didn't allow his son to innovate vigorously.

Oris had the ability to put aside his music score on the piano and violin to improvise. But Dad would be furious and let him stop playing impromptu, "Looking at the fucking score!!! Did you hear me? You are a fucking stupid dog in Pyrenees!!! I'm enough of this fucking strumming!!!"

"But you hear, It's more gorgeous than the fairy nebula!" Oris prayed to the stars and moon.

The answer was always, "You can't give a whale shit for improvising right now!!!"

"But it's really so beautiful!"

"What the shit motherfucker!!!???"

Pa pa! Two slaps on soft cat face.

Whenever parents failed to quarrel against you, they would hit you.

There was a great musician who had listened Oris's piano performance, he excitedly said, "Someday, the art of this kid must shake the world!"

But even so, Oris's dragon scale spruce piano in home at sunflowers-sea beach, it was Dad begged from his classmate ten years ago.

Saw the horror and cold of Oris's family , saw his bitter hard, saw his art talent as brilliant sukura, that kind classmate gave the old piano to Oris.

Every day after school, Dad took Oris to pick up some bottles and junk in dustbin and sell for a little money.

On the mottled wooden wall in home, that rose blood Alpine maple violin, it was Dad picked up from the garbage dump at the Art Institute three years ago. The violin and the old piano were the only holy shining luxuries of their poor cold house.

Everyday, Dad's face was miserable like a Fuego octopus, repeatedly said to Oris, "Our family is very poor! You whale dick must work hard! Our family is really fucking poor!!! We are too poor to eat an apple honey pizza even once each month, and every two months we just could drink once the three bowls of Hungarian seafood soup!!! We gonna the garbage heap every day to pick up some bottles, pick up some junk, then we can buy the medicine for your Mom, do you understand?"

Because of these words, Oris never dared to look up in front of other kids.

"Because I'm a fucking poor on the Fairy Mountain!!!"

The school had compassion for Oris, so he had no tuition and didn't pay for meal at school. But when the class was dismissed, rich classmates went to buy fish parrot gorgeous colorful snacks, once came into the classroom, a group of little girls instantly surrounded the rich boy for this and that.

Some girls even chased a kid of rich family into the store after class.

Poor little Oris stared at it all, but could only hide in the snow-storm cave of Iceland volcano, just silent and cold, nobody's eyes were burning at him.

Because of poor, because the grades were bad, because of inferiority, Oris was bullied every day by demons' poison claws.

Being forced to eat dry feces, liquid poops, eat blackboard eraser and dirty window cloth, pressing his head into the urinal that shit explosion. Walking down the stairs, dragging his feet, banging his head on marble steps.

Burning his arm with cigarette butts. Lifting him up and down, or kicking him directly down the rock stairs and rolled over thirty lava cake rolls.

Every class break, a dozen little demons around him kicked and beat.

Oris was afraid to go out of the classroom, even if went out, he would be against the wall. Desperately lowing the head, very feared of being seized by little bat, then drew a group of pig-nosed bat big demons and be kicked again.

If had to go out of the classroom, Oris must hide behind the door of other classroom, didn't dare return to his own class. Until the bell ringed, he just moved cautiously into classroom and sat down in glacier cave at the last row.

went home with the ice cold aurora despair mood, Oris would crazily play dozen burning Canon. And he often felt chilly ice, often felt the aurora of despair. So, Canon was the most brilliant summer sakura sunshine tune in his violin playing.

Little Oris, only ten years old, at the grade five of primary school, day and night tempered art talent in father's brutal hell fire.

But, Oris's parents didn't want their son to be a truly great musician who truly created happiness for the world.

Parents only wanted Oris could be used to make money as a art prodigy! Just to fish a lot of money!

But Oris really hated this nasty art of instant success just for money!!!

Fucking hate it!!!

Dad also wanted little Oris to have a good grades in school, for Dad's red devil octopus face.

In fact, before the grade three, Oris's grades was at the top of list, but he never got a smile from Mom and Dad.

So I wasn't fucking gonna learn any class!!!

Even if teacher praised Oris, Dad would give a thorny ice, "The teacher just was polite to say that! Don't I fucking know how many

FLORAS ATHENA

pounds you have? You big stupid egg yolk jellyfish in Aegean Sea!!!"

In grade four, Oris tried to practice the piano for more time, so he had the bad grades in final. When Oris came home from school, he held the report to Dad.

"Fuck you!!! Go fuck your fucking pink dolphin's turn around fart!!!"

Dad kicked his son into Iceland volcano and kicked over the table! The china bowls was breaking all over the floor just like ice dragon eggs.

Oris was so scared that suddenly knelt down, Mom pulled Dad's trouser leg and cried to Oris, "Quickly promise Dad that you must be back in the top in the final! Or you're gonna eat rhino fire shit and choke yourself to death!!! Quickly!!!"

"I promise I must go back to the top!!! Woowoowoowoowoowoo...... Or I'm gonna the Sicilian beach to eat blue whale poops and choke myself to death!!! Woowoowoowoowoowoo......"

Dad just said, "Fuck your rhino blue whale shit!!!"

Report card and exam paper were ripped by Dad into purple angel dandelions all over the dark house.

And Mom, Mom never gave Oris any shelter of sakura and sunshine.

Mom only could cry and lament, "My whole life had really been worse than a mirror lake's swan with her bloody wings, than a nightingale that wings were broken by devil cat's mouth! I gave up singing dream and dancing dream! I gave up all the dream of art! I gave up everything! Anything! Only hard work to earn money to support our family! It's all for you! You know what, kid? Now Mom's leg has been broken, just like a mermaid in glacier, nothing can be done...... Nothing can be done! Everything in the future is counting on you, kid! Do you understand???"

Every time Oris listened this ice dragon shit, a big Iceland volcano must press on his little lemon heart.

There was a feeling of magma, "If I can't get the good grades, if my piano playing can't earn money, I really should eat a Danish unicorn and choke myself to death!!!"

This also always gave him a damn thought, "I breath, I play the piano and violin better, I do well in fucking exam and get the fucking good grades, the fucking biggest purpose is not for me, but for my mother!!!"

Even get the good grades, Oris never won any praise and smile.

Because, mother's swan eyes had been staring at other people's damn kids. Other people's kids all could fly in the sky and bite eagle, all could gonna sea and catch sharks and fuck the blue whale, just so omnipotent.

In Mom's witch eyes, I'm a fucking boy who could only drink crocodile urine, eat blue whale poop, anything I do is just jellyfish urine, anything I learn is just starfish poop, and I'm just a big stupid turtle egg!!!

Mom taught Oris to sing opera, but she joked, "I heard an mallard that asshole is blocked with Finland tigers cactus, just wailing like ghost and howling like wolf! Ah ha ha ha ha ha ha ha ha ....." Therefore, for so many years, Oris never dared to sing even just a narcissus song in front of people.

Actually, he was secretly singing in the flower sea by mirror lake.

The housework done by Oris, mother often forced him to do it again, because he didn't do as what she wanted.

Mother had never praised Oris since he was born.

She only would stare at him like an ostrich and bullshit, "Like your Dad said, you're a big stupid turtle who only can drink crocodile urine, eat blue whales poop, and fart pink dolphin's wind!!!"

Oris hadn't grown up in the warm since childhood, this had already been a kind of Alps ice and snow injury.

Playing the piano well, I thought my parents would love me. But what I got was only ice negative in deep black aurora sea, only swan blood on the polar bear's paw, and only the Cinderella-housework like the tiger sharks that biting you into the fire sea and ice sea.

Grade one, two and three, Oris's grades had always been ranked the head of unicorn, but his parents never gave him any cream roses on the sweet warm affirmation and colorful sunflower shining inspiration.

When got the good grades in class, parents just said, "My friend Lucy's kid was fucking more excellent! Why didn't you do better? You big shit worm in hippo dung!!!"

When desperately got the better grades, parents just said, "Motherfucker! Why don't you get full scores? My colleague' son that ostrich python egg, he got the full scores in every exam!!!"

No matter how hard Oris tried, how obedient he was, how well behaved he did, his parents never recognized him, or even gave him a warm eye.

At home washing the dishes, scrubbing the bowls, and having something Oris forgot to do or did badly, parents must satirize him, "Can't do this well! Can't do that well! Can't do well in the exam! Can't earn more money! Why weren't you drowned earlier by rhino dung? Roll the hippo dung beetle are better than you!!! You are really a thorn forest big dumb snake who can only eat crocodile eggs!!!"

All of these bloody dragon tusks had made his cherry heart more sensitive than peafowl guppy and more fragile than macaron. Always afraid that I haven't done everything well. Always feared that other people had a little whit chocolate mousse unsatisfied and cookies unhappy given by me.

Had long suppressed his volcanic emotion under the Greenland glacier.

Had no rose butterfly sense of security under the daisy sea.

Always felt superfluous as flowering sakura.

Often desired to bath the aurora and meteor rain and fly to the golden paradise with unicorn......

In addition to the piano dream and art dream, Oris had a biggest blue star brilliant dream since childhood, the dream was having a happy warm family with Dad and Mom who really love him.

If he had his own family in the future, he would give his kid the family love and warm care, never let him experience a bit of the ice spine injuring he had experienced.

He would praise his kid, encourage his kid, affirm his kid, let him feel the warmth like blooming sakura tree and the golden sunshine of affection.

If only he could live to that day.

Chapter 2

CULTIVATING OF TALENT

*I*n fact, the real most important root cause of the conflict with school and parents is, more and more he thought he was wasting time studying in school, cramming and doing exam problems!!!

Really wasting time!!!

Oris totally could use all the time to refine his art and develop a more comprehensive self-education.

Before a great scientist died, he lay on the sickbed and asked, "why our school is always unable to create the great?"

Now, we reply,

The reason why no great is born,
it is we neglect the process of forming the great soul.

It is because our education has neglected the growth of great so that our education has produced no great.

To Oris, dreaming to be a great musician and artist just as Mozart, Beethoven and Joe Hisaishi, he must understand the forming process of their souls and talents, he must pay the same or even more time and effort.

But in our education, it takes us a lot of valuable time and energy to force us to cram and practice exam every day.

From ancient time to the present, there are no worthies or greats

in all fields, like our children nowadays, wasting a lot of precious time and energy to cram, do exam problem and practice exam.

From ancient time to the present, the great talents and greats in all fields have devoted most of their time and energy to the cultivating of talent and the accumulating of knowledge.

Cram and doing exam can neither train up excellent talent nor accumulate a great deal of knowledge.

So, we must get rid of most of the time we cram and do exam problem, and then spend more time and energy on what we love.

Cultivate talent and accumulate knowledge.

Only in this way can we stand out in the fields we love.

If we love music, we need to know about Mozart, Beethoven, Chopin, Lester, Tchaikovsky, Wagner, Pavarotti, Michael Jackson, Taylor Swift, Katy Perry, Vitas, every kind of Korean musicians, Jay Chou, Yanni, Kajiura Yuki, Ayumi Hamasaki, Joe Hisaishi, and the most outstanding talents and greats in this field, what they did in each growth period.

If we love painting, we need to know about Da Vinci, Rafael, Michelangelo, Giotto, Titian, Rembrandt, Monet, Van Gogh, Disney, Stan Lee, Terryl Whitlatch, Disney, Hayao Miyazaki, and the most outstanding talents and greats in this field, what they did in each growth period.

If we love sports, we need to know about Jabbar, Jordan, Kobe, Durant, Bailey, Beckham, Messi, Ronaldo, Boulter, Lining, Yao Ming, Zhang Yining, Bruce Lee, and a lot of Olympic champions, and the most outstanding talents and greats in this field, what they did in each growth period.

If we love martial arts, we need to know about Mohammed Ali,

Tyson, MMA champions, UFC world champions, Buakaw, Tony Jaa, Jackie Chan, Jet Li, Donnie Yen, Bruce Lee, and the most outstanding talents and greats in this field, what they did in each growth period.

If we love literature, we need to know about Shakespeare, Goethe, Schiller, Green Brothers, Andersen, Dickens, Romain Rolland, Pushkin, Tolstoy, Tagore, Haruki Murakami, Kawabata Yasunari, Yukio Mishima, Selma Lagerlf, J.K.Rowling, J.D.Salinger, Hemingway, C.S.Lewis, John Ronald Muriel Torkin, and the most outstanding talents and greats in this field, what they did in each growth period.

If we love drama and film, we need to know about Shakespeare, Wagner, Chaplin, Audrey Hepburn, Marilyn Monro, Schwarzenegger, Stallone, Jim Carry, Rowan Atkinson, Bruce Lee, Jackie Chan, Jet Li, Donnie Yen, Stephen Chow, Daniel Lee, Ang Lee, Stanley Tong, James Cameron, Stan Lee, MARVEL studios workers, DC studios workers, Disney, Joe Hisaishi, Hayao Miyazaki, and the most outstanding talents and greats in this field, what they did in each growth period.

If we love science, technology, computer and internet, we need to know about Da Vinci, Galileo, Copernicus, Bacon, Franklin, Newton, Leibniz, Pascal, Descartes, Einstein, Planck, Edison, Nicola Tesla, Oppenheimer, Mrs.Curie, Von Neumann, Zuckerberg, Bill Gates, Jobs, and the most outstanding talents and greats in this field, what they did in each growth period.

If we love military, we need to know about Alexander, Hannibal, King Arthur, Attila the Hun, Caesar, Charlemagne, Machiavelli, Frederick the Great, Napoleon, Gen Gi Khan, Trotsky, Stalin, Montgomerie, Braton, Zedong Mao, and the most outstanding talents and greats in this field, what they did in each growth period.

If we love politics, we need to know about Cicero, Caesar,

Charlemagne, Gen Gi Khan, Louis XIV, Peter the Great, Ekaterina the Great, Maria Theresa, Roosevelt, Washington, Franklin, Lenin, Stalin, De Gaulle, Zedong Mao, Obama, Trump, and the most outstanding talents and greats in this field, what they did in each growth period.

If we love philosophy, we need to know about Socrates, Platon, Aristotle, Lao Tzu, Taoism synthesizers, Buddhist philosophy synthesizers, biblical philosophy synthesizers, Koran philosophy synthesizers, Descartes, Leibniz, Newton, Bacon, Rousseau, Schopenhauer, Nietzsche, Dewey, Marx, Engels, Lenin, Mao Zedong, and the most outstanding talents and greats in this field, what they did in each growth period.

Draw inferences about other cases from one instance.

Their biographies, related works, lives, every word, every action, we all need to know and understand, take the essence, discard the dross, and keep pace with the time, combine with our own situation, make hard effort, learn widely from other's strong point, make integration and innovation.

Isaac Newton said, "If I have seen further, it is by standing upon the shoulders of giants."

The great scientist Isaac Newton, his greatest contribution is fully integrating and refining the individual breakthroughs of Galileo, Descartes, Kepler and many scientists, finally he summarized them into his own fire-new scientific theory.

The great martial artist Bruce Lee said, Jeet Kune Do advocates intangible, as a result, it can adopt all tangibles, Because it has no fixed style, so it is suitable for the style of every hue. As a result, Jeet Kune Do uses a variety of methods, but without any kind of limitation. Jeet Kune Do use a variety of technology and means to

achieve their purpose. In Jeet Kune Do technologies, the utility is the most important. Jeet Kune Do can use a variety of methods of every faction, and not be limited by any limitations. Jeet Kune Do makes good use of all skills, and all means for its use. Jeet Kune Do covers all things, but is not covered by all things. Use no way as way, have no limitation as limitation.

So we said, "Think of bee as model, very widely reading, practice our own inventive mind, melt all the flowers into our own nectar. All has the origin, but all has new hue."

Absorb the methods and efforts of outstanding talents and greats, at the same time, we must keep pace with the times, with the new era, with our own special circumstances, then pay the same amount, even more time and effort, and then learn widely from others' strong points, make integration and innovation.

Only in this way can our education create more and better talents and greats. Genius is not only the result of self-effort, but also the highest achievement of education.

The French philosopher in the age of Enlightenment Helvetius said,

The spiritual differences we see between people are due to the different circumstances in which they live and the different kinds of education they receive.

Helvetius is a leading proponent of the "Universal Theory of Education". He believed that the difference is because the human intelligence environment and acquired opportunities, and education caused by the different, even think that education can create a genius.

Helvetius thought,

The starting point, everyone has equal talent.

Reason and knowledge are from hard work and education.

Genius is the creation of effort and education.

Everyone should have the right to receive secondary and higher education.

Edison said, none of my inventions came by accident. When you see a worthy effort, material resources need to be met, I will do the experiment again and again, until it is reality. This is due to the final 1% inspiration and 99% perspiration.

But we would say,

Any talent, and any achievement, is due to 1% education plus 99% of our effort.

Inspiration doesn't come out of nowhere, but by the outbreak of a large number of accumulated ceaselessly.

And a great deal of accumulation comes from a great deal of effort.

The excellent musician Joe Hisaishi said in his autobiography *Touching, So Created*, "Fleeting inspiration seems mostly to occur in the unconscious. Although it is the unconscious, but not entirely without trying to think, but how to make our works totally perfect, will continue to process yourself to the limit. That is, in the subconscious mind at any moment in thinking about the creation of the situation, a good idea suddenly surfaced. This process does not have a fixed pattern to follow. When and how to emerge, and what kind of inspiration they appear, change with different circumstances."

He said, "As for the creation, the emphasis is on sensibility, but what is the so-called sensibility. Calmly analyze and sort out the content of the word "sensibility", and the results also include the feelings of the individual. But we can imagine, more importantly, the basis of the feeling, in fact, is every bit of accumulated in the past."

So we said, "Excellent works and remarkable talents, their births have never been accidental. Inspiration is emergent, but for this emergent inspiration, we often have to do a lot of work."

Education is to provide a good environment and resources for our efforts to cultivate.

With good education and great effort, anyone can become a genius and anyone can achieve great achievement.

Genius is never born.

Genius that makes great contributions to mankind and world is the product of effort, suffering and education.

Everyone is different because of the degree of effort, which leads to the difference in the size of talent.

Everyone is on different paths just because they are in different fates. But everyone is different from achievement, totally not because of talent.

The growth of talent people and great in every field can prove it. Every great talent and great, their talents are made up of effort, suffering, and education.

We can totally ignore the talent problem.

There is much more talent in diligence and misery than in talent given by talent.

Most of all, we firmly believe that in terms of spiritual and intellectual talent,

All beings are created equal!
All beings' talents are created equal!

We firmly believe that every genius, what he or she needs to do, is simply the use of hard work and education to develop the talent, to make talent's wings fly.

Whatever it is Mozart, Beethoven, Da vinci, Rafael, Michelangelo, Napoleon, Einstein, Bill Gates or Jobs, Bruce Lee or Joe Hisaishi and so on.

English philosopher Locke said, "Everyone comes to this world like a blank sheet of paper, and then the circumstances in which he lives begin to color him, and what his circumstances are ,and what he will be."

Bruce Lee said, "People tell me that a genius can create their own opportunities, in fact, a person's deep expectations can not only create their own opportunities, and even create their own talent."

English word "education", derived from the Latin "educere", composed of "ex" - "outside" and "ducere" - "lead", its original meaning is "guide the abilities of the human mind".

The school, is derived from the Greek word skhole, meaning "leisure time, free time".

This is the first school created by Aristotle, let the students to read books in leisure and free time.

So, Art Fairy said,

All beings are created equal!
All beings' talents are created equal!

As a country, the biggest purpose of education is to cultivate outstanding talents and great more and better.

Personally, the biggest purpose of education is to make us work hard to grow successfully into outstanding talents and great in our own field.

Therefore, our education method should be summed up in the development of outstanding talents and great in various fields, instead of taking cramming and doing exam crazily.

We should always remember,

**The reason why no great is born,
it is we neglect the process of forming the great soul.**

The advanced education system, must give All beings to provide a good environment, abundant resources, and a lot of free time, so that we can successfully cultivate talent, healthily grow.

The advanced education system, will not force us to waste time on rote learning and do the tests.

The most important point is still the current educational environment and school, cramming and doing exam question take up 80% of our effort time, a lot of valuable time to should to cultivate and accumulate knowledge is squeezed out.

And cramming and doing exam can not cultivate talent, nor can it accumulate much knowledge.

This is the fundamental crux.

The quality of the education system determines the quantity and quality of the talents.

A good education system can train the talent with the highest

percentage and the relatively high quality in the population base.

And the number of talents trained by the bad education system from the populations base is relatively small, and the quality is relatively low.

So, we must try our best to get rid of cramming and doing exam, and use the methods of outstanding talents and greats in all fields to learn and work.

Only in this way, as long as our children strive for self-improvement and struggle hard, our education will continue to cultivate more and better talents and great on the source of energy.

Oris wanted to be like Mozart, Beethoven and Joe Hisaishi as a great musician, artist, but Mozart, Beethoven and Joe Hisaishi at the time of Oris's age, were not wasting a lot of precious time and energy in cramming and doing exam, they just spent a lot of time and energy in refining their art talent and accumulating extensive knowledge!

Mozart told friends in 1787, "Almost all the works of great musicians, I have been thoroughly researched and perused regularly."

And he said, "No one studies as much as I do about composition."

Mozart's father Leopold said, "I have no what can teach my child, he was completely beyond me. Later, my child must accept the teachings and practice this time each of the master, and my responsibility is just to help him to seize the opportunity to learn, accumulate more knowledge."

Leopold wanted Mozart to be at the top of the world's music heaven at least.

With this in mind, have to come up with some true skill and genuine knowledge.

So in the end of Mozart for 3 years in Germany, Britain, France, Holland and other places after the travel show, dad at home earnestly to let children learn a counterpoint, and the works of Bach, Handel, Ebeling Hasse and so on.

Studying repeatedly, imitation, combination, and innovation.

At this time, Mozart just was 5 years old.

In December 23, 1768, the Mozart family arrived in Vienna.

When Mozart and his piano prodigy sister re-entered the palace, they are no longer the kind of children who feel new and know nothing about the world.

Their pace is so sophisticated, their eyes are just looking ahead......

Beethoven loved self-study, reading the works of the greastest thinkers hungrily and thirstly , he spent a lot of time and energy in poetry, drama and opera.

In 1809 he wrote a letter to the Leipzig music publisher Brett Kopf Haertel, "From my childhood, I seek to understand the thoughts and methods of outstanding masters and intellectual people of every age."

Beethoven accepted the so-called formal education, only in primary school, and there he was just a "bad" student.

Joe Hisaishi said,

Extend the antennae to various fields, let yourself look, listen, read more, walk, try and feel, and try to increase your knowledge and experience.

Reading music from different composers is a good study, and we can derive considerable inspiration from it.

Today I wanna go beyond yesterday's me, and tomorrow's me will be better than I am today, in order to create better music, and constantly surpass myself.

(Joe Hisaishi, *Touching, So Created*)

Not just music and art, but other fields have the same principle.
The ways of absorbing knowledge in different fields will be some differences, but never cramming and doing exam.
How can we cultivate knowledge and absorb knowledge in different fields? We must look for the lives of talented people and great in every field.

The reason why no great man is born, is because we neglect the process of forming a great soul.
The reason why we can not cultivate outstanding talent is because we neglected the process of cultivating outstanding talent.
We must understand the growth of great and outstanding talent.
We must understand the process of training outstanding talent, we must learn and practice the method of talent's cultivating.
So, what's the method of talent's cultivation?
We would say,

Read   Practice   Think

The growth of the amount of reading, practicing, thinking, is also equivalent to the promotion of talent.

But different fields have different proportions and contents.

This requires us to gonna the lives of outstanding talents and great in all times and all fields to find.

At this age, books are so numerous like sakura sea, at the internet age, information is so developed like galaxy, I believe we will always have many ways.

So, Oris really hated school, really hated cramming and doing exam problem! Only music and art! The only things that made him mad and melted his blood! Made him glow like a flame!

Every day when the bell ringed, he rushed out of the classroom and ran to the dance room or the auditorium to practice the piano.

He didn't laugh with classmate in the hallway like mad apes, or played with classmates like crazy baboons. He didn't gather in the side of the teacher with cram-exam madman lurk and sneak around like ghosts.

Even in class, Oris was holding the music score of Bandari, listening the melody in dream of pure light.

He loved Bandari's music very much, because they are pure and beautiful as the Alpine snow fairies.

The music creators of Bandari dedicated the talent from the Alps to the whole world.

They never appeared in the media, once they started planning new music, they would secluded in the mountains in the Alps, until the music completed.

Being in the mountain forest let Bandari has an endless stream of creative inspiration, and also remained a natural and pure style of music.

Every sound of insects, birds, petals drop and waters flow,

creators are deep into the mountains, lakes, visited to Switzerland's the Alps, mirror lakes, rose peak foothills, Jungfrau, and other places to draw from the real field.

One of the Bandari's creators Oliver Schwarz said, "Bandari's music is a combination of vision, touch and hearing, the creative inspiration from nature will continue to the hearts of audiences all over the world. It's not only a new century music, but also a spiritual nutriment from nature."

Bandari's music has come to perfection, not just because of the tireless efforts of the creators, more important, it's because the creators keep away from the secular world, close to nature, and never be polluted by the profits luring of this world.

Bandari merged with nature to extract the essence from all creatures of nature, thus created the incomparable pure elegant music of nature, of happiness, of heaven.

Leonardo Da Vinci said,

If the artist will look up to as the standard work of others, so this artist's works will not be worth a farthing.

But if he can learn from nature, his effort will be fruitful.

The painters we see after the age of Rome are a case in point, they imitated one master after another without stopping, and their works from generation to generation became into the decline.

Through such a recession, Giotto di Bondone was on the stage of history. He was born in a remote mountain area and nature led him into the palace of art.

At first he painted pictures of sheep on the rocks, then he used the same method to draw all the animals he saw in the country.

In this way, after a long period of painting and research, not only did he surpass all the masters of his time, and he has transcended all the masters of the past.

After his death, art went back again, because all the painters are imitating the works of masters.

After so many centuries, art was still going backwards. It was not until the arrival of another florentine Tommaso that changed this situation. Tommaso, also known as Masaccio, proved the futility of other painters with his perfect work.

For that painters did not realize that nature is the master and ruling goddess of all masters.

Those who know only the works of masters, and ignore the creatures of nature, they are grandsons of nature, not the sons of nature.

nature is the master and ruling goddess of all masters.

I hate those idiots, they blame nature's apprentice, and in this way to defend the masters, but they do not know that the masters themselves are nature's apprentices.

Painter, if you wanna achieve the highest painting achievements, please understand this point, your works will not bring you honor and achievement unless you put your art on a solid foundation of nature.

But, if your foundation is hard and solid, and know how to innovate, then your works will be better and more, and can bring glory and generous benefits to you.

When an artist's work transcends the artist's ideal goal, this artist can no longer make progress. When his work is lower than his ideal goal, his works will be continuously improved. Unless he gets greedy, becomes too ambitious.

A student who can't exceed teachers is a bad student.

Those who boast of his work are poor masters, but those who are dissatisfied with his works are on the road to perfect art.

(Da Vinci, *The Notebook of Leonardo Da Vinci*)

Beethoven's Pastoral Symphony was also born in the fairy singing of nature.

Beethoven had a natural passion for nature, he spent a lot of time traveling around the countryside. He frequently left Vienna to work in remote rural areas.

He said in letter in the summer of 1808, "How happy I was when i was walking among shrubs, trees, lawns and rocks! Because the trees, the flowers and the rocks can give me empathy."

In his notebook in 1803, people found such words, "the bigger the river, the more heavy the melody is." It shows he draws inspiration by observing nature.

The Pastoral Symphony was written by Beethoven on his own happy experiences in the countryside.

Of course, none of these great works can be done in school or in exam.

In fact, in this world, there are many dreams, there are many artistic dreams, in the time of cultivating talent, they have an explosive conflict with the dirty money that for quick success and instant gain, they have an explosive conflict with doing exam with breaking head and bleeding.

There's a conflict! And very fierce!

Chapter 3

SNOWSTORM
AND ICEBERG

a cold winter morning of the fifth grade, Oris became onto an ice rabbit to escaped of the classes one day, for gonna the piano recital contest held by the conservatory, and easily won the gold medal laurel. In the evening, as soon as he entered the house, the atmosphere was instantly cold and piercing to the bone.

"My son," said father, with an unusually sweet face, smiling at him like a grampus, "How are you getting on with your studies recently?"

"That's it. If I can't count on the bottom second, I'll go eat killer whale shit and choke myself!"

He was trying to take out the splendid trophy hidden behind him and appease his parents, unexpectedly, Papa kicked him a shit!

"Ah!!!!"

Malnourished deer weak boy flew straight away three meters away.

"The head teacher called fucking home!!! Where the hell did you fucking escape one day and go mad??? Fuck you raccoon cubs!!!"

Papa rushed to son then kicked, hit and scolded fire-dragon shit, "Grades are bad as demon parrot shit! Every time the parent's meeting let me get into the flame of fire squid face! Music! Music doesn't make any money! You ice dragon poop have been learning music for so many years! Why don't you rush along with the band to make more money for me, and let me buy more Remy Martin to drink, buy more German cigar to smoke! You useless stupid jellyfish of the Sicily! It's really because I beat you less, hit you light, that you just so fucking idiot!!!"

"Papa, don't hit me! Please don't hit me! Please! When you hit me last time, the wound on my arm hasn't healed yet! Please don't hit me! Please!!! Woowoowoowoowoowoo..."

Oris seemed as a aurora ice rabbit rolled over in hell fire and burned through the skull, broke into violent lamentations.

Only helpless! Hopeless! Powerless!

Just weeping wail, waiting for death.

Finally, Papa was too tired to beat son, like an African bison bitten legs by an African lion, he was straight panting.

"Papa...Papa..." he was dying, with a deer tongue, "I went to the piano contest, I got the gold trophy!"

"Gold trophy or bonus???" Papa's eyes were full of shark urine, spew dolphin shit excitedly.

"Gold trophy, no bonus..."

"I fuck your mother!!!"

Papa kicked his son again, like a wolf grins hideously, "I thought it was a bonus! Take a lousy goosey trophy, can change a hippo shit??? Can change a hippo shit!!!??? The gold trophy is not made of gold!!! And I don't have fucking money to send you to conservatory!!! On, no! Did you steal my money and find someone to make this goosey trophy??? Fuck you!!! Honest confession!!!"

Papa kicked again. Kicked Oris thirty rolls of mango doughnuts and seventy lava chocolate Iceland cake rolls.

"Don't kick our kid into a Finland fox dog!" Mama was on the bed like a cat or fox cries.

Woowoowoo...Mama does really love me!

Oris wiped his tears and iced crying.

Just a smile bloomed on the boy's face like an pink rose bud in sunshine, but Mama said, "Maybe we can take a leash and bark at him husky!"

"Wa!!!"

Just crying! Then Oris was beaten into a husky with broken legs.

Mama was always more cruel than the deep sea dragon.

I remember, once Mama dug a spoonful of watermelon, but not steady and dropped on the floor, she picked up and stuffed it into my mouth.

Saw the son surprised at her, she smiled suddenly, "Oh! I thought you were just a baby..."

My heart was instantly cold to the horror teeth of the dragon fish in deep dark sea.

"Son, do you know why I didn't divorce your idiot dad who was hatched with crocodile eggs?"

"Is it because of me?"

"Because no one fucking wants your parenting rights!!!"

"......"

"Mom, I have a headache!"

"That's your Corgi brain is sick!!! Ahahahahahhaha....."

"......"

Christmas Eve of grade four, Oris was cutting the roast chicken with a knife in the living room, Mama was mopping the floor, but Oris accidentally cut his hand and blood gushing!

He cried, screamed, and visions of fairies were in front of his eyes.

Mama heard it, hurried to see and said, "Hold your rose dolphin blood in your hand!!! Don't spill the blood on the floor I just mopped!!!"

Biological mother!!!

"Sure enough!!! You stole my money to make the trophy!!!"

Papa took out his wallet and found nothing left.

"Damn! I must hit you today black and blue!!! Beat your head and break the blood flow!!!"

Papa tugged at his collar and pulled him up, gave him a lot sharks slap, week deer boy was slapped over to the ground. Then, Papa pulled his belt and beat son madly. As if pink six angle salamander was roasted by the hell fire, the crying and screaming of the cutting heart spread outside.

The neighbors heard it and called the police directly!

The police burst through the door, the hands mutilated the son of Papa were still flogging cruelly, not worried about the police's awe-inspiring righteousness.

"No more spanking!!!" Policeman pushed the dung beetle man who became a Sahara mad cow.

"My son stole my money, why can't I hit him???"

Then Papa rushed up and ready to trample on Oris, but was forcibly stopped by the policeman.

On the glacier floor, Oris like a Arctic hare overlay the Hell-fire cliffs and huddled, all the body overflowing withe rose blood, the footprints are dirty, the face was still burning like dragon fire disembowelled a fairy cat.

Looking at Oris, the policeman's eyebrows twisted into Florence croissant, he turned and yelled ate the man, "Is this your son? You beat him like that? Neighbors have reported that you beat your son every day!"

"This is my turtle egg son, I wanna play it as I like, can you manage it?"

The policeman took out the handcuffs, "Hit the kid again and you'll follow me to the office! In the office, the rice is served! There are fresh husky poop let you eat!"

"I don't play! I don't play..." Papa quickly put away the belt.

"Poor boy..." The policeman uncle helped Oris up, "Don't be afraid. I think your father just eats too little husky stool. If your father hits you again, call me, I must put your father to the police station and let him eat the husky stool of ten days before with Corgis."

Oris nodded like a Norway forest kitten.

But as soon as the police car left, Papa flew up his ass and kicked his son to the ground. Before the belt had been waved down, Oris climbed up his cat body and rushed out of the house.

Smashed the searing Canicula trophy!

In the snow with sakura tears and night sky, he was running away.

So far, far far away! Never looked back even just one time......

With the cat eye little match girl together froze to death in the new year night?

Wearing a thin butterfly feather sweater, Oris shivered in the ice heavy snow for two hours. Finally, he went home desolately, just as in the past.

No matter how cruel my parents are, after all they are my biological parents......

I used to roll around in the trampling of my Papa's buffalo hoofs, I used to cry in my mother's crocodile abuse on the Iceland River.

I've done my best to mop the floor, wash the dishes, and brush the bowls, but I can't win your praise. I have been very careful to wash clothes, but also can not change your encouragement.

I am so depressed! I never seem to walk out of this fire-cold dark!

Papa, Mama, sometimes I really wanna die! Really desire to die......

But, Papa, Mama, I don't hate you, even though I can't get your love now.

**I love every flowering life of this world.
Even if they hurt me,
I still love them!**

Papa, Mama, the afterlife, I'm still willing to accompany you to reach hoary hair together!

But when Oris got home, he found that home had become a hell-fire sea.

Just now after Oris ran out, Papa saw the brandy on the old piano and patted his head, "Oh! My silly turtle son, he didn't steal my money! I bought a bottle of brandy and drank! But beat him, I am more carefree!"

"Drink drink drink!!! Fuck you!!! Drink to die!!! You stupid fucking gorilla!!!"

Mama cried and cursed, then behoove became the Sri Lanka mango punching bag of Papa.

Mama was crippled and unable to walk, Papa abruptly pulled her Nereus flower long hair, drop her on the ground, kicked and hit, played and scolded.

"You useless starfish! Only can sit on the bed crying day by day! Why don't you jump into the Aegean Sea and suck the vampire squid? If you die, I would not be so poor! It's all your fault! It's you lying in bed all day without making money, so I can't drink more brandy! It was you stupid fish that made me so miserable! The thing I regret the most in my life is marrying you! You fucking big foolish glacier mermaid!!!"

Papa hit Mama's head out of the rose blood with a violin.

Hit tired, and just drank, Papa went to bed, immediately sleep like a dead ape.

Mama had despaired......

She made every effort to climb to the piano, prop up the body of falling cherry blood, strove for the last blossom of cherry power, threw the bottle of brandy into the blazing fireplace!

The dark broken house quickly became a sea of fire!

The rag, broken clothes, inferior wooden table, wooden amber piano, as well as the dusk moonlight violin in wooden house, are all snapped and swallowed by the hell-fire!

The blazing fire in the boy's face was cold and tender like a flying bloody dragon.

A drop of summer cherry tears from the boy's cat eyes, dropped with a fire butterfly.

The house was burnt to pieces.

Mama and Papa flew to paradise in the hell-fire river.

On the day of the funeral, Oris hid in the auditorium of the school, on the piano, he was playing the Requiem of Mozart's posthumous music that written before he flew to heaven. In the dark, Oris was quietly wiping the glowing sakura tears.

Once, in Papa's abuse and poison hit, Oris's art talents made rapid progress. But now, he no longer forced practicing.

Even if I wanna be forced by Papa, I never have a chance......

Never!

Forever!!!

Cleaned the house after the fire, Oris lived in it again.

"Or lead a vagrant life in Alps? This is my only sunflower-family..." sitting beside the piano of flowering moon queen tulips after fire baptism, Oris spoke to himself in all violets fading.

The disable grandmother came all the way from the rose snow

mountain to take care of Oris. From then on, Oris and Grandma depended on each other.

Every day after school, Grandma will do Oris's favorite chive cod and windmill bread. As soon as he came home from school, he could eat delicious cod and bread as soon as he dropped his bag.

"Eat more, baby, Grandma doesn't wanna eat, Grandma isn't hungry."

Grandma always said she was not hungry. She always said so.

Grandma used to take Oris to the garbage cans to pick up bottles and junk, sold for money, then bought Oris good food, bought music score.

But at school, he ate a devil crisps and had to hide with a cacomistle, lest the little devils lay out the leopard's claws without shame.

Today, he came to school early, the teacher hadn't come yet, then, he was snatched by a group of pig nose bat demons one pack of small panda crisps.

"You give it back to me! This is my grandmother braved the snowstorm and hard to pick up the bottles in garbage and bought it for me! You give it back to me!"

Oris rushed up for a fight like a deer, but he was turned over to the ground by the crocodile demons' tails, they also carried a mop that had just dragged the toilet into his cat mouth.

Oris only could be helpless! Hopeless! Powerless!

He could only let his head hit ground and cry loudly!

Every time Oris was abused black and blue at school, as soon as returned the glacier home, he roared at Grandma like Venice's lava burst, every time he angered Grandma downed bed and cried bitterly, fire tears danced in the ice river.

"My grandson, why do you hurt me? Why are you so angry? Do you know how sad Grandma is? Woowoowoowoowoo..."

Although Oris was guilty, he never comforted his grandmother and said, "Grandma, don't cry, it's all my fault..."

At that time, he was helpless, hopeless, powerless with his own misery!

At that time, he did not know how to cherish the sacred time his grandmother could accompany him.

At that time, he didn't understand love, and he didn't have the ability to love.

Most of the time, as soon as talked about Oris's Papa, Grandma must cry.

"When your Papa was a child, his favorite is onion cod, windmill bread and alpine blueberry cake roll. Your Papa, he...he...Woo...Woowoowoowoo..."

"You don't cry!!! OK???"

The more he roared loudly, the more Grandma cried hopelessly.

"Woowoowoowoowoowoo..."

"Can you stop crying? Can you? Can you!!! Can you!!!!!! Woowoowoowoo..."

So, he was domineering to roar himself to cry.

A small empty house, but only the old Grandma and the kid crying with sakura falling blood, bone cut out the heart.

In the class, Oris saw that the rich students could drink canned sakura milk every day, he really envied to the Rafael's Frauenkirche tip.

In fact, he also liked drinking sakura milk, but every time to gonna the supermarket, he never dared to reach out his angle kitten hand.

Because of poor. Because he had no money.

So he went to pick up bottles and pick them up after school.

When he saved enough money into the door of the supermarket, but saw Grandma awkwardly holding a box of sakura milk.

"My angle, Grandma bought it for you, when Grandma pick up more bottles, I must buy more for you."

Oris looked at his wrinkled grandmother and smiled like a cherry blossom in full bloom.

Smiling and smiling, but wept deeply.

Oris was not good-looking. Actually, he is very ugly.

On Halloween, he accidentally knocked a girl's textbook onto the ground, the girls yelled at him like a porcupine in front the whole class, "You are uglier than a Christmas deer, and fucking dare to touch my textbook! I am so fucking sick of eating one hundred Arctic blue dragonflies!!! I'd rather have ten thousand Somali magic mantis squeezed die in the textbook than you touch a finger!!! Hideous!!!"

Oris returns fire, "Have you ever eaten an Arctic blue dragonfly???"

"eat your fucking beluga shit!!!"

A fat snake swallowed ten thousand pounds of beluga shit, he kicked Oris out of the classmate, and then, a group of sharks under the Caribbean coral island rush forward......

A moment later, a boy gasped and ran to the next classroom shouting, "You gonna tell the teacher!!! I'm afraid Oris will be killed by them in the toilet!!! Today they use mops and tiles!!!"

But no matter how the teacher criticized, they can not stop the huskies eat shit and rolling balls of dung beetles.

Every time, they just criticized those huskies and beetles of rich and powerful families.

As soon as he came out of the teacher office, those huskies and beetles nipped Oris's arctic fox neck, roared like a purple boar, "If next time you dare tell the teacher, we'll roll you into the big shit ball at husky camp, let million dogs dismembered you in ten seconds!!!"

"I didn't tell the teacher!!! I didn't!!! It's not me!!! Please don't make me roll into big ball shit throw to ten thousand huskies!!! Please!!!"

Several dragon shit boys still glared at him, they also waved fists to throw fire octopus shit like baboons.

"Ugly dickhead!!! Even husky sees you as so ugly as shit that doesn't dare lick you! You're so hideous! You must have been grown up with eating blue whale droppings!!! Which girl's giant lizards ostrich eyes are blind that she would love you corgi shit???"

"Poor dolphin dick!!! We just robbed you of one pack of small panda crisps, and you cried like a polar bear shit! Tell your stupid Grandma to pick up more bottles, so next time I can grab you Oreo."

"Idiot dragon pussy!!! You play a foolish piano all day long, can the piano make money??? Does the piano make you the first in the grade??? In our grade, even the most ugly gorilla feces fat can not love you short poor dwarf!!!"

When they finished the scolding and leaved, Oris was leaning against the wall, one parrot step by one parrot step carefully moved back to the classroom.

As soon as got home, he burst the Iceland volcano to Grandma.

"Grandma, why are you so useless? Everyone else's children are so happy, why do I have to be so miserable!!??? Grandma, I hate you! I hate you! I really hate you!!! Woowoowoowoowoo..."

Oris knelt on the ground and cried like a moose.

"My angel, why are you so mad at Grandma? If Grandma die by you anger, how do Grandma make chive cod and windmill bread for you later? Do you know how scared Grandma is, is afraid won't see the day when you grow up...Do you know how much Grandma wants to see you happy and grow up happily...Grandma has done the best, Grandma is also helpless..."

"Woowoowoowoowoo..."

Grandma cried, even Christmas Rose trees are distressed by withered.

"Grandma, don't cry! I didn't mean to anger you! I didn't mean it! Today! Today a girl in my class said I am hideous than a Christmas deer!"

Oris fell in Grandma's embrace and continued the pink dolphin rainstorm crying.

"Woowoowaawaa...They said! They said, even chimpanzee would not like me! No one in the world will like me! No one will like me! Why am I so ugly! Why am I so hideous! Why!!!??? Why..."

Woowoowaawaawaa...woowoowaawaawaa......

Grandma gently stroked Oris's parrot fish forehead, "Don't cry, don't cry! Oh, my angel, don't cry...My angel, you are the most handsome and beautiful in the world! The most handsome and beautiful! The people who will like you in the future must be more than the petals of the cherry blossom sea! Sure! Must! So, don't cry, angel. When see you cry, Grandma is so sad that can't breathe. So don't cry, OK...?"

Grandma was gently as cat wiping Oris's glowing meteor rain tears, gently like swan stroking his little deer angel shoulder.

"Grandma, I don't be crying! But I really think I'm really so ugly!!! Really so hideous!!!"

"What a nonsense! Grandma said you are the most handsome and beautiful, you are surely the most handsome and beautiful! Do you hear?"

So, crying and crying, Oris suddenly laughed out of the blue whale song.

"Well, hey hey. Grandma, you are so kind...I love you, Grandma..."

Latughing and smiling, Oris fell asleep in Grandma's embrace and became a fairy Nebula angel cat.

In Grandma' arms, I always felt very relieved.

Even the sunshine blue butterfly dreams in lilies sea, were so fragrant and beautiful.

He did not say he was abused.

He was afraid of Grandma's butterfly fish heart will ache that couldn't breathe.

Every day, Grandma went out and picks up the bottles in garbage, then sell the money to buy Oris roast mutton chop and sakura milk.

Sometimes Grandma brought him to pick bottles, but on rainy days and snowy days, Grandma didn't let him go out.

"You play the piano well at home, home is warm."

"Grandma! It's so cold outside and so heavy snow! Be at home! Don't go out, OK?"

"Grandma is not afraid of cold. When see you eat and drink well, see you play the piano happy, Grandma is as warm and happy as sitting on the Swan Nebula and holding a luminous white star."

Grandma always said she was not afraid of cold and snow.

She always said so.

Bought delicious food, Grandma never wanted to eat.

She only ate vegetables, the roast mutton chop with mayonnaise, shrimp lily salad and sakura milk, all left Oris to eat.

"Grandma doesn't like mutton." Grandma always said, "Grandma doesn't wanna eat shrimp either. You eat more. Are you full? If not enough, Grandma make an alpine blueberry cake roll for you."

But every time in the late night, he looked at his wrinkled Grandma struggled to eat cold lilies soup and hard lava bread sticks, he could not restrain his burning sakura tears.

Outside the snow fog window, with Oris's hand flowing sunshine violin melody, Grandma's fairy deer silhouette disappeared in the cold plume snow.

Then, the melody on the piano was dancing with the golden angels.

Playing and playing, he couldn't help crying star tears like snow sakura.

Grandma, I love you forever...

Forever forever!

Grandma went to the market outside 1000 meters every afternoon to buy meat for cooking.

If Oris wanted to eat pasta and egg tart but Grandma can't do it, then the morning before gonna school to tell Grandma, she would stagger to the Christmas bakery outside 2000 meters to buy Oris's favorite cherry rose egg tart and oyster wine pasta, I could eat into my cat mouth as soon as enter the room.

Grandma was difficult to walk, every minute she has to stop, holding the waist, breathing like a lacerated deer by dragon bloody teeth.

Oris never knew that the journey was harder for the old Grandma than the stairway to paradise, and longer than the path to heaven.

However, for Oris as soon as entering the room can delicious cherry rose egg tart and oyster wine pasta, even farther tired and hard, even on the road more dangerous and crazy car, Grandma is willing to keep walking.

Yes! Keep walking......

But, the snow covered Christmas night in grade five, Grandma went out, and never came back......

"She must gonna buy me cherry rose egg tart and sakura milk."

Oris lapped his mouth like a Norway forest fairy cat, he had eaten sweet egg tarts hundreds and thousands of times in heart.

Practiced for two hours piano and violin.

Still couldn't see Grandma's deer silhouette.

"Such a big sakura snow, Grandma has not come back yet."

Oris's stomach was hungry as an alpine avalanche.

Suddenly! Aunt broke into the house!

"Grandma is in a car accident! She's in the hospital now! I'll give you some money, go out and have dinner yourself."

Oris froze into a column of ice crystals.

"Before, your Grandma fainted on the way home from the grocery shopping, but she was brought back by a kind person. This time she was hit by a motorcycle when crossing the street."

Oris was dumbfounded...

The ice pure cat pupils were shocked by this new into cherry petals plume snow.

Grandma was sent to the operation room. Three hours later, she finally was sent out.

She was laying for a long time.

Two hours later, Grandma woke up suddenly.

Her mouth was humming as the wings of hummingbirds all the time, aunt leaned her ear, "You speak slowly, I am listening."

Grandma was sore and blurred, thinking she was about to fly to heaven, so she waved desperately as if she were looking for the white violets of the Irish castle. She couldn't say a word, she was at aunt hand gestures of a name, everyone finally understood.

She was calling Oris.

Oris approaches with star tears and fire butterfly.

Grandma was very weak and spoke very hard, "After school, I

gonna cooking for you, do your favorite chive cod and windmill bread. I am gonna cooking for you..."

Grandma tried to climb up, but she couldn't flower a small cherry blossom.

"I can't give up...I...I can't die...As long as I live, there is hope in Oris's life...so long as I live one more day, Oris's art dream will come true one day earlier..." But at last, Grandma could only fall into bed, only gasping, only coughing.

Oris's cat eyes instantly burst ten millions of Cygnus flower in meteor rain!

"Grandma! Grandma, you must get better hurry up! I can't live without you!!! Only you are the best to me in this world! Grandma, I can't live without you! Grandma!!! I can't live without you!!!"

Grandma! I can't live without you......

Long long ago, the nightingale was singing in the mirror lake forest, but Oris's grandfather had died in the singsing of beautiful nightingale and katyusha era.

Now, in this sakura snow world, only Grandma is the holy and pure sunshine angel who really loves Oris.

When Oris was 3 years old, in order to treat his ballet Mama's legs, in order to buy him better foods and expensive music scares, 63 years old Grandma climbed the steep snow mountain every day to collect tulip Queen roses, iceberg roses and sakura blood roses, then went down to collect Miss Catherine rabbit eyes lavender.

In the winter snow sakura, other villagers were reluctant to climb the snow mountain, Grandma still insist on the mountain.

Even if on Christmas and New year's day, Grandma didn't rest at home, but hobbled up the snow mountain early in the morning.

"Walk on the snow cliff, is the nearest place to heaven. But I prefer to adopt more adventure, to collect more tulip Queen golden roses, iceberg white roses and sakura blood red roses. Because only in this way can we get more money. My angel Oris, only get more money, you can eat more delicious food and buy more exquisite music scores."

Grandma used to say so.

Then Oris cried over the tree, fell red whale goldfish and sakura rain all over sky.

For Oris's artistic tragedy, 63 years old Grandma blossoms a glorious hope of heaven flowers with her selfless sacred love and the sanctity of the summer sakura power.

"Grandma, don't go, okay...You don't go...Please, Grandma...I beg you, don't leave me alone...Don't leave me alone......"

"Grandma won't leave...Grandma will not leave you alone......"

On the hospital bed, Grandma had no narcissus power to speak, she was so weak but tried her best to hold Oris's kitten paw.

Grandma's smiling face bloomed with one after another pink cherry angel roses, then a difficult but happy sigh was in her throat.

Relatives discussed the accident and court with joy and eloquence. When they discussed the how to divide the claims of soul reapers, they looked like the Sahara crocodile was grabbing a little watermelon.

But Oris felt that the sigh of Grandma was particularly stinging and icy.

Three days later, after trampled and kicked by demons at school, Oris hastened to climb up, clothes footprints and snow are too late to shoot, he ran as a cat to the hospital to ask aunt, "Grandma...Is Grandma still here...?"

"Grandma...She's gone......"

So Oris hid in the icy sea of aurora, sobbing out the meteor rain, crying out the mermaid whale tears.

Once I love sakura milk, and my Grandma often bought it for me. In fact, I have been tired of drinking it, but Grandma had always insisted on buying it for me.

The last time I saw Grandma, she talked about the most, is she couldn't cook for me, couldn't buy music scores and sakura milk for me.

Grandma! I love you! I love you forever!

Forever, forever......

Forever!!! Forever!!!

On the way home, Oris saw faintly Grandma's quivering weak holy deer silhouette in the heavy snow of daisies.

He saw Grandma just to collect more bottles, just to buy him music scores and good food, so carry an angel lamp to cross the road.

Unfortunately, since then, He would never eat Grandma made chive cod and windmill bread.

Couldn't eat forever!

Forever!!!

"I didn't mean to bump into you! I didn't mean it!"

There was a weak wronged injured deer's whining from roadside.

An old woman was shouted by a fat orang woman with magnificent scarlet.

"Do you believe I can plug your mouth with husky shit!!! You red boar dick!!! fuck your mother!!! You're dressed dirtier than a red boar rolling over the Nile, how dare you fucking bump me!!!??? How can you fucking afford my ferret coat!!!???"

Oris was curious as Scotland's cat all over the world, what education would their daughter and son be received by this rich and powerful ostrich Titan python bastard.

He ran over and looked up at the woman, "Do you believe I'll put a big rhino in your mouth and choke you to die! You chimpanzee littering with dung all over the world!!! How could you say that? Granny didn't mean to bump into you!!!"

The old granny sobbed, "I'm a cleaner, usually pick up some bottles to sell money and buy some good food for my granddaughter. My granddaughter is deaf and dumb, she can only hear a little bit of music, her mom and dad abandoned her alone, My granddaughter very wants to learn violin now, so I'm saving money to buy a good violin and music for her. I wanna pick up some more bottles to help my granddaughter achieve this dream. As long as I earn more money, so my granddaughter will not be bullied at school, what others can eat, I really hope she can eat too. Just now I squatted down to pick up the bottle, when I got up, I bumped into this lady. Would you help me beg the pardon from this lady? Don't let her anger, I really thank you!"

This was another tragic family which is deplorably struggling for art.

"She is not intentional!!!" Oris's sun tears were burning his eyes.

The fat baboon woman is really not letting this go, "Fuck you! A cleaner picks bottles! She must bump into me? She saw a dirty bottle is anxious like a husky that couldn't eat fire dragon shit for hundreds of years!!!"

When the woman said so, Oris burst into meteor tears!

"You can't say that about her! I think that you are a husky fire shit! No! You are a lump of Alaska ice shit!!! Smelly and cold-blooded!!! Granny, she is a working people! She is for her little granddaughter can eat well, good at school without grievance! She is for her little granddaughter can play the violin happily just so hard!!! You can't say that to her!!! You can't!!! You can't say that to her!!! Woowoowoowoowoo... You can't!!!"

Oris was out of breath with sakura tears.

"I'll give her three or four for her tattered dress! I am so mad! Do you fucking know?"

"She didn't mean it! She didn't mean it! She didn't mean to bump into you! She just is a working people!!! Woowoowoowoo...It's because she's hard to pick up bottles there, so she wants you to understand her! I hope you understand her! She didn't mean to bump into you!!!"

Oris was incoherent.

"She bumped into me just now! You know what? She spilled all the dirty water on me!"

"That's because she's here! I saw her standing here just now! She turned her back on you, so she didn't see you! She didn't really mean it!!! Please forgive her! Please! Please!! Please!!!"

The woman was speechless.

What Oris said seemed to make the woman who swallowed the ostrich suddenly recognized his own snake tooth fault.

A kind people often wakens the purest kindness of others.

The woman squatted down and wiped Oris's glowing tears, she stroked his Siberia forest kitten shoulder, "OK, honey, angel, don't cry, I know I'm wrong! Don't cry..."

But his blue cat eyes are still tearing the meteor rain and sunshine.

Granny cried, too.

"Don't cry! Don't cry!" She ran over and crouched down, hugged Oris and said, "Thank you! Don't cry! Thank you! My angel, thank you! I don't want you to get hurt for me! Oh, Thank you! My angel, you are so kind!"

But how could Oris's sun tears stop?

Granny gently wiped away his sunflower tears, "Don't cry! Grandma love you so much! Grandma love you so mach! Don't cry! Thank you! I'm so sorry, for Grandma, you suffered so much wronging!"

At the moment, granny's face and tears are more clear and holy in the heavy snow.

"Not at all!" Oris's sakura tears and cat eyes suddenly blooming daffodils sea and pure warm smile.

"Even if I am wronged, I don't let you be bullied or insulted! Grandma, I am not afraid of being wronged!!!"

"Thank you! Could you tell Grandma why you did that?"

"Because I sympathize with you!"

Oris cried again.

"Because my Papa and Grandma used to pick up bottles in garbage and sold them. In a heavy snow day, my Grandma just died in a traffic accident because she in order to pick up bottles to buy me good food and music scores."

Oris wiped the lily queen pink flower sea tears.

"I used pick up with them many days, so I know the pain, so I'm not sympathizing with you! I just...But...Because when I was young, my Papa and Mama told me we don't have money so we picked up those things, because we are poor, so I just......"

Choking with sakura tears.

"Well, I'm poor, my work is a common cleaner. Others scolded me, I can bear it."

"It shouldn't be this! Grandma! Saw Grandma so hard, I really felt heart ache! Grandma, I don't want you to be wronged! I don't want you to be bullied!"

"Angel, you are so kind! Grandma's clothes are dirty, or Grandma really wanna hug you. Little angel, you are so kind!"

"Not dirty! Not dirty!"

Then he hugged Grandma.

"Grandma, you are not dirty at all!"

"Thank you! Thank you for being so nice to Grandma!"

"Grandma, you're not dirty at all! You are really kind and beautiful!"

The old granny and the kid embrace each other, crying loudly, and wiping their sunshine tears each other.

"Grandma, you are working there so hard, so I'm sure Grandma never bumped her on purpose! Absolutely! Grandma' clothes are dirty, but Grandma, you are so kind and beautiful in my eyes!"

"My little angel, thank you! Grandma love you!"

"I used to pick up the bottles with my Grandma. As soon as we saw the bottles, we would go up and pick it up, so I can understand granny's special hard mood. Saw Grandma pay so much for your granddaughter, I do not think Grandma dirty! And Grandma is not dirty! Grandma is very kind, very beautiful, very clean!"

"Grandma thank you! My granddaughter loves the violin, but the violin and tuition are so expensive. I have to pick up more bottles and earn more money to afford it. For my granddaughter to be happy, Grandma no matter how hard it is! I believe your grandmother in heaven must know my feelings."

"Well, If there's any chance, I'll teach your granddaughter the violin free of charge! Free! But I will do my best! I must teach her with my best!!!"

"Thank you, my angel! My clever poor little granddaughter often tell me with sign language, if she learned the violin, she must play the most luxuriant melody for me. I am looking forward to one day, I will alive to hear my granddaughter with her violin melody......"

Oris cried again!

Yes, Grandma had never heard of my seriously playing of the piano and violin, but in a hurry to the far heaven.

Oris was seeing Grandma' sunshine again, the holy deer figure of Grandma that picking iceberg roses and sakura blood roses.

Oris was seeing Grandma' sunshine again, she was cooking chive cod and windmill bread for Oris, because they were Oris's favorite foods.

Oris was seeing Grandma's holy light again, the holy figure of Grandma that picking up the bottle in the sakura snow and then bought Oris sakura milk and beautiful music score.

The pathos of heavy snow was so beautiful as flowering sakura!
The pathos of flowering sakura was so beautiful in the heavy snow!
My dear Grandma, where are you......
Grandma, where are you......
If I call a "Grandma" still could get your response, then how happy I should be......
How happy I should be......
How happy I should be!!!

From then on, Oris ate at aunt's home. Every day, Oris endured a vulture sarcastic and shark teeth ironic vulture because of freeloading.

After dinner, he went back to his own empty cold home, writes homework, washes clothes.

Then he played the flower fairy Canon with the phoenix violin and piano.

Out of the melody, thousands of bright little angel was flying and dancing!
Hymn lights up the night!
Holy light shines all over the world!
Only music! Only art! Can save his wounded soul!
Only music! Only art! Can save his miserable fate!
Yes! Save!

Every time a splendid melody flies, he can hear the singing of nature's rescue! With the wings of melody shine, he flies to the beautiful world of the great artistic soul!

There are pure mirror lakes!

There are many great arts!

There are the glorious smiles of the flowering sun!

There are elegant singing of the sacred sunshine!

There are the holy light and brilliance dreams!

There is a strong refuge of the Art Sages!

There is the light of salvation of the Art Fairy!

Some people say, "I have never seen the beautiful and holy Art Fairy. And I have never heard the Art Fairy's hymn."

In fact, the Art Fairy has been watching over us.

She loves each of us.

She cares for each of us.

She watches each move of us, each sorrows and joys of us, each misfortune and happiness of everyone.

But only those who are kind, who have dreams of loving life, loving art, can hear the Art Fairy's holy song!

Only those who are for art, for the happiness of all creatures, burning own lives and dedicate to the world, can deserve Art Fairy's powerful asylum, can earn Art Fairy's glorious rescue!

Art Fairy loves each of us forever!

She is with us forever!

Forever! Forever! Forever!

Listen......

Chapter 4

MIRROR LAKE AND FLOWER SEA

*T*hree thousand years ago, butterfly forest, side of the mirror lake.

A long-haired boy that wearing a snow long dress was walking in the fairy flower sea, a exquisite lyre in his hands flowing the brilliant melody.

A florid butterfly was gyrating and dancing with the melody.

The butterfly's wings shined with gorgeous blue blaze, fantastic beauty like a beautiful dream.

This butterfly, was the daughter of forest.

The flowers, glasses, trees and little animals called her Flora with fairy language.

Flora loved music.

When dancing, the ice blue blaze on her wings were rippling, just like the seven shining golden strings in boy's hands.

When met favorite music, Flora would dance with the melody.

And this beautiful boy on the side of mirror lake, could play the most beautiful melody in the world!

However, his music was also the melody of death!

Every time the melody of beautiful boy bloomed as wind fairies, then all the flowers around were falling, all the grasses around were withering, all the trees were wilting......

So, Narcissus was his name given by gods. He was the son of moon fairy, and his father was the god of poetry and music.

Narcissus's favorite thing was playing his lyre. So, wherever he went, it's full of desolation!

This beautiful deep art forest still didn't wither rapidly, just thanked to the blooming magic of Flora, the daughter of art forest.

Every time Flora was dancing gracefully, all the falling flowers would come back to lives, all the grasses would come back to youth, all the dead trees would bloom the brilliant flowers!

Even a hard cold marble column, also could bloom ten millions bright snow roses with sakura heart.

And Flora was deeply fascinated by Narcissus's gorgeous melody, so she forever followed him, looked at his pure glittery eyes, danced elegantly.

He was falling the flowers.

She was blooming the flowers.

Indefatigable.

Never stopped!

Although all the trees in forest were afraid of Narcissus, all the flowers disliked Narcissus, and all the little animals hated Narcissus, but every young girl who had seen him would love him deeply, and every girl who had heard his music would wanna have him.

Because, besides the artistic talent, this beautiful boy who named Narcissus, also had a comely gorgeous face just as a narcissus sea.

A pair of pure eyes like butterfly orchids, so every girl who stared at him could hardly move her view.

And his bright red lips like sakura in sunset, were more vivid than Venus morpho dancing in the summer sunshine, and softer than the narcissus immersed in the dragon's blood.

Every girl who saw him couldn't help falling in love with him!

Of course!

Flora, daughter of the art forest, following Narcissus and dancing elegantly every day, also loved him silently......

The beautiful boy who named Narcissus, had the most gorgeous and attractive face in the fairy world, also had the most florid and touching art skill in the fairy world.

But nature is fair.

She also brought a terrible curse to Narcissus.

Although the melody of Narcissus's lyre was extremely magnificent, it's also the melody of withering, the melody of blooding, the melody of dying.

Thus, except all the infatuated girls, the boy named Narcissus was unanimously opposed by all the flowers, grasses, trees and little animals in the forest!

When walking, tripped by snow jade wistaria.

When jumped off ice rock, hit by the ice rock and injured knee.

Picked up the iceberg roses, stabbed by thorns.

Drinking water by the mirror lake, just slapped by the tail of a flame carp.

Similar things couldn't avoid every day.

If it wasn't Flora's helping and shielding, Narcissus had been dead in the forest! Flying like blood petals! And no bones!

But nature is always fair!

Only when Narcissus falls in love river, the curse of death melody can be melted.

But nature is so fair that she won't let Narcissus fall in love easily!

Narcissus had a gorgeous face, but he was dismissive of all the beautiful girls! No matter how those girls giggled and flirted to attract the attention of Narcissus's moon eyes, he was so indifferent and ignored them.

Narcissus only loves the girl who has the most beautiful singing! Narcissus only loves the girl who understands his music!

But those girls who loved him were ignorant of music and art at all! So Narcissus was blind to them.

In this world, only the girl who has the most beautiful singing can understand the fairy melody of Narcissus.

"Such the girl, I have never met. Maybe she's not born yet!"

While playing the lyre, Narcissus smiled and self-talked.

"This butterfly dancing on my shoulders every day and never tired can understand my music, her dance always fits my melody, I'm so happy! But it's a pity, she just is a butterfly! How good it is if she can become a beautiful girl! How I long to fall in love! Then my music will turn from the cold ice and snow to the sunshine and spring! The world will no longer wither, thousands of trees will bloom brilliantly......"

Alas! Narcissus sighed, went on playing the death melody of withering flowers.

And the beauteous ice blue fairy butterfly, still dancing with the flowers blooming!

Flowers Bloomed and fell.

Flowers fell and bloomed.

Day after day.

Never ceased and rested!

One summer morning sunrise with soft wind and beautiful cloud, Narcissus was playing his death melody with scampering, and Flora still was behind blooming the flower sea.

But a tragedy had happened!

A gorgeous blue jacaranda tree just withered by Narcissus's melody, and before Flora revived her, a huge wilting branch fell heavily!

A terrible scream!

Just saw a tender snow deer under the tree fell in blood lake.

"Ah!!!" Narcissus covered his mouth and scream, burst into tears in a flash! He threw out the lyre and ran away!

Flora didn't catch up. Because she found that the place Narcissus's tears poured over, withered flowers and grasses had come back to lives!

That's the first time Narcissus shed tears.

The tears of kindness and mercy!

But looked back and saw that tender little snow deer with dropping blood, Flora couldn't help dropping a butterfly's sunshine tear......

The miracle happened!

The butterfly's sunshine tear dropped into the wound of little dear, the wound healed quickly! Even just one scaur you couldn't find!

Soon, the little snow deer jumped up! As usual, she went to eat leaves and run. That withered jacaranda tree also returned to bloom miraculously! The pure blue flowers bloomed full of tree in a flash!

Flora also bloomed a comforting smile.

She turned her head.

Reached out a hand.

Wanted to call back Narcissus.

But suddenly found, her pure feet had stepped into the soft daisy sea......

Unbelievable......
I become a girl!

A soft breeze suddenly sprang up behind.

Turned around, the sky poured out the golden gorgeous dazzling light, Flora covered her eyelids with hand, smiled and looked at the fairy coming slowly from brilliant clouds.

Flora had never seen such a beautiful fairy!

Her colorful long hair just like the waterfall of bellflowers that woven by the sunshine in summer!

Her eyes were fantastic than the blue parrot tulips, brighter than the Andromeda stars frozen in glaciers.

The pure gorgeous melody was flying all over the sky, that's the singing in flower sea blooming from the fairy's sakura lips!

Those kind people who love art,
you don't be sad!
Merciful Art Fairy will shield you forever!

Those persistent people who burn the life for art,
you don't despair!
The great art pioneers and art saints will shelter you forever!

Those devoted people who fully suffer the misery for art,
you don't cry!
Nature has sent me to save you!

I am the Art Fairy Florithena!
I am with you forever!
Forever! Forever! Forever!

Art Fairy Florithena fell lightly in front of the girl, a merciful pure smile bloomed on Florithena's gorgeous face.

Flora was still bewildered by suddenly changing from a butterfly to a girl.

She asked with devout eyes, "Merciful Florithena, why did I become a girl?"

"Kind daughter of art forest, because you will save this holy forest."

"Me? Save?"

"Yes." Florithena's eyes were serious.

"Why me?" Flora's big eyes that became from butterfly orchids were twinkling as butterflies, dancing as flying orchids.

"Because all the girls in this world, only you love art, only you devote the heart and soul to art. All the girls in this world, only you can understand Narcissus's music. Only you, can stop Narcissus from destroying this holy art forest!"

"Oh......"

Flora looked at the brilliant moon lyre that thrown away in the narcissus sea, nodded thoughtfully.

"But Narcissus will only fall in love with the girl who has the most beautiful singing voice in the whole world." Florithena said, "So, I turned you into a real girl and blessed the most beautiful singing voice to you. Thus, Narcissus will fall in love with you, the death curse on his lyre will fall in mirror lake with wind, then disappear just as falling sakura petals."

"So......" Flora's eyes were pious, "What's the price of exchange?"

"Nature is fair forever. All the excellence and beauty in the world need to pay for equal price. Nature gives you the most beautiful voice, and only you sing every day can you retain the beauty of singing, can you keep the most ultimate beauty! Kind daughter of forest, will you?"

"Yes!" Flora's eyes were full of hot tears, she nodded desperately, "As long as I can save this holy art forest, as long as I can let Narcissus fall in love with me, even the most brutal price of this world, I'm still willing to pay! I'm willing to sacrifice! I'm willing!!!"

Seeing the girl so firm, Florithena couldn't help blooming a holy, merciful, and pure smile.

"Who's that? Why is my lyre's melody? Why her voice is so beautiful? Why her melody can bloom full of trees, and blossom flowers all over the ground?"

That song was not a human language.

That song seemed to be the prayer of fairy.

That song seemed to be the holy light of heaven!

Narcissus couldn't discern the content of that song, but he could deeply appreciate the kindness and great dedication pouring from the song.

It's the song of salvation that all the creatures of nature can touch and understand.

Narcissus came near the lakeside and discovered that it's a radiant and enchanting girl! Narcissus looking at the girl and forget all flower seas and fairies all over the world!

He never looked straight at such a beautiful girl ever before!

And never heard such gorgeous singing!

The bright sunshine in Narcissus's big pure eyes had already told the world, he, already deeply fell in love with her!

When heard the fairy high singing of the girl, Narcissus had already palpitated with love! In the moment of seeing the girl, he had already fallen into love with her!

Suddenly, a little snow deer scampered and came in an elegant posture, then leaned against Narcissus's arm. She lovingly kissed Narcissus's hand, gently sniffed his fingers, so close that almost magic.

"This......This is the little snow deer killed by my death melody? So......So you didn't die? You didn't die! Really great!"

Narcissus squatted down, hugged the little snow deer's neck and smiling with tears, all over the heart filled with gratitude warm stream.

"Really great......Really great!!!"

At this time, a singing flew from the lakeside.

Narcissus raised his head.

It's just ten sakura trees between her and him.

That little snow deer ran to the girl whose face blooming pink sakura, she gently touching the deer's downy head and soft ears, and the deer snuggled comfortably at her waist.

"You are the forest goddess?" Narcissus's face was full of excitement.

Flora was silent, just bloomed a saintly smile.

"Your singing is really gorgeous! Even the nightingale fairy who has the best singing talent can't compare with you!"

The girl smiled fairily, gave the lyre back to Narcissus.

Narcissus took the lyre, blinked and said, "Oh! But in this world, no one can play the lyre better than me! My art talent is a godsend! No one in the world can compare with me! Not even you!"

Then, Narcissus's proud chin poked into Lyra star.

Flora just smiled and looked at him, then nodded.

A stream of sakura blossoms and helpless flowed from her smile.

Narcissus never knew, what a terrible price Flora paid for the contract of Art Fairy!

"Kind daughter of art forest, now I give you the most beautiful voice of this world, then Narcissus will be infatuated with you and dazzled by you! But in exchange, nature will take your language."

"Take my language?"

"All the beauty and excellence has to pay equal price. From then on, you can't speak, you can only sing the most beautiful fairy songs. And you must remove Narcissus's death curse, fall in love with him, then save this holy art forest. Kind daughter of forest, would you do it?"

"I'm willing! As long as I can save my forest mother, as long as I can remove Narcissus's death curse, anything I'm willing to do!!!"

Flora didn't hesitate!

Looking at the girl's firm beautiful face with sunshine tears, Art Fairy Florithena was suddenly touched by the kindness and selflessness of the girl.

Florithena gave the girl a brilliant contract woven by tulip fairies.

"This is our contract. If someday you feel sad, burn this golden contract! So you can change back to the butterfly, still as carefree as ever, happy day by day as ever."

"Just burn the contract?"

"Yes, but not with fire." Florithena said, "This contract, only your tears can melt it. You must remember, only sad tears can burn this contract, and just one drop."

"What if the tears of happiness?"

"The tears of happiness would only bloom pink tulip sakura on the contract."

"Well!" Flora nodded firmly.

At this moment, Narcissus was looking at Flora lovingly, he reached out his hand and said, "Beautiful forest fairy, would you like to be with me? I really love you!"

Flora smiled. Smiled more sweetly than the colorful freesia.

She nodded.

Then Narcissus took Flora in his arms and kissed her!

When kissing, Flora shed a drop of tears from her eye. That's the sunshine tear of happiness.

The flower fairy beautiful boy that all the girls were longing, he couldn't help falling in love with the daughter of forest!

Flora was so happy! So happy that almost gone back to the butterfly and melt into Narcissus's soft glowing kissing......

Flowering tear quietly shed as butterfly, a pure tulip-sakura was quietly blooming on the brilliant contract that woven by sun fairies.

Narcissus and Flora, just be together!

After fell in sunshine love river, Narcissus's curse really flew away with wind as sakura petals!

Every time his lyre bloomed melody, the light of youthfulness just fell from the sky like sakura rain! The whole world instantly flowered everywhere! Thousands trees were blooming brilliantly!

Every time his music sounded, grasses no longer withered! Flowers no longer fell! Everything became bright and beautiful!

Every day, Narcissus and Flora would walk on the flower sea of lakeside, played with the little squirrels, little snow rabbits, and little flower deer, laughing and running, really enjoyable.

When tired, Narcissus and Flora nestled in the lily sea.

He played the lyre, she sang the song. The wind fairies and tree fairies were silent. The thousands of birds were devout. Only gorgeous melody flying in the sunshine sky!

All the creatures in the forest stopped flying and running, they perched on the flowers, leaves and branches, listening silently to the most beautiful and touching melody in the world!

In such a beautiful art, all the creatures in the world would forget all the worries, forget all the sorrows, forget all the pains.

Forget all the misery and suffering!

Only warmth and happiness permeated the body and soul!

Only the beauty and sacredness suffused mirror lake and flower sea!

Of course, this holy forest had always been coveted by evils and demons.

Every grass and every tree all contained the great power of nature, even just eat one petal of tulip-sakura tree in the art forest, also could make ice fire dragon's wings bigger and more powerful, make his ice and fire fiercer and more terrifying, also could make wizard's magic more destructive, make the monsters' fangs harder and longer, make the demon's sickle longer and sharper.

And the brilliant crystal diamond mountain in the forest, was also deeply secretly desired by the greedy demons.

A dismal cold ice morning in early spring, a chilling twinkle flashed!

A thick pine fell heavily!

At the same time, there was a squirrel head fell with blood stream flowing, her tail still hung on the branch, and half of her body was swaying in the cold wind.

At this time, a ray of golden soul flew from the little squirrel's neck that dripping with blood, soon tucked into a dark bag by a demon.

Little birds and little animals in the art forest had never seen such a horrible demon! His head was a rotten skull, and there was still a bloody skin on his face. Two snot green eyes embedded in the bone snail, burning the thrilling snot green fire.

The demon named Acheron, he came from the distant devil forest, he held a huge sickle, everywhere he went, all living creatures were in blood and fire, blood fog were all over the sky!

"I'm gonna reap all the souls in this forest! I will reap the souls of Flora and Narcissus! So I can have the most beautiful voice and the most beautiful music of this world! And then play the dirty music to pollute all the souls! I wanna pollute all the pure souls all over the world! I wanna pollute the holy lands all over the world!"

Acheron waving his sickle, five little snow rabbits' rose blood of their heads instantly incarnadined a resplendent golden tulip sea.

So, Acheron cruelly plundered five pure bud souls again.

As Acheron grinning evilly, suddenly! A full-blown waterfall-sakura tree rained a splendid holy chant.

All the demons must be punished!
All the dirty souls must be purified!

Acheron hadn't looked up, but was kneeling at the five little snow rabbits' corpses. Because the song just sounded, Acheron's bloody leg flowered thousands of sakura sunset crimson fire lilies, snow pure moon narcissus, and sunshine gorgeous butterfly orchids.

When Narcissus's lyre sounded, hundreds of flower vines breaking out from the earth, climbed along the Acheron's dirty legs, twined his head, until Acheron turned into a heap of golden dust in desperate scream.

The wind was quiet. The trees were silent.

Narcissus's melody gradually flew away as butterflies, Flora's singing also fell as sakura.

And on that heap of golden dust, there had been blooming millions of fantastic flowers.

The squirrel and five snow rabbits that been beheaded by Acheron, had also connected their bodies, then jumping and running with rebirths.

The art forest that polluted and withered by Acheron had flourished again. There was still a fairyland! Thousands of trees were still blooming brilliantly!

So, Narcissus and Flora hand in hand, side by side, dancing, running, frolicking with little animals in the forest, really enjoyable.

Just like every year and every day in the past.

Every spring and summer. Every autumn and winter.

Every sunrise and sunset.

Midsummer night, firefly fairies dancing on the Milky Way's reflection of the mirror lake, the moonshine like crystal waves in lake, and the moon glistening in the dark sky. Where stars gathered, just like blooming bright tulip-sakura seas one after another.

In such a peaceful night, the forest should have been immersed in a sweet sea of dreams, but......

The calm lake was suddenly broken by a little snow deer who's escaping!

The moonshine was also broken into a stream of sakura petals. The panic deer's crying and screaming woke up all kind creatures of this forest!

The succubae had appeared at the lakeside. She named Sirena.

All the little animals in flower sea had fled!

Sirena dressed in silver moonlight dress, except two long pointed ears, except the evil spirits light pervaded all the body, in fact, she wasn't very different from human beings.

However, Sirena's enchanting face, would make all men watcher her possessed by ghosts. Even if lightly glance her just one eye, also could love her until death! Those men who loved Sirena were searching the women who had beautiful voice every day for her.

After Sirena flayed and swallowed them alive, her voice would become more beautiful, so that all the men of this world were entranced for her! Obsessed and possessed by ghosts for her!

Of course, conceited cruel cold enchanting Sirena, also had a sudden moment of heart attack.

Except the beautiful boy Narcissus, was there anyone who could make vicious Sirena thirst for? But Sirena's voice still wasn't beautiful enough, so Narcissus was sneeringly dismissive of her!

It's said that a girl who had the most beautiful voice in this world was born in this holy pure art forest, and she fell in love with Narcissus! This really exploded Sirena's blood sucking eyes!!!

The jealousy fire was jumping and spurting crazily!

Shrill screaming!

Wailing like ghosts and howling like wolves!

Crying amuck! Insanely!

Along the way, Sirena killed every woman she saw, ate them no residue left in the bones, then she ripped their faces into pieces of dark elves!

Now, Sirena had stepped in the mirror lake.

But she didn't sink!

Sirena's butterfly steps were light, every place she stepped on only the shallow ripples rippled in the moonlight, even the slightest moon shadow in lake wasn't disturbed.

But Sirena's voice was so horrible!

"I must catch that ugly Flora! I must snap her neck brutally! I have to dig her dirty eyes that stared at Narcissus obsessively every day! I'm gonna eat Flora's body even without one drop of blood! I'll take the rock and smash Flora's bones one after another! Amuck! Insanely! Then use her bones to refine art magic and hammer-harden my voice!!!"

The little animals all covered ears in horror and hid in bushes and tree holes. Sirena's voice was so terrible! So harsh! So horrible! So raucous! No wonder she always longed to temper her voice to be beautiful.

At this moment, Flora was smilling on a waterfall-sakura tree at the other side of mirror lake, mercifully and sympathetically looking at the Sirena.

As soon as saw Flora's smilling, Sirena went mad in a flash! In Sirena's eyes, Flora's merciful and sympathetic smile was full of pride and complacency! Full of triumphant! Full of contempt and disdain!

"Ah!!!!!!"

Sirena screamed! Her hands gathered two blood red fire, then crazily rushing to Flora across the lake! On the waterfall-sakura tree, Flora's legs was swinging gracefully in the air. Saw Sirena went mad, Flora just gently rose her mouth.

As Sirena rushed into the middle of lake and the bloody fireball in her hands grew larger and larger, but the sakura tree rained thousands of holy flowering prayer songs!

All the hatred in the world must sink into lake!
All the envy of the world must be purified!

Resplendent fluttered like butterflies, thirty-three flame carps with bizarre splendor leapt out of the mirror lake, firmly snapped Sirena's feet, wrists and dress, dragged her into the bottom of mirror lake.

It's too late to fight, it's too late to scream, Sirena just disappeared with the pure light of flame carps in the darkness of lake.

On the sakura tree in night, Flora looked at the tranquil lake and moonshine, eyes flowing the merciful holy light, mouth shining a kind smile, and then sank into the Milky Way of dream.

In the days after, every time Narcissus brilliantly played the lyre in the starry night, there was a enchanting little carp emerged from the mirror lake.

She was full of silver moonlight, spat bubbles while swaying gently tail, listening thirstily to the music of Narcissus.

See......

Narcissus's gorgeous figure, was reflected limpidly in the carp's eyes that bright as plenilune......

So beautiful pathos, but so heartbreaking......

This forest Flora lived had a range of mountains, every mountain was covered with diamonds, gemstones, aquamarines and gold. Every peaks were composed of pure diamonds, looked far away, just bright like glacier and snow that shined by the morning sunlight.

In the flowers under verdant trees, also decorated with sparkling gold and shining gemstones. When the sun shined, every mountain's light were gorgeous than the Milky Way and hundred suns, resplendent than ten million crowns with thousands of jewels!

So, every year, there was a lot of rapacious robbers came to plunder the wealth, but before stepping into this holy forest, they were just burned to ashes by the sunlight refracted from the diamond peaks.

Because every rapacious heart all glowed the cold dark light, it would attract all the light to the greedy man, and when the burning sunlights refracted by the hundreds of diamond peaks in this forest were together, it was enough to melt a marble castle into sakura petals and star dust just in one twinkling!

Once there was a fancy knight, he wore the toughest gold nail in this world, thought that he could steal the gold and precious in this forest at night, but when he went through some trees and exposed in the moonlight, seven diamond peaks burst and rayed in one flash!

From the heart, until the bright silver sword and golden armor of the knight, all melted into lava!

With the shrill screaming, this knight was purified by fire and holy light! Even his molten golden armor, also disappeared with the clear sakura creek in depths of the forest.

After the knight died, no more mammonist or greedy man was so crazy enough that dare close to this holy land.

The man who is addicted to wealth always likes fancying himself clever.

Just like this conceited knight, perhaps he would think he died in the burning moonshine, but he would never understand that the moonshine is also the sunshine in the night sky.

And the sunshine is always with us.

The evil people who covet wealth and wish to defile the art holy land, they will never understand that the holy pure art forest is sheltered by the great and merciful nature forever.

The people who covet wealth will never understand that how strong nature is, in front of the forces of nature, how small and fragile these ugly buffoons are! How fragile and small!

Yes!

Really small! Really fragile!

But desire and greed also have powerful forces of self-destruction.

A rainy day in cold autumn, a lone-haired wizard stepped into this holy art forest.

He named Styx.

He had evil thoughts in heart, but he didn't be burned into ashes in the fierce light.

When the cold rains came, it was the weakest of the sunshine.

And Styx also held a mirror shield, he reflected all the conflagrant condensed sunlight into all directions.

But Styx wasn't assured. Just saw he was chanting curses, and his body was covered with full mirror crystal! Even his eyes also turned into aplysia rubies!

So he was unharmed.

Except being thirsty for wealth, Styx still had greater ambitions.

"I'll make Narcissus and Flora be slaves under my feet! I'll rule this forest with the power of their music and singing! I wanna be the richest king in this world! I wanna be the most powerful emperor in this world! I want all creatures of nature to die for me! I want them to fight with gold swords and shields! As long as Narcissus plays the military music! As long as Flora sings the fighting song! All creatures will be the strongest and fiercest army in the whole world! And I! Ha ha! I'll be the richest and most powerful emperor in this world! The greatest emperor ever! Ahahahahahahahah!!!"

Styx laughing loudly and rushed into the forest!

Because the mirror crystal of his whole body reflected the dazzling aurora, all the little animals couldn't see him directly, they all were frightened into the caves and on the trees, watching Styx in terror.

But the hearts and souls of little animals were immaculate, so they were not burned by light.

A little rabbit quietly whispered in a little chipmunk's ear, "I heard that Styx had used crystal to freeze the hands and feet of all the living creatures in a city, and then controlled them to fight for him, killed people, built palaces, made sakura cheeses, blueberry jam, grilled ocean bread. The most terrible thing is to wash his dirty cloth! And even...... wash his stinky socks!!!"

"Wow!!!!!!"

The little animals were terrified and hold tightly together!

"Really awful! Really disgusting!!!"

Obviously! No one wanted to be Styx's slave and wash his smelly socks every day......

At the moment, everyone was worried about Narcissus and Flora! So they followed behind Styx to see what he wanted!

"Looking at this exquisite face, I think I've found the fool I'm looking for!"

Looking at Narcissus on the lakeside of mirror lake, glowing crystal Styx raised his hands and prepared to release the curse.

"Your face is beautiful, but it doesn't bring great power and wealth. What I want is your music and art. Do you understand?"

Narcissus smiled like soft feathers and said like sakura, "Don't fight. Lovely little animals will be terrified."

Narcissus still was smiling, smiling mysteriously and kindly.

"Follow me!" Narcissus just smiled, "I take you to see the diamond mountain, if you love it, dig it away! I won't stop you."

"Don't think about playing any tricks!"

The crystal chains made by Styx's magic was grinning and waving claws.

"Otherwise, I can put you in the crystal cage at any moment so that you can't eat or drink but play the lyre all day! Then control the little animals to dig diamonds and gold for me! I'm gonna build a diamond palace!

An altar made of colorful jewels! I'm gonna be the most luxurious emperor in the history of the world! And you? Narcissus! You are a big idiot who just can play the lyre! You will be in my crystal cage for your stupid art!!!"

The crystal eyes of Styx were spouting the thirsty fire that the characteristic of mammonist or greedy man.

But Narcissus just smiled, then turned around and walked towards the nearest diamond mountain.

Styx followed behind, keeping an alert distance.

The mountain road was steep and rugged, if without the guidance of Narcissus, Styx couldn't find the way up the mountain. Turned into a crystal body would resist the burning of the holy light, but Styx also temporarily lost his ability to fly.

If he went back to human body, he can sit on the owl demon and flew directly up the mountain top, but a moment he backed into human, he would also fly off as sakura petals in the burning holy light.

So he could only follow Narcissus step by step.

Along the way, so much golds and colorful jewels big as rocks were all around, Styx was dizzying that almost blinded!

He cut cut here, dug dug there, he filled the whole body with gold and jewels, so heavy that every three steps he needed to stop and breath.

Finally arrived at the top!

The diamond mountain top near the sight were much bigger than looked at the foot of the mountain! At least big as thirty castles! And autumn rain made diamond mountain looked more gorgeous!

Styx completely forgot all the fatigue! He ran mad at the huge diamond peak! The gold and jewels on his body spilled all the way!

"Just this diamond mountain is enough for me to build thirty castles! Ahahahahaha!!!"

In the horrible laughter, Styx stretched his crystal hands to the diamond mountain, dreamed to dig a large diamond and comforted his greedy dark vulturine heart.

But surprisingly, when Styx's hands mercilessly hit hard diamond mountain......

"Pa la!"

His crystal hands in one instant broken into a sakura petals creek!

"It's over! I suddenly remembered! Diamond is the hardest thing in the world! Oh! No! Narcissus you big liar! I must cut your head! Break your hands! You'll never play the lyre again!"

But Narcissus had disappeared without one trace.

At this time, five little snow rabbits and five little squirrels together lifted a large piece of gold, then threw to Styx hard!

"Pa la!"

Styx's two crystal legs was smashed!

As he wanted to change back to the human and escape, but on the peak of diamond mountain, Narcissus's music sounded grazioso.

Then gorgeous sunshine poured all over the world!

Holy light and flower rain!

And Styx's body had melted half.

Then, he was desperate! He gave up!

He no longer struggled, no longer fought, just waiting for death......

At this time, the diamond mountain suddenly opened a gap, a sacred force sucked Styx's crystal body and crystal fragments of his hands and feet! And then the gap closed in a flash!

In the huge diamond seal, Styx's body miraculously returned to perfection! Just forever sealed in the diamond mountain.

The crystal wizard so reckless with greed, just sank into the dream of flower sea. He would always go on sleeping.

Spring and starry sky in summer. Hundreds and thousands of years.

The little squirrels and the little rabbits took a long breath and wiped their sweat on their forehead. Just now, that big piece of gold took their great efforts to lift it up the mountain!

They are really great! Right!?

Yes!

In fact, nature didn't wanna hurt the ambitious creatures just like this wizard. But! Nature will never tolerate evil marauders run amuck!

Those careerist who wanna loot nature into an empty field, but ultimately looted everything by nature! Even if you dream to swallow everything of nature, nature will eventually devour your everything!

This stupid and pathetic wizard, let's keep him sleeping with the diamond that he crazily craved forever!

To be in harmony with nature, might be his best ending!

And Narcissus, he still snuggled with Flora at the lakeside, playing the lyre and singing with little animals, everything was really carefree.

The boy still was so free and narcissistic, so joyful and so happy.

The girl still was so merciful and beautiful, so kind and so nice.

Autumn gone and winter came. Sakura snow was falling heavily.

Pines and cypresses knew how heavy the snow was. The birds of thousands mountains had flown off.

Thousands of ice flowers bent the branches down. Snow river just like thousands of blooming pear flowers.

Frozen mirror lake was quiet surprisingly.

Suddenly, a huge fire flow from the lake side rushed to the other side, thick layer of frozen instantly melted away!

Then, a terrifying roar resounded through the forest! The ice flowers on branches, and the snow on Narcissus and Flora's shoulders, were all shaken to the ground.

A huge dragon dark as night queen tulips flying and roaring overhead! The huge shadow just like husky eating the sun.

The huge dragon flying over the forest, blotted out the sky and covered the sun, really invincible.

He spat out the long long black fire, large tracts of the forest were burned into ashes! Not even a blade of grass grew!

Everywhere was scorched earth! Every life was ruined!

Numerous pure little snow rabbits in the tree caves were burned without bodies and bones!

This huge dragon's biggest hobby was to destroy all the creatures!

He didn't love diamonds, nor gold, nor art!

He only loved to destroy all good things and kind creatures!

Suddenly, the melodious music and high war song came from end of the forest!

Thousands of diamond fairies flew down from the hundreds peaks of diamond mountains, they were full of flame, attached to all the flowers, trees and all the little animals, turned into hard armors.

On the foothills of hundreds of mountains, thousands of gold flown down, they were full of spirituality, and melted into thousands of swords, shields, then gently fell into the hands of little animals.

Thousands of colorful star gems flew out from the mountains and forests, they all embedded in the swords and shields in the hands of little animals, gave them the courage and strength of nature!

Wearing the diamond armors, the dragon's flame never hurt even one grass or one tree, even one flower or one creature in the forest.

The little animals also made up the most powerful, greatest, and the most kind holy light army in the world!

But in front of the evil dragon huge as a snow mountain, after all, pretty cute little animals were still a little weak......

In fact, all creatures living in this art forest never grow up.

They kept the most simple, the most lovely, the most tender and the most pure appearance forever.

Blooming youth forever.

Forever and forever!

But all creatures were not afraid of evil at all!

When the fire dragon fell heavily, even the earth was shaken by his huge claws, the forest's four sides poured thousands of little squirrels, little white rabbit, little snow wolves, little tigers, little chipmunks riding on small white horses, and fairy kitties riding small unicorns......

All the great and kind warriors rushed up!

We desperately climbed the evil dragon's body and fought like hell!

But the dragon skin was very hard, even though the gold swords couldn't hurt it at all!

However, the little animals of art forest were endless, they climbed the dragon's body and so dense, they blocked the snot green big stupid eyes of dragon. Even a few little flower rabbits held the dragon's thick eyelashes just as vines and couldn't stop dangling!

Suddenly, a little snow rabbit thrust into the dragon's right eye!

The huge dragon thundered, tyrannously twirled and thrown off the little warriors on his body, next flash, just flapped his bat dragon wings to the sky and fly to the end of forest.

The music and singing, were just pouring the holy light from there!

"I'll grind all the stupid creatures who can play the music and sing! I'll destroy all the holy art land!"

The dragon was thundering, flew to the last diamond mountain in the forest.

That was the end of the forest, the Flower Fairy Palace of Flora and Narcissus, located in the flower sea that surrounded by diamond mountains.

The palace was built by Flora's magic. No matter the pillars or walls, no matter carpets or tables, all made up of blooming flowers and all cuddled by myriads of brilliant flowers.

The dark green, virid and verdant vines twined the skeletons of palace, and the hundreds of flowers were palace's gorgeous dress.

The flowers were so dense that neither raindrops nor dewdrops could drop in.

But when the sun was bright, thousands of gorgeous sunshine poured through the flowers gap of palace.

Every day, this palace was flowing the colorful lyre music.

Every day, the holy forest hymns of heaven were danced and flew over the palace.

Every day, inside and outside of the palace was full of little animals, they were chasing and playing, frolicking and laughing. They lived together with Flora and Narcissus, all creatures bloomed the happy and beautiful smiles just like the flower seas on their faces.

Now the blooming snow like flowering sakura, outside the palace, only a few little snow rabbits were jumping here and there, the cute footprints behind just flooded instantly by the sakura snow.

The falling snow was mystically silent. The snow falling could be heard clearly.

Suddenly! A horrible thundering destroyed this peaceful world!

Dark ruby dragon flew closer and closer, and his huge dark shadow scared the little snow rabbits into the tree holes under the palace!

Narcissus and Flora walked slowly from the depths of palace.

As soon as saw them, the huge dragon roared and spurted a huge fire river!

At this time, a song of prayer was quietly blooming on Flora's lips, a chord ripples was shining on Narcissus's hands.

Any evil creature that wish to hurt the art angels,
must be hit heavily by nature!
Any evil power that wish to destroy the holy land,
Must be swallowed and purified by nature!

Then, the fire river hadn't touch the steps of the Flora's palace, just became a sakura wave, immediately fell in front of Narcissus and Flora.

The sakura waves along the fire river to the dragon, and immerged the dragon's terrible tusks, eventually, immerged the whole body of dragon!

The dragon's body was purified by the sakura sea from inside to the outside. Even the beating heart just became the sakura heart that hugged by petal fairies.

The huge dragon didn't die. He was just turned into a sakura dragon by Flora and Narcissus.

But the dragon didn't give up, he fiercely spurted out the fire to Flora, but just spurted out a sakura wave!

In a flash! The red sakura and pink sakura flying and dancing just like butterflies all over the sky!

Gradually, the fire dragon felt no more evil in his heart.

That sakura heart, was full of blooming buds of kindness and mercy.

Large and sharp fangs also became bellflowers and purple wisteria.

Butterflies and birds gathered around the flower dragon and fly to the pure sky with him!

"Really great." Narcissus smiled like morning sunshine.

"Really great." Flora smiled like sakura snow.

From then on, every day you could see a huge flower dragon that even his wings were flowers, he carried the boy and girl, and countless cute little animals, flew up the hundreds of mountains and forest, then soared to the pure sky!

When they fell into the flower sea of the lakeside, the flower dragon lay in the flower sea and ate the petals, Narcissus and Flora still played the lyre and sang with little animals, they chased and played, frolicked and laughed.

The pure art forest still was peaceful, trees and winds were still quiet, fairy songs were still gorgeous.

Every creature in the forest still was so merciful and kind, so happy and beautiful.

Chapter 5

BLOOD OF THORNY ROSE

"*W*hat is the most morbid place in our educational environment?"

"The kids who have the bad grades are just bad kids!"

Oris's grades were never over the top three countdown as koi.

His homework wrongs as a hornet's nest.

His exams was messed as crazy big monkeys.

He always took a wrong dictation on the blackboard like devil salmons in the Caribbean.

Therefore, he never received every teacher's good wolffish face.

"Oh my fucking Oris White, how much did you pay for your kindergarten diploma? You can't fucking write a 'thorn'?" The teacher roared like a tiger-shark, "I don't think you should be called White Oris! You just named White Idiot!!!"

The classmates burst into a monstrous ridiculing side of Styx.

But Oris just froze on the platform like a moon jellyfish.

One day, the math teacher talked about the Fan area fucking calculation, after finished, she asked, "Oris, do you understand?"

"Yes! I understand!"

The small moon fish Oris full of confidence there nodded, he was ready to stand up and answer, then receive applause and admiration.

"Well!" The venomous tiger fish teacher nodded, "Even if you idiot disability of intellectual fool can understand, so I'm absolutely relieved."

The whole class laughed and bombed the teaching building!

The eyes of everyone were looking at him poured with burning laughter of the lava flowing waterfall.

But sun-fish little Oris just was silence like a snowing sakura on the lakeside, his eye were just like sunshine stream.

One day, the old teacher screamed as a demon husky, "In English class, Oris idiot you hold a music score thicker than a zebra's droppings and bigger than a hippo' face, can you fucking study by your pig legs? I think your head is being shot by a wild roar! It's always you have not finished homework! It's always you war criminal with all students dog fights dog, pig bites pig! It's you drag on our grade's hind legs! You you Always is you!!!"

Oris just winked his the Iceland owl eyes, "Is our grade a wild roar? How does it have forelegs and hind legs? I'm the second of count backwards still drag on our grade's hind legs, so, does the first of count backwards pull our grade's boar tail to straight?"

"Ahahahahahahaha......" The whole class laughed to become proboscis monkeys.

Pa!

The teacher broke his textbook and rushed like a rhinoceros, she took Oris's *Music Score of Joe Hisaishi* that thicker than the sunflower parrot, bigger than Alaska eagle wings, then hit Oris's Iceland owl head hard.

Pa!

"Don't you want your corgi face that fucking by Chihuahua? Don't you? Don't you! Don't you!!!"

Pa! PA!!!

Oris's deerhound head twisted.

The teacher was hitting and hysterical, "You can do fucking anything, right? Don't need to fucking listen to the teacher, right? Right!? Right!!!??? What a fucking whale shit!!! It's really a hideous monkey makes many mischief!!!"

Right! I'm certainly ugly! I'm certainly hideous!

I am certainly hideous than Madagascar blue eyes lemur!!!

So no matter what I say, what I do, all other people have a baboon shit face and despised that I'm a fucking whale dung, I'm a hideous monkey make many mischief!!!

Pa! Pa!! Pa!!!

After hitting, the teacher threw the music score out of the window.

Splash splosh! Splash splosh!

The exquisite music flew down, like a ice glacier flamingo fell to sharks sea.

Oris covered his burning polar bear face with cat paw, but even a little meteor tear can't be seen in eyes.

The teacher was really not letting this go, She poked Oris's rainbow parrot temple with her wild boar roof, and roared like her dragon fire dung exploded, "It's too cheap for you to stay in this school without tuition! Our school is full of good atmosphere but you lead an evil member of the herd! Oh no! You are a mess of fucking ice-fire shit! You are A zebra's stinky droppings! Rex constipation feces! You are fucking smelly! Hard to swallow! Oh no! Difficult to eat! Oh no! Whatever fucking......Anyway, if you dare to do any fucking thing in class, I'll ask you parents to roll you back! Our school don't want you zebra droppings at school! Really saw you poor and took you! If you don't wanna learn, you can roll the fire shark shit and go away! Everyone say, right?"

"Yeah!!!" All students swallowed the ice dragon shit pie. Immediately, there was laughing of spurting shit that tore heart and cracked lung.

Hahahahaha~Belch~Hahahahahaha~Belch~

Oris bowed his head, still keep silent as dead butterfly.

He bit his lip to bleed the rose fairy.

You can call my parents! You call! You cal!!!

I don't have Mama and Papa anymore!

I don't have!!!

I don't! Don't!

The bell rang through the clear sky and campus burst into a sensation.

But the teacher said, "I speak fucking more two minutes!"

Then she spoke directly to the bell rang again, the campus suddenly froze silently.

"Which raccoon wants to go the bathroom, hurry to go!"

Oris rushed out of the classroom running toward the playground and went down his knees, he handed the music score back to the arms, in the glorious morning glow bath, he smiled and lit up with the colorful sunflowers.

The brilliant smile, even the sun was shined and hid in the whirlpool of galaxy, listening to Oris's sakura smile with all the shining stars.

10 years old, Oris naturally obsessed a sun starfish deep sea jellyfish girl.

Her childish face is like summer sakura and clear snow, elegant ice, limpid fire. Her roses pupils are more splendid than the spiral of nebula

40 million light-years away. Her grades were in the top three, always is the boar foreleg top one in grade.

Everyday she went to school and leaves school has a snow white Ferrari to pick her up.

Her name is Cynthia.

Since first grade, Oris had been adored this proud wasp jellyfish.

Oris would wait at the gate of the school early every day, and then pretend to meet her casually.

In PE class, he waited for her to come out of the classroom, and then silently followed her and went downstairs with her.

Every day, when he stepped into the classroom and moved out of the class room, his first glance and last glance could not help looking into her seat.

But Cynthia never looked at the ugly hideous sea star Oris even one shark glance.

She was too lazy to glance at him.

This was better.

Because the sight of her made him feel inferior.

That's the way he grew up.

In the carps crowd, he didn't have the colorful dazzling sense of existence as carp scale. Meeting the person he likes, his first reaction is to feel inferior like a starfish.

For those we like, we always try to pull her braids, kick her bench, shake her desk, when she seriously copies the new words, hit her arm, then she throws her pen angrily and turns over your desk.

Who the more we love, who the more we love to anger.

Who the more we like, who the more we love to tease.

But Oris never dared to pull Cynthia's braid, neither dare to hit her arm and let her draw a ice shit on the exercise book and screaming.

He never dared! He was afraid of being killed!

He just went into the dance room or the auditorium after class, then as Cynthia passed by, he quickly played the most brilliant sakura melody.

But Cynthia just laughed and chased with a group of boys, dismissive of Oris's beautiful music.

There was a poser dick in class, he is also infatuated with Cynthia's torpedo octopus.

His name was Lancelot.

His appearance was white crystal and clear than carefully peeled steamed ostrich egg. Anyway, he looked better than Oris, better than Oris too much!

Lancelot's parents were both enterprise manager, he's so rich, richer than Oris. Anyway, Lancelot is richer than Oris too much!

From grade four that girls beat the boys all over the class, Oris and Lancelot were the worst enemies as tree cat and corgi.

On the shark shit math class of grade four, the teacher said, "I wanna ask the Nile ostrich who didn't raise his hand at once! Hmm...... Lancelot!"

There were always a few Saharan ostriches in each class, the teacher told them to pull their heads out of the desert and answer the questions, then the whole class must laugh and become into ten thousand huskies.

Lancelot rose slowly in the wolf laughter of everyone.

"Now there's a Belgian milk chocolate, You, Cynthia, and Oris, everyone really wants to eat. To be fair, we have to divide it evenly, but only cut once. Lancelot, how do you think should be done?"

"Pu Hahahahahaha!!!!!!" Lancelot burst the scary laughter as a shadow dragon had constipation that couldn't shit cactus, "One knife hack Oris that pink dolphin big idiot!!! Then share it with Cynthia!!!"

Suddenly, Lancelot, Cynthia, teacher, and the whole class laughed and asshole exploded! Their head, eyes, ears, nostrils and mouth all spew the fire dragon shit, they were convulsed and rolling with laughter. They were laughing. Their eyes were covered with Tyrannosaurus and Rex's dark shit.

Only Oris's aurora star face was lowering slowly below the glacier.

He looked at Lancelot. As if looked at a ice dragon's big poop.

"Looking at me is for fucking your mother!!!???" Like swallowed ten thousand fire dragon poops and choked to death, Lancelot's devil face was fucking ferocious, "Kill you a flamingo egg big idiot after class!!!"

When the bell had rung, Lancelot and Oris were sucking ink and spraying each other as whale in the doorway.

But teacher Grace's tyrannosaurus face had emerged from the window.

At that moment, Lancelot threw the straw and drank the ink, he closed his eyes and tried to spill shit.

But teacher Grace's forehoof had entered the classroom......

Just heard his mouth "Poof"!!!

The whole class froze.

Teacher Grace washed her face three times with soap, changed her clothes, then kicked them both away.

I thought she would spit, spit, and scold hideously, however, teacher Grace was uncharacteristically kindly smiling, She helped Lancelot clean up his clothes first, helped him tie up the bowknot again second, then shot a crumb of bread on him. Just when Oris marveled at the teacher's mercy......

Pa!!!

Teacher Grace slapped in Lancelot's husky face!

Lancelot twisted his Chihuahua neck, then slowly turned his corgi head.

"You drink ink?" Teacher Grace's long face was instantly ferocious, "Why don't you eat raccoon shit?"

Lancelot saw teacher Grace with a nameless porcupine eye, then turned away.

Teacher Grace' face changed greatly! Quickly let Oris see what Lancelot gonna do!

"Report!" Oris ran back as deer and gasped, "Lancelot didn't gonna the dark forest to eat raccoon feces! He was pressed on the blackboard by girls, they pulled his pants, hit his ass with a broom! Unfortunately, he seems to have diarrhea today! Two pounds of ice dragon shit were ejected! The scene was out of control! Now our classmates are mopping the floor!!!"

"Well......" Teacher Grace's mouth was full of lava fire, "Oris, you write 300 words self-criticism here in one class."

"But I......"

The bell suddenly rang as husky ghost.

"I'm gonna class! The next class, I come to see your self-criticism! If you dare to write one wrong word, just one, I promise you will eat the dictionary with baboon shit!"

Then, Teacher Grace held her textbook, went with twisting her hips.

"Teacher Grace' thinking is always so twisted and farting fire! What the fuck let me do this? I didn't drink alpaca shit and spill her!!!"

The word "self-criticism" was written on the paper but nothing else.

Really suffering from ennui, I turned over to her desk, I cut off the three keys on her calculator, broke two steel nibs, and tore her dictionary dozens of pages. Suddenly I wanted to gonna the bathroom, so I took away a large box of toilet paper on the table. When my shoes and bottoms were wiped clean, the toilet paper was empty.

After that, I drew a Madagascar lemur on her work note, his small claw is holding an exercise book, two words on it, "examination questions", another paw is holding an earth, painted a mess of five continents.

There are some big words written on the earth.

"doing exam questions is no damned use at all, just like shit ball!!!"

The bell rang, after about 5 minutes, still can't see teacher grace's baboon shadow. She is always like this, always loves delaying class. And always because she asked student after class, "Had your mother been fucked by an Amazon rhino???"

It's almost time for fucking class, I'll play the piano for Cynthia next music class. I can't wait, so I go back to the classroom with the cacomistle.

But as soon as the music class was over, teacher Grace kicked me to the guard room on the first floor and forced me to write the fucking self-criticism!

Specially arranged a security guard to take care of me!

Damn it!!!

Teacher Grace was absent during the lunch break, and teacher Medusa took care of us. She teaches English.

In this school, everyone need to sleep in the noon.

Before flowering hair and body were turned into a ice snake by Swan goddess, teacher Medusa was really beautiful, however, the poison fire snake crime she did, Oris is unforgettable all his life.

There were always some gibbon students who can't sleep during the lunch break, Lancelot was the first one bitten out by teacher Medusa's bloody teeth.

Lancelot and Oris was roaring each other like two hippos, when Oris didn't speak and Lancelot' butt was bitten out.

"Lancelot you're a fucking big ass pig!" Teacher Medusa said, "Stand up and catch who is speaking!"

"Fuck!!!" Lancelot's boar face was ferocious, as if his lantern fish asshole was fucked through by the Atlantic blue marlin, "Oris!!! What the fucking are you talking about? Stand up!!!"

In fact, Oris didn't speak at all.

"Ahaha…" Teacher Medusa laughed gently more than the boa of dead butterflies forest, "As a punishment, you two idiot raccoons slap each other."

At first, Lancelot and Oris didn't dare to slap.

But teacher Medusa said, "If you don't slap, then stand until the end of break. There are still two hours, fucking stand forever!"

No way, just start slapping.

Squirrel monkey students are watching, asleep spider monkeys are also wake up.

Oris gently slapped Lancelot one time.

"Exert yourself!" Teacher Medusa ordered.

Oris slapped Lancelot again, still didn't exert himself.

But teacher Medusa is cruel as a scorpion was fucking a snake, "More harder! Take out all your usual power that eating dolphin poop!"

Then, Oris had to slap Lancelot more little harder.

He didn't wanna exert himself, for fear of hurting Lancelot's pup corgi face.

But after all Lancelot is a wild fucking husky.

"Now Lancelot slap Oris."

Lancelot's slapping was more violent than husky grabbing baboon shit! You can hear clearly the cookies crashing on his cat face, "Pa! Pa! Pa!"

"slap more!" Medusa said.

Pa! Pa!! Pa!!! Pa!!!!!!

Meteorites burst! Badly mutilated!

When Lancelot finished slapping, Oris felt ten thousand salamanders with bloody fangs was biting his cat face and creeping everywhere! The whole face was sore as meteor rain explosion.

Lancelot this Akita dog is so ungrateful!!! In order to let his corgi face not pain, Oris slapped him gently than husky licking fire shit!

But Lancelot! His flame cactus almost slapped Oris's head to roll to the ground, and "GuluGulu" rolled into Iceland waterfall!

So fucking damn it!!!

However, the most hateful one is teacher Medusa who is beautiful than Medusa, this snake idea was broken from her Titan's python eggs.

Repeated slapping three times.

"Still fucking talking?" Teacher Medusa smiled as a devil orang.

"It's he talking first!!!" Lancelot covered his face and argued.

"Huh? Want slapping???" Teacher Medusa had lifted her leopard cat bloody claw.

Lancelot immediately beg, "No no no no no!!! We really don't talk anymore!!! Even if put our heads in the rhino's asshole, we will never dare talk any shit!!!"

"All right, just listen to me. After eating rhino feces, you must remember to catch the Styx jellyfish beside the mermaid sea and drink two coconut jellyfish urine, or you'll choke to death with rhino shit. All right, gonna sleep."

So the owl Oris and husky Lancelot were staring at each other and back to the snow nest and kennel.

What really drives Oris mad is, when all classmates read the text in unison, Lancelot' butt as if bitten by an Australian ghost sake, he always loves fucking being faster than an ostrich! In the sound of neat reading, only Lancelot's harsh voice like a ostrich fucking stood up in cats!

The head teacher Grace's ears seem to have been stuck by the ghost octopus, she seemed never knew Lancelot's voice that his asshole bitten by lizards, jammed by cactus how terrible is! Or she just letting it go!

Fucking Damn it!!! Damn!!! Fucking Damn it!!! Damn!!!!!!

In order to be uniform, everyone was forced to speed up to catch up with Lancelot, so, the faster Lancelot read, the faster all read! The faster all read, the faster Lancelot read! Damn it!!!

Reading a three or four page text, everyone was out of breath as being come up to the top of the Alps by ten thousand mad huskies! Damn it!!!

Today read the *moonlight*, a text about Beethoven.

More than 200 years ago, there was a great musician named Beethoven in Germany. He wrote many famous music. Among them, there is a famous piano music called Moonlight, this is its legend.

One autumn, Beethoven went on a tour around the country, he came to a small town by the Rhine River. One night he took a walk on the quiet path, hearing the staccato piano sounds from a hut, it was his tune.

Again, Lancelot read with his dirty voice as he swallowed ten thousand Sahara hedgehogs! This is an insult to Beethoven!

Lancelot is really should be fucked by ten thousand devil huskies!!!

Beethoven is Oris's most revered musician!!!

Oris never forgive!!!

when they read the text half way, "Pa!", Oris put the book severely hit the wooden table that the fire of hatred!

"Pa!"

Lancelot also hit his book on the table for entering the jungle challenge!

when read again, Lancelot continued to run against the Nile ostrich, but Oris slowed the panther pace in the Amazon. So everyone's reading wavered between the ostrich and the panther.

Oris and Lancelot was staring at each other while reading!

Lancelot climbed like a gorilla in the upper right-hand corner of the first row in classroom.

And Oris was like an eagle perched in the last row of the lower left corner.

The meteor explosion point of view, it's on Cynthia reading carefully in the middle of classroom.

For 3 years, Oris's position has been in the last row at the lower left corner of the glacier wind hole.

Parents are high-ranking officials, or family is wealthy, or good-looking or well-grade children, they can sit in the first row of the volcano throne nearest to the blackboard just like Lancelot.

Well, how does a good man turn into a bad man?

When he feels unfair.

After class, Oris peed in a green tea bottle and then screwed up the cap.

Back to the classroom, Oris said to Lancelot, "You crocodile dinosaur egg! You are fucking dead! Teacher Grace call you to gonna office!"

as soon as he left, Oris put Lancelot's green tea changed, just as the Akita dog changed Shiba inu, husky changed snow wolf.

When teacher Grace was halfway through class, just heard the "Oh!" in the back of the classroom. All class turned round.

"How does this green tea taste like urine? Fucking you tyrannosaurus rex dick!!!"

Teacher Grace scolded, "You drink urine and eat dick in class, how much black whale shit do you wanna put on the young pioneers' face? Take the textbook and roll back like a dragon shit ball!"

"Ahahahahahahaha......"

The whole class laughed with trees and apes. Among them, Oris's laughter was the most magic as snake rattans.

As soon as the class was over, Lancelot went into jungle war with Oris.

Oris kicked Lancelot's trousers fall to pieces, then Lancelot told the teacher.

"Teacher Grace, Oris tricked me into drinking snow lion urine! And he kicked my ass! Kicked my whale shit out! He broken my pants too!"

"I swear I must provide Lancelot with some rags to keep off the wind. Whatever." Oris said.

So Oris back, Lancelot write 300 words self-examination.

Teacher Grace never dare Oris write an self-examination in the office.

Lancelot wrote that he felt so wronged and cried sadly.

Deserved it!

From then on, as long as read the text aloud, Oris and Lancelot must gone to the vulture war.

Once it comes for Cynthia, Oris and Lancelot must haved collided with the antelopis coenua.

Afternoon recess, Cynthia was kicking a fairy light ball in the hallway, Lancelot hit her as a mischievous bull, the fairy light ball flew out of the balcony, dived down from the four floor, as a grin sea-gull that choked to death because ate too many lemon sharks.

"Hum!!!" Cynthia glared at boar Lancelot like a lion, "Get the fuck down and pick it up!"

as soon as Lancelot ran down the stairs as a boar, he caught the giant bear teacher Grace.

The bell was suddenly crying as a ghost husky!

"Why do you always gonna the toilet when the bell rings! Afraid your mouth won't catch the seagull's hot feces? Damn it! Get back to the fucking classroom!!!"

Teacher Grace scared Lancelot back.

"The next class I'll pick it......" Lancelot said to Cynthia, "Here coming the old teacher Grace......"

"What if it's picked up by somebody else!?" Cynthia almost cried, "That's a fairy light ball I love most!!!"

But teacher Grace had riding mammoth tusk and trampling over.

Suddenly! A figure rushed downstairs!

"Oris! Are you afraid you can't catch the polar bear's hot feces!!!? You fucking get back!!!" Teacher Grace roared as a furious dragon at that figure.

Marching on the bell, Oris rushed from the four floor to the ground floor and knelt on the ground, He grabbed the fairy light ball and as a leopard jumped on the four floor.

But the students had already the third paragraph of *Moonlight* in chorus.

As Beethoven approached the hut, the sound stopped, and someone in the room was talking.

A girl said, "How hard this tune is! I've only heard it a few times. I can't remember how to play it. How I wish to listen to how Beethoven plays, how nice that would be! "

A boy said, "Yes, but the concert tickets are too expensive, we can't afford it."

The girl said, "Oh, dear brother, don't be sad, I just talked it......"

heard this, Beethoven pushed the door open and walked in quietly. A candle lit in the hut. In the faint candlelight, the boy was making leather shoes. There was an old piano in front of the window, a 16 or 17 years old girl sat beside the piano, her face was very pure and beautiful, but her eyes were blind.

The shoemaker saw a stranger coming in, he stood up and asked, "Would you like a pair of shoes, sir?"

Beethoven said, "No, I come to play a tune for this pure kind girl."

Cat-shark teacher Grace stared at guppy Oris by the door, until the reading was end, she tore his fins.

"Heaven has ice shit but you don't eat, hell without fire shit but you take a bowl coming! Did you run down and grab the polar bear's hot shit?"

"No...I went to pick up something..." Oris whispered as a parrot.

"What the fuck did you pick up??? How many shark dicks did you pick up???"

"It has been picked up by other......"

"Oris did you fucking eat too many Iceland owls??? Why don't you hornbill choke yourself to death???"

"Ahahahahahaha......"

all class laughed as the sea pigs of Antarctic.

Oris's grades was last raccoon and he was always undisciplined, teacher Grace never sees him as pleasing to the cat shark bloody eyes, as long as there's a chance, she must bite Oris with fangs and abuse him as a eruptible volcano.

"Why do you always come late? why coming late is always you? why you are always coming late? Do you still have the Alaska old dog face? Grades grades you drag our class hind legs! Discipline discipline you are late everyday! During the class, you can only giggle and smirk, or become a husky and stare blankly! I think you got ten thousand pounds of beluga shit stuck in your head! Hurry to roll home, don't let me see you idiotic shit tub every day! Who do you eat shit for? Who do you study for? Just look at you idiot, I know you grew up with drinking shark urine, eating blue whale shit and farting spirally as a pink dolphin! Just listen outside this class! Get out!!! One! Two! Three! Still don't roll???"

"Ahahahahaha......"

The whole class was laughing as crazy apes and baboons!

Saw the white feathers out of Oris's pocket, Cynthia's smile was overflowing with a fiery stream of proud.

For Cynthia, Oris was always not afraid of touching sharks.

Even if Cynthia wanted an iceberg white rose of fairy spark mountain pass, he must brave the cold plume snow, search cliff and fall blood, then pray to the snowberg Flora gift him one.

Even if he should pay the Flora is his own life, Oris will be most willing to go ahead.

Every day, Oris would get up one hour early and wait for Cynthia on the way, silently and mirror lake follow her together.

Every dew steps Cynthia turned round and scolded.

"Idiot!!!"

But Oris giggled as a daisies sea.

"Hideous!!!"

But Oris was giggling as canterburybells.

"Poor!!!"

Oris was still giggling as sunflowers.

Once, Oris stayed up late and stressed the cold, hid in the quilt to help Cynthia painting pictorial, but Cynthia gave it to Lancelot.

In the cold of aurora star flame, Oris cried for a whole snow night.

New year's party, Oris played the piano and violin on stage, and the solo of bel canto.

"I dedicate my solo and singing for Cynthia!"

Instant springbok sensation below the stage! In the Madagascar rainforest, the lemurs on the deer' eyes trees was screaming! Leaves left and flowers danced!

Melody was on the alpine cypress, Flora danced as flowering sakura sea. Singing was dreamed sun as a cloud butterflies in the flowers sea of Poland forest.

After playing and singing, a deep bow, applause instant exploded galaxy! Cheers volcano rained all dawn!

After a long long time, when cheers destroyed as stars, Cynthia said loudly to Oris that laughing as a whale on the stage, "Idiot! Hideous! Poor! Only big howling monkeys and dog raccons in cloud forest would like you this only can play the piano and sing but poor and hideous, and grades are bad as tiger cats' hind legs of Caribbean! You unicorn whale big idiot!!!"

Instantly! The auditorium dead like Lyra stars......

Even so, Oris refused to sit on the butterfly petals and give up.

One day after class, Oris put a nebula love letter into Cynthia's hand, then turned cat head and ran away.

Cynthia was shocked and frightened, but also glad and proud.

There's a music lesson next.

Oris was singing on the Siberia cedar, Cynthia was admiring a Cygnus love letter with ocelot besties.

On the stage, Oris felt one hundred small ice volcano of Pluto burst on his cat face.

"Cynthia......" The parrot fish girl beside spat a few aureliaauruta blue bubbles to Cynthia, "Teacher Grace has been watching you for one minute at the fire-fiend octopus hole......"

Teacher Grace was free and had no turtle eggs to hatch, so she was coming to patrol the music class again.

She came in, walked over to Cynthia and put out a flame tentacle.

Her octopus mouth that swallowed crabs shut and say no fire shit.

Cynthia lowered her butterfly tail goldfish head. For a long time, she didn't dare to spit a pink flying elephant small octopus bubble.

After a dozen small rose aplysias swimming in front of eyes, trembling, Cynthia handed Cetus love letter to teacher Grace's flame tentacle.

On the platform, in front of the blackboard, Oris's dolphin sound was scared to the Canadian aurora forest, completely out of tune!

As soon as end singing, Oris hurried to run back to his seat and put the bear head under the arm of flower sea forest. He never dared face the aurora ice age again.

Teacher Grace opened the Pegasus love letter and looked, suddenly cheerfully said, "Oris, It's the first time you polar little sea meerschweinchen write article not disgress!"

She rode a warhammer shark swam to Oris's desk.

"Put your sea meerschweinchen head up!!!"

Oris put his little polar bear head, "Teacher Grace, I'm not a meerschweinchen!!! I'm not!!!"

"Fuck!!! you dare talk back with snout???"

Teacher Grace stabbed Oris's little bear head with a flame tentacle, sat on the stool and swing, so Oris fell behind the sun coral garbage can.

So Teacher Grace asked students carried Oris with bucket into the mouth of cachalot.

In fact, Cynthia has no raspberry swan cake roll interest in poor and poor grades Oris at all, but Oris never knows to give up and die with the white parrot tulips.

One day, on the star-spangled way home from school, Oris plucked up the glass cat courage of five years, expressed love to Cynthia personally.

"Finland snow fox dog, Siberia snow cat, sunflower phoenix parrot, which one do you like? "

"Finland snow fox dog."

"Haha! Me too! Hehe..."

Cynthia tilted her head and looking at Oris.

Oris lowered the kitten head in snow sun, in a flash he raised his head again in the ice morning sunshine.

"Cynthia! I......I! I really like you!!! Even if I head into Arctic sun-glow jellyfish, I really wanna be with you!!!"

"Haha! I'll never be with you poor idiot in this life!!!"

As soon as Cynthia said so, Oris began to cry.

"Unless......"

"Well??? Unless what???"

Oris suddenly laughed as butterflies flew and sakura danced.

"Unless you buy me a sakura princess dress! Lancelot invited me to eat Caribbean blue ringed octopus pizza yesterday! You guys who is the best to me, who the fuck will be with me!!!"

"OK!!! I'll buy it for you!!! Even I sacrifice my Finland forest kitten life, I will buy for you!!!"

The poor ugly little Oris promised with his cat mouth.

As a leopard, Oris ran all streets of the city and looked for a place to play the piano and earn money.

For love, Oris even began to take art for money.

But this really is a hopeless act.

He needs money!

But his magnificent art is not for money! His magnificent art is to create beauty for the world, to create hope, to create courage, and to create happiness for the world.

This difference, just like Cetus and whale, Lyra and lyra of Flora, Andromeda and fairy's difference.

Each artist must consider how his art can be transformed into earthly happiness.

But first of all, our art must create beauty, hope, courage, and happiness for others.

The grand pianos of many hotels are sealed in the coral volcano of the Aegean Sea, is completely empty like the red sea coral tree ornament, just see the butterfly fishes come and craspedacustas go.

In the lobby of hotel, 100 dollars per hour for playing the piano, but there are several international hotels with music shut Oris out.

"Would I play the piano here?"

"Not everyone can play here. The degree must be more than master can play in our hotel, and we don't recruit primary school student, not to mention you farting brat!"

"I don't have any qualifications. I just really need this job......"

"Every night we invite people to play here, so we don't need anymore."

"But......"

"Go! Go! Don't block the guests at the gate!"

"Oh...I'm sorry..."

But Oris refused to sink into the Styx medusa's ice pupil in Antarctic, he refused to throw the mermaid into snow and ice.

He hopped as a deer across the street all forest cafe.

"Do you have a piano here? Do you need someone to play the piano? Don't you need......Oh......"

"Would I play the piano here......Just need girl? Oh......"

"I never mind how much money! Even if let me work here, and I will play the piano for free!"

......

Finally, Oris found a quiet mirror lake cafe of Bohemia forest to play the piano.

40 dollars per hour.

Play in a broad circular table under the rotating sakuragi ladder.

Alpine snowy white grand piano.

The crystal lamp overhead poured brilliant light, underfooting, the marble floor was resplendent as Phoenicis Cluster stars.

First time played crazily, Oris was scolded as shotted by sheep shit emmagee by a guest who was a vulture that tore African antelope.

"You dead raccoon cub!!! I fuck you Atlantic puffin spiral fart!!! Did you eat so many fire-breathing fishes and can't pull out the fire shit??? You are playing raspingly than ten thousand mad fire belly woodpeckers!!! Even I can't hear what I'm talking!!!"

The guest made a direct fucking complaint!!!

Cursing, and he almost became a woodchuck to give sloth bear Oris a good beating!!!

The manager tried her best to console the guest with koala good words, and gave him a cup of wine with cherry Babara dew as a present, then guest changed the shape of devil bird, as quiet as griffin.

Fortunately, the manager as kind as flying elephant octopus, she didn't use the mammoth nose to throw away little arctic fox Oris.

Oris admitted, saw more and more guests, he really had a bit of a show off, so he's playing all were passionate melodies, and exerted great strength than the snow lion that head was full of hornets collided lemon tree.

Oris's legs were cute and shorter than Irish little corgi, and the pedal of grand piano needs more power than vertical piano, so everytime he footed the portamento vigorously and heavily than the Danube gothic church. He was afraid that the whole hall couldn't hear his humming-bird art talent.

However, he never thought that he can't play crazily and arbitrarily.

He had no idea that playing must consider the feelings of audience and occasions.

At least the quiet mirror lake cafe of Bohemia forest is not suitable for the iceberg explosion.

"Play softly." Beautiful manager softly touched Oris's parrot head, "It's a new feeling to play a soft tune passionately, and there will be a new beauty that play a passionate tune softly."

"Well!!!"

So, Oris was playing soft as cats, more cats, more cats, more fairy cats......

The whole cafe was finally cozy.

Clear moon stream melody blended with brilliant flowers, and sakura creek flowed limpidly.

Everything was beautiful as entered the golden rose sea......

A whole cherry snow winter vacation, 6 hours every day.

One month later, when Oris put a 7000$ white sakura princess dress in front of beautiful sakura fire proud narcissistic Cynthia, snow wolf Cynthia snatched the dress, but gave Oris a husky milk white gLancelot.

"You bought me a summer dress in winter, was your head squeezed by mammoth asshole!!!???"

"Didn't you want me to buy you a princess dress?" Oris whispered as a nightingale, "I played the piano for a whole winter, ran a lot of clothing stores, it was difficult to buy this kind of sakura princess dress......"

"Hum!!!" Cynthia's chin flew to the sun, poked the sun out of ten thousand flowering meteor rain, "This grade of dresses are fucking stuffed my armoire into constipation!!! One more will be gonna shit explosion, do you know???"

"So what exactly do you really want???"

"Lancelot bought me an Apple yesterday, if you are a true man, buy me a bigger one!!!"

"Apple!!!???" Oris's cat eyes lit up the magic hope of Cygnus stars, "I'm gonna to the supermarket to buy you one hundred kilos of big apples now!!!"

As speaking, Oris became into a unicorn and flew to Pluto!

"I really can't be hardhearted to look straight at you idiot!" Cynthia laughed that her mouth sprayed ten thousand crimson glass butterflies, "I said Apple Plus!!! Oris you are really a flamingo egg big idiot!!!"

"Plath apple?" Oris turned his cat head and blinked his moon eyes, "Prague apple??? Or wonderland apple of sky city Laputta???"

"You fucking go back to your Laputta let the fairyland apples kill you!!! Rolling rolling rolling!!! Shit idiot!!! You shouldn't have rolled out of the egg at all!!! Get into flamingo's asshole and roll back to your Narnia forest!!!"

Finished, Cynthia hugged the dress and turned away.

"But you promised to be with me as long as I buy you a dress......"

"Oh! My fucking Caribbean Oris whale!!! Fart your fucking Styx jellyfish!!!" Cynthia turned head and sniffed, "When the fuck did I fart this red light jellyfish???"

"But you promised me......" Oris almost cried out candy fairies.

"I've changed my mind now!!!" Cynthia's chin rose and broke the heart of sun, the solar system instantly exploded and turn into stars sea, "What? If you have any starfish opinions, quickly climb out and let me fucking trample a thousand times!!!"

"No! No......No any starfish opinion......"

"Hum......I know you don't have any starfishes in your cat mouth. I'm prettier than pink dumbo octopus, of course everything I say has jellyfish truth!"

"Well......" Oris lowered his head and wiped out the sea butterfly tears, "You rejected me, is because of my poor or my ugly? Which one exactly?"

"Oh fucking a glass octopus giant grampus!!! You are not only poor!!! You are also hideous!!!"

"I......How hideous am I......?"

"You are so horribly hideous!!! Crazy Norway deerhounds see you are afraid to bite you!!! Wild boar, porcupine and sea pig see you are scared to ride shark and flee as numbfishes, roll as crabs and creep as lobsters!!! Saving pink pigs see you are scared to instantaneously explode, golds silvers coppers fly with clang all over sky!!!"

"Well......What kind of boy do you like exactly......"

"In fact, girls are the same, all like the handsome boys! But Oris you are an exception!"

Heard this, Oris was happy as a peacock in his pride, so he quickly asked, "you also like who's not handsome like me???"

Cynthia gave a crocodile smile and shook her head, "You poor idiot like a Christmas deer, Even if you become a swan elf, I won't like you at all!!! And besides, You will never be a candy angel!!!"

"Oh......I see......The fairy whose wings were destroyed by Phoenix meteors was really no longer beautiful......"

Oris nodded his snow rabbit head silently, turned away with the Raccoon's best friend little panda.

On the stage of the auditorium, morning sunshine passed through stained glass, twinkled as flowering sakura and bathed the forest.

But Oris was hiding in the cave of the volcano under the piano, thousands of candy fairies in the sun tears were flying with sakura.

Looking at himself in the wide mirror, Oris can't bear to look straight!

"If I become Cynthia, I will not like myself."

From the bottom of heart, he think so.

Pa la!

Oris smashed the small mirror in his hand! Broken glass such as stars rain!

Every sakura shard reflected his face of narcissus with glowing tears.

This ice sea elf, because felt hideous, so even if he was sad that fairy tears flew as dead sakura, he still dare not let others see.

Which laws do you think they are impressive and instructive?

The fucking law that everything depends on the fucking grades.

The fucking law that everthing depends on the fucking money.

The fucking law that everything depends on the fucking face.

In PE class, Oris saw the meteorite scene which made him completely hopeless.

On the stone steps in front of the auditorium, Cynthia's head laid softly upon Lancelot's alpaca shoulder, they were eating a Bobbi cake one by one, they also holding the alpaca hooves hands!!!

They laughed happily more than two Akita dogs that assholes were blocked by centipede globular cactus!!!

When everyone was up the stairs, Oris immediately rushed into the auditorium and roared wildly as a bloody deer!

Then he laid on the empty glacier stage, and his little deer head was crashing into the aurora marble floor!

Dom! Dom!! Dom!!!

Pom! Pom!! Pom!!!

Again and again! The meteorite collided!

Roaring crazily! Crying hard!

Such helpless! Such hopeless! Such powerless!

Suddendly his cat body climbed up and playing the piano wildly!

Crying while playing!

Stars tearing!

Ears blooding!

Fingertips flowering sakura!

smashing the glass piano!

Alpine volcano exploding!

Backed home, he playing the violin wildly again!

Destroying the entire Reinhardt rose princess forest!

Clewing the sun!

Tearing off Lyra rain!

Angels breaking wings and fairies bathing fire!

Pulled off three strings!

Crying all night!

Two cat eyes cried into blue giant star volcano of Andromeda nebula! Pillow was wet as rosestar sea of Lyra!

What the fuck that the boys who play football are the most handsome, and the fucking boys who play basketball are the most handsome, all the fuck are fucking farting egg yolk jellyfishes!!!

As long as you look handsome, although you fucking bomb husky fucking milk pupil glass ball are still handsome!!!

Ugly plays golf is just like shoveling the indigestion shit that Rex swallowed a panther!

What the fuck gentle girls have charm, what the fuck girls no make-up are pure, all the fuck is farting devil king squirrel's chestnut!

As long as you are pretty, you fucking sell dark chocolate cakes that others will say you are cake princess and sweet heart! You fucking eat a Halloween demon lollipop will turn into invincible candy fairy!

Ugly playing a piano is like a Parkinson's seizure!

Ugly playing a violin is like a cretinism cramp!

I have fucking seen thoroughly this fucking ice dragon world!!!

Many people think that this fire dragon shit is the fulgurite truth.

Maybe I'm really ugly! I'm really hideous! I'm hideous that arrived at Delphinus fifty thousands of light-year away!

Head is bigger than angel octopus! Neck is shorter than ramos prawns! Eyes are more oblique than parrot's mouth! Nose is more round than whirlpool nebula of Delphinus! Lips are thicker than Iceland's Christmas fairy deer!

I'm so ugly! I'm really hideous!!!

I'm a poult running in the tulip sea of Alps foothills, I'm so horribly hideous!!! Crazy Norway deerhounds see me are afraid to bite me!!! Wild boar, porcupine and sea pig see me are scared to ride shark and flee as numbfishes, roll as crabs and creep as lobsters!!! Saving pink pigs see me are scared to instantaneously explode, golds silvers coppers flew with clang all over sky......

Grandma! Grandma! Where are you? Let me lie in your embrace and cry, OK...?

Grandma, where are you? I just wanna hear you say, our Oris is the most beautiful little angel in this world!

Grandma, where are you? Where are you? Where are you!?

Grandma, please take me away, OK......Please take me away!

Grandma! Please take me away! Please! Please! Please......

Lying on the last row of glacier desk, Oris burst into tears as a blaze rabbit.

Cried all the day.

Looking up, Lyra fairy snow was dancing out of the flower window.

At noon on the second day, queuing in the classroom to hold lunch, Lancelot was already at the end of the line, but he rode a swordfish of the Great Barrier Reef and directly stuck in the whale head of whole line.

"Today, fruit salad is my favorite, so I must be the fucking first!!!"

Everyone didn't dare to confide any colorful jellyfish little opinions.

"Don't fucking jump the queue!!!"

In the last row of the team, Oris broke out the whale roar of justice!

"Lancelot! I've endured you for ten thousand years! You always made a foul in playing basketball but rather eating dragon ghost shit than avowing!!! Every time the examination papers were handed down, you fucking took my papers at the first time as smelling the husky's fire shit, then blew shit and sought the flies!!! Teacher! See! Oris didn't write 'Solution'! Teacher! See! Oris didn't write 'Answer'! Teacher! See! Oris didn't write answer's period! 60 grades just passed, but you fucked it to 59!!! And now you jumped the queue, why are you fucking so dick than king of huskies!!!???"

Volcanic rage of five years under the Arctic ice once erupted! Oris's roared exploded three galaxies!

"Fart you fucking mother dust tornado!" Lancelot's rage eyes as a flame bear, "Fuck you mother!!! Are you so dick to say more one word!?"

"I fuck your motherfucker!!! You hear me? Fuck your motherfucker!!! I can kill more than 300 dick huskies like you motherfucker!!!"

At this time, Cynthia said rightfully, Lancelot had already helped her with a full plate of fruit salad, "Mr. Oris, have your quality been rolled into cat shit island by dung beetles? Even if Lancelot jump the queue, you can't speak foul language so loud! My fairy ears feel like poured one hundred fluorescent squids, almost shocked to a deaf by you whale shit idiot!!!"

Criticized by the beautiful girl that he obsessed and humble to the Aegean seabed, sought but fail to get, sea hare Oris finally unbearable!

"I said it! How the fuck!! How many dicks do you want!!!??? Cynthia who do you think you are!? Are you fucking in charge!!!??? Do you think you are the rose princess and decree the whole world??? Do you think you are a candy fairy with infinite magic??? Do you think you are a anemone princess and radiant??? No!!! You are fucking not!!! You are a fucking peach blossom jellyfish liar!!!"

Cynthia was speechless as asshole blocked by the chrysanthemum starfish, in a flash, shark tears filled her fire eyes.

Wronged and swallowed hundreds of sun starfish before she uttered a shit, "You are a big peach blossom jellyfish asshole!!! And when did I say I'm the little candy fairy??? I don't say I'm a candy fairy, but you have to know, I am!!! Hum!!! Woowoowoowoowoo......"

Suddenly, Cynthia dropped the little rose coral spoon, and rushed out of blue bubble coral classroom.

A group of New Zealand clown fishes besties ran after Cynthia and put her in a circle, tried to comfort her. Then they all look back, breaking the window with fire glare, angrily staring at rainbow nudibranch Oris.

"Oris you wait to jump into mermaid sea and die!!!" A Lancelot's blue ringed octopus small evil party laughing as his head crushed by a tiger shark, "Lancelot can put your head into the cachalot's asshole and kill you!!!"

But Oris went straight to the first row, and brutally snatched the rose coral big spoon of Lancelot's hand, handed it to the first mermaid girl in the front row before.

"What the fuck fire turtle eggs do you do!!!???"

With saying, Lancelot pushed Oris, Oris took a backward step.

"What the fuck one eyed shark eggs do you do!!!???"

Oris pushed Lancelot down to the ground!

The plate full of fruits Lancelot had chose leerily "Pea Lee Pa La" fell like meteors over the ground!

"Everyone sees that!?" Oris point on the cat eyes coral floor, "Lancelot forcibly occupied so much watermelons, pineapples, blueberries, bananas and kiwis, originally, these are less than Holland cucumber and cherry tomatoes, the last thing everyone wants are little cucumbers and mini tomatoes! The students in the back always can't even eat cherry tomatoes, only could pitifully nibble at a few Holland cucumbers, or wait for the duty students, they ran from the four floor to the big kitchen on the first floor and hold food again. But this kind of waiting felt like longer than climbing from the foothills of the butterfly flower sea to the top of Alps! And saw other students were playing as crazy husky, but he sat alone in the classroom just for eating some fruit salad, this feeling was more miserable than thrown into the new year snow night and died of hunger and cold with little match girl! Do you fucking know that!!!???"

Then Oris said, "Every time ate fruit salad, cranberry souffles, Rome shield biscuits and shell jam cookies this delicious of candy fairy wonderland, Lancelot you must fucking crash queue as a swordfish!!! Although everybody never dare to speak as Guinea pigs, but today I must enforce justice on behalf of Heaven!!! Lancelot you were at the back of the line! Today, you never wanna touch a small piece of Sahara watermelon until everyone has held the fruits!!!"

"Wonderful!!!"

Every students cheered enthusiastically!

Looking at Lancelot that bottom first ate the Sahara watermelon of the ground, whole class burst the shrill crazy laugh as chewing one hundred violins.

"Hahahahaha......Hehehehehe......Cicicicicicicici......"

Sat on the ground and trousers are all wet, At this moment, Lancelot was thoroughly irritated by classmates' laughter!

"Oris you are fucking dead!!!!!!" Lancelot poked finger in the direction of Oris and roared as porcupine, "Don't fucking leave from school afternoon if you are a true man!!!!!! I must let you eat ten thousand Arctic blue dragonflies to choke you to die today!!!!!!"

"I will not fucking leave!!! Who scares who??????"

Oris roared too! He has had enough of Lancelot's oppression and abuse of eating shit by force and mauling cats!!!!!!

"I've fucking had enough of it!!! Enough!!! Enough!!! I will fucking let you eat one million red glass butterflies and choke you to death!!!" Oris dropped his plate and roared angrily as a fire dragon!

"All right! Wait for me after school!!!"

Lancelot pointed at Oris with his porcupine hoof, then jump up as husky, patted his ass and ran out to comfort Cynthia.

In math class of afternoon, Lancelot privately changed his seat and sat down at Oris's desk, wanted to take revenge on Oris.

"You'll be dead if you dare to take off my chair!!!" Lancelot gnashed his boar croc teeth in anger, "As soon as after school, I must put your head of New Zealand's eunymphicus cornutus into Iceland's volcano and keep your bones alive!!!"

Oris just had a snow owl smile.

Lowered the laughing owl's little head.

Continued to study the big white rose parrot piano scores.

Later, the teacher wrote a blackboard full of ghost spiders, scorpions with red paws and math problems, then she turned back, but found Oris holding his fairy kitten head in the last row, she thought he was sleeping soundly and dreaming fishes, so immediately shouted as sea lion, "Slap that dead sea pig for me!!!"

Since Oris has devoted most of his energy to music, so that his grades was backsliding as bears falling off the cliff, he has always been a spider in the eyes of math teacher, or a scorpions in skin, bees on tongue, snakes in mouth, even everything all right but find Oris some big tiger sharks and little troubles.

Lancelot turned and stabbed Oris with wasp octopus' tentacle and whispered, "Teacher told you fucking to go up and clean the blackboard!!!"

Oris looked up, found that teacher was glaring at him angrily as a shark, he ran up to the platform and pick up the blackboard eraser without any word......

A whole blackboard full of snakes, scorpions, bees, spiders and math problems instantly became fire ashes!!!

On the side, teacher was stupefied and had been a great white shark on the Caribbean beach.

So, in the student's gulls laughter, Oris was kicked out of the small coral classroom by teacher.

After three lesson, the bell chimed as wind-bell broken ice.

Under the aurora cold night, the playground had been annihilated with snow plumes, beautiful poignant sakura waterfall and pure snow all over the sky were slowly burying the world.

Each grade's dick bullies were tightly around Oris.

Succuba Cynthia stood in front of Oris.

She angrily glared at Oris, deep ice disdain was on her devil face, as if Oris was a blue cat of Siberia that just climbed arduously from glacier to the Iceland volcano.

"Kneel down for her! Hurry up!"

Lancelot roared as a snow wolf, throwing basketball between left and right hands.

"I! Will! Not! Kneel!"

Poor can not move Oris, and force can not bend he at all.

"Look! He gave me a low-grade dress!"

Cynthia roughly pulled out that sakura princess dress from her pink bag.

"This low-grade dress can't match me at all! Lancelot and I ate a blue ringed octopus pasta and fire squid pizza can buy more than a dozen! Poor Oris! You look so sad and so hideous! I'd rather be fucked by ten thousand unicorn pigs than be with you! Your family is so poor! I advise you to play your shit piano! Remember it every day! Poison dart frog never dare to lick white swan! Little low chick never dare to kiss fire phoenix! Really such fucking disgusting!!!"

Cynthia boast without shame! And waving that sakura goddess dress, which cost Oris's 6 hours every day for a whole winter, which exchanged with Oris's art, heart and dignity.

"You are so poor and hideous, and your grades are poor! What capital do you have to like Cynthia?" Lancelot said with doom in his husky eyes.

"I just love Cynthia! I am poor! I am hideous! I have the poor grades! So that I can't have love???" Oris's chin flew up to the top of church in Vienna forest, "Do you fucking......Ah!!!!!!"

The basketball hit his face before finished speaking.

Lancelot was the first to kick Oris to the ground.

Then a group of dick devils rushed to step tyrannically on the fairy deer boy of mirror lake!

Hitting while kicking! Kicking and cursing!

Oris was rolling like a little snow deer that had been burned alive by Iceland's volcano lava, the rock fists were bashing in his deer's soft face and body but Oris couldn't do anything!

This fire deer child fell in hundreds demons' trampling. He was short and thin, skin was white as snow, a cold look as stars creek in big eyes.

Deer face twisted and frowning.

Lancelot rode on Oris, hard slapped him twice, then trampled him as a boar.

Then Oris was kicked aside by three devils and three hoofs, but Lancelot continued chasing after Oris and trampled his little deer head, so others rushed up again and kicked Oris's belly.

After kicking, they picked Oris up and pressed his Norway forest cat's arms.

"Oris! I want you to see who Cynthia really loves!!!"

So, in front of Oris face, Lancelot kissed Cynthia!

And put tongue in her roses thorns mouth!

She responded to him!

"See how I kissed her? Did you see??? Did you fucking see!!!???"

Oris was dying and looked up.

Lancelot kissed a few again, then spat out his tongue and crowed, "Oh yeah!!! You can't kiss her! Can't kiss her! You can't! You can't!! You never!!! Ahahahahaha......"

As if eyes were bit by crazy wolf spiders, Lancelot was shaking and dancing as a silly Shiba Inu.

"Cynthia, burn the fucking dress he gave you to ashes!!! Decimate it!!!"

"Good idea!!!"

Just like a dark ice night queen tulip blooming in devil castle, Cynthia smiled proudly.

The muffin vanity idiot girls like Cynthia, boys buy her something is a golden glory for her as crowned aquamarine laurel by Pope.

Seeing two boys were jealous and fighting for her, that even is a Troy glory of self-styled flower goddess.

So, in front of Oris's face, Cynthia burned the flower goddess princess dress that concentrated his art, his blood, and his dignity!

Burned! Burned!!!

The horrible snowy night fire, madly jumped as demons on these little devil's twisted laughing face.

They were laughing wildly!

They were dancing crazily!

But Oris's burning sakura eyes with fire tears, also burning with fierce hate and bone inscription in sakura snow all over the sky!

Burning! Burning! Burning......

The flame was beating the deer's heart!

The fire tears was gnawing the cat's eyes!

The blizzard of whole world cannot quench the flames of hatred in his eyes! The bright sunshine of whole world cannot cure the scale injuries and sakura scars of his fate!

"Roll to home! Don't say we beat you shit! You dirtied our hands!"

Then, Lancelot held Cynthia's shoulder, left with those dick devils.

"Pu!!!"

Oris spit a mouthful of sakura blood, many Flora red roses flowered one after another on the pure snowfield......

"It's easy to bully him, he never resisted, many students like to bully him. But we didn't expect to really kill him! We hit very light...... Who knew he's so weak......?"

The second day, as a husky, Lancelot sobbed to the policeman.

"What he feared most was the class break, every day must be beaten cruelly." Said one student.

"This was not the first time he had been hit. In grade three, everyone saw Oris devoted all his time and energy to music, so resulted his grades to be worse, then he was often bullied by his classmates, every class break he must be slapped or boxed and kicked." One student said.

"As soon as after class, those bullfighting bully dog boys must pulled Oris in toilet and hit him violently. They forced him to eat the dry shit a few days ago, and dilute shit shat just now. And stuffed the blackboard eraser covered with chalk ashes and dirty cloth into his mouth." A classmate in the next class said.

"They threatened to kill him, so he dare not tell teachers." A girl close to Oris's house said, "His father, mother and grandmother were unable to protect him while they were alive! Now his most loved ones have died one after another, no one can protect him anymore......"

"Because introverted, poor, coupled with poor grades, he was recognized as a doormat. People bullied him, sometimes because of a bad mood, sometimes just boring to have fun."

"The classmates have got used to bullying Oris. Someone hit him with feet, someone hit his head. I often saw Lancelot and them pulling Oris's hair, hitting his head against the wall and knocking at the corner of the table."

"Lancelot was the first to bully Oris, is bullying the most. As long as Lancelot was in a bad mood, he must bully Oris."

"Once before a music class, Lancelot wanted to change seat with Cynthia's deskmate, but that deskmate refused. Then Lancelot got angry, he turned and rushed to Oris's table and slapped him, kicked him, vented his spleen on Oris."

"In grade four, Oris would cry as soon as Lancelot walked up to Oris's desk." One of Akita dog classmates involved in the abuse said, "Because I had been bullied by Lancelot, saw him poor, and I also wanna help him. But once I helped other kids who were bullied by Lancelot, then I was hit hard by Lancelot in PE class. Eventually, I had to choose to stand on Lancelot's side and take part in the assault."

But Lancelot told the visiting journalist, "I bullied Oris, most are directed by other students! Every time I hit him, other students would run to see, and sometimes come up to help kick two feet......"

"He lied! Obviously he took the head in bullying Oris! Obviously he took the lead!!!"

A girl cried as she spoke.

When the police asked five students why they abused and bit Oris, they answered that,

"It's fun and easy to bully."

In fact, Lancelot had also been bullied.

"Once I saw a group of older boys trying to bully a little boy, I reported to my teacher that they had been stopped by the teacher. But as soon as teacher went away, I was kicked and trampled on the ground by those demons."

Lancelot cried abjectly than the husky whose hot shit snatched by Shiba Inus!

"Then I thought, I must protect myself! Before grade four, I would only slap someone, but in grade five, I could kick someone hard......"

Lancelot cried as a husky with shit bombing.

"I just took Oris to practice my hands and feet......I was really never willing to kill him......Woowoowoowoowoowoo......"

"Those who have poor grades, or you can fight, if you can't fight, you need to hide." The students told reporters.

"Every time was beaten, Oris thought about telling teachers. But every class break Lancelot must gonna Oris's seat, all the time Lancelot was asking Oris had sneaked or not, and threatened to force him to eat fire dragon hot shit, then kill him."

"Once the other students saw Oris in the toilet, they were hitting him with tiles and bricks. Then he ran to next class and shouted them to tell the teacher. But as a result, Oris just got out of office and hit by them again, they kicked several feet."

"Previously, Oris had looked for help to head teacher, he said that his textbooks had been thrown away by someone, but he dare not say directly who thrown it. But the head teacher just said, 'I know, find it somewhere else.' "

"Once Oris's piano scores was gone, he was shouting wildly in the music class, 'where is my piano scores? My scores! This class is not gonna work! Where is my music!? My music! My scores!' At that time, all students were laughing crazily, but Oris cried so sadly, so desperately......"

"In fact, Oris's music was thrown into toilet by Lancelot. Later, Oris went to toilet to pick it up."

Oris's front desk girl told reporters, "After beaten, Oris had told the head teacher, but the head teacher thought Oris was pretending to be ill."

"No! I didn't!" The head teacher denied this matter.

"Since grade three, Oris had no deskmate all the time." Front desk girl said, "There were 27 people in class, so teacher arranged for him to sit alone in the corner of last row."

"No!!! I didn't!!!" The head teacher denied the matter again, "I just thought he was the more one, I couldn't arrange a table mate for him."

"But obviously there were classmates who wanna sit by Oris's side with three people!" One girl said.

But the head teacher Grace mercilessly stared at her, she was scared to shiver, instantly remain silent.

Many students told reports, "In fact, we all have suffered from school violence."

A student in grade four said, "Many times, I just walked through aisle, happened to touch someone, then I was punched right away."

A little partner beside also said, "Once I scored a lot of three-points when playing basketball, then I was hit by a senior student I didn't know."

"Every new student would be felt out to throw pebbles or dead rats to see if he was sensitive."

"If he found out quickly, It was difficult to make a surprise attack. If he didn't respond, they could trip over him with rope on the way. If he still hadn't responded, and nor reported to teachers, they could basically judge he could be bullied. Because Oris is very kind, so it aggravated the bullying."

"Most of students who was bullied have poor grades. Therefore, who has poor grades, you must fight or you can dodge."

Several parents told report, "Nearly ten students dropped out of school every year because they couldn't bear the school violence."

"It's so heartbreaking. The children have learned to hide from each other. Until seven days after the incident, the school knew the whole process that Oris was bullied to die. Though we asked before, but no one said."

The headmaster told the reporter, "Either the perpetrators or victims, they are all left behind children, all without love. These children's parents either work outside, or are busy with work, the children were brought up by grandparents."

The teacher in charge told reporters, "60% of the class are left behind children. Always I wanted to call and communicate with their parents, but I can't get in touch with them. Now these students have more irritable characters, it's difficult to supervise. When encountered something, they just like slapping others, but very little communication."

The girl front Oris's desk told reporters, "Oris used to tell me that if he was bullied at school, he never told parents. After his mom and dad died, he neither told grandma. Because even told them, he would still be bullied again back to school."

"Every day we get home from school, our parents usually only care about three questions. What do you eat at school? What do you play at school? How many grades do you get at school? If more, they wouldn't pay attention. In fact, most of our parents are so careless."

Some parents argued, "Asking is useless, the children wouldn't say!"

"Saying is useless!!! You only care about grades! Only know comparing kids!!! Whether we grow up happily or not, you didn't care at all!!!"

"The schools, teachers and parents who just care about the grades are all sea turtle eggs!!! They all should be fucking burned alive in Iceland volcano!!!"

"In school, you have to get good grades, anything else is useless."

"Aha ha! Is it???"

"As a student, what's the point of living without good grades? Just like an adult, if he has no money, what's the meaning of living? It's best to die."

"Aha ha!!!"

So Oris was killed.

So every alive day, he did deserved to be more inferior than a husky.

Such helpless!

Such hopeless!

Such powerless!

What about Lancelot? Lancelot had the law for the protection of minors, as well as powerful mother and father. They cleared up all kinds of relations for their son, and bribed many officials.

So, Lancelot not only did not get any sanctions, but also still immensely proud every day, and got dizzy with success. Even, he got more little girls' adoration.

After all, he was a kid who had killed someone!

How dick! What a dick!

So dick into the hell fire!

Ha ha!

But in the last time of that miserable world, Oris leaned against the ice marble wall and spat rose fairy blood one after another, flashes of old scenes was flashing before his cat eyes......

After all these years, when bullied at school and came home, mom and dad were always indifferent, they would just became aggravated to bully Oris.

One day in grade three, Oris was accidentally broken into the palm of his hand by a nail on a broken table, then also brought the nail down.

He cried and found for dad, but dad helped him put it out.

Instantly, Oris's palm gushing forth in fountains.

He cried harder!

He thought that dad must take him to the hospital at once, but dad suddenly had a bright brain wave, he only put the nail back again!

After that, Oris couldn't play the piano with his right hand for two month.

And mom wasn't good enough to gonna Cassiopeia.

"Oris, would you like to go out and play today?" Asked mom.

"I'm so ugly that I don't wanna go out."

"What absolute drive! The uglies' hearts are all kind."

Walking out on the street, Oris asked, "Mom, am I really hideous?"

"How many times have I told you? Don't call my 'Mom' in public!!!"

When at home, mom asked Oris, "why don't you go out and play?"

"Other children have money to play in the playground, and buy fairy lollipops for girls to make them happy. But I don't have money, anywhere couldn't go."

"Silly kid, you still can gonna die!"

In this ice world, grandma is always the only one who loves you most!

When grandma was still in the world, Oris's clothes were all washed by grandma.

Remembered last December winter, with snow flying, grandma's hands soaked in the cold aurora water, washed a jacket, a sweater, washed pants and socks one after another for Oris.

"Grandma, aren't your hands cold?"

"Not at all! Grandma is not afraid of cold!"

So, Oris always thought grandma's hands were not afraid of cold.

Until after grandma died, Oris first washed the clothes, he was keenly aware of that, how icy and piercing the cold water in winter is!

Then dropped the hot tears of love.

Crying while washing!

Washing while crying!

Pitied himself in the world!

Pitied grandma in the heaven!

Before grandma died, she bought two cans of sakura milk for Oris with only a little money for curing, and a Alps woolly sweater, a pair of small swan boots.

"Grandma......Grandma......Why don't you buy some good food for yourself with this money? Why......"

Oris choked with sobs.

"Silly kid, Grandma is willing to do anything for you. Last year, saw you were forced by your father to practice the piano, your shoes were not warm, your clothes broken so many holes......As soon as remembered that you were cold and hungry at the piano, my heart still hurt until now......"

"Grandma!!!"

Hugging grandma, Oris burst into tears!!!

"Grandma! Don't go! Okay!!!??? I still wanna eat the chive cod and windmill bread you cooked......Don't go......Don't leave me alone!!! Okay......? Woowoowoowoowoowoo......"

It was the last time, the last time Oris hugged Grandma.

Tightly hugging Grandma......

After grandma died, there was no one who loved Oris.

If I could still get a response when I shouted one "Grandma", how happy I should be......

How happy I should be!!!

Every day in school was just like haunted Halloween.

Went to the platform and handed over the fucking homework, accidentally tripped up by the husky classmate.

Walking in corridor, accidentally fucking overturned by the Shiba Inu student, slammed as a kitten eating whale.

Grade four, sat in the last second row, every time answered the questions and sat down, accidentally taken off the chair and fell down as asshole ate rhino horn, crying in pain as a wounded deer.

Then the whole class laughing as tore hearts and cracked lungs.

"Poohahahahaha!!!Hawhehehehehe......Woowawawawa......"

In the mad laughter, Oris just stood up with a silent sakura face, then sat down, buried the head, went on studying the brilliant sakura music of Mozart, Beethoven, Joe Hisaishi, and countless great musicians.

As soon as Grade five began, Oris was like an owl perched in the las row.

So far hadn't moved the snow nest.

Grandma risked her life that collected iceberg whit roses and Sun Queen golden roses at the cliffs of snow mountains, then, step by step, stumbled down the snow mountains and sell them, so that she could buy exquisite piano scores for Oris.

However, the music he placed in desk pocket was often throw downstairs and throw in the ladies room by some husky classmates, then Oris searched for everywhere and cried out of breath, tears just like cherries in storm.

Yesterday, Oris's Mozart music went missing again in the music lesson.

"Where's my piano scores! Where's my music!!!" Oris was crying with little pink doll dragon fishes.

"Fuck me!" One little guinea pig evil party laughing as husky, "Oris is mentally ill again!"

But Oris went on crying as a whale, "This lesson is fucking over!!! Fucking over in dragon asshole!!! Fury get out!!!"

Miss Fury was music teacher.

"Ahahahahaha……" Everyone laughing as became into ten thousand big meteorites shit balls.

And teacher Fury also laughed as the mouse lemurs jumped and ran madly on her face.

"Laugh your mother shit!!! Get out!!! Get fucking out!!! Where's my music!? That Mozart music!!! I miss my music!!! I wrote my name!!! No one saw it!!!??? It fucking gone!!! Gone!!!"

"You should be quiet first." Said the commissary in charge of discipline.

"Who can be fucking quiet!!! My music!!! Where's my holy music??? My piano scores!!!!!!"

"Ahahahahahahaha……" Everyone laughing as pigs rolling and shit sprayed from their eyes, noses and mouths.

At this time, a classmate handed Oris a music grading test book.

"What's this fucking shit!!!" Oris threw it to the ground, "I said my Mozart music!!!"

"Too fucking dick! Fuck me……" One classmate marveled as a bobac.

"What whale shit do you want? That's the teacher gives you!" The disciplinary committee came here and said, "Where's that test book?"

"On the fucking ground!!!" Oris roared as eagle and leopard, "Pick up by yourself!!!"

"Is he shit mad?" Lancelot said laughingly.

"I've lost my music!!!" Oris roared as a swan.

"Really shameless!" Said the disciplinary committee.

One classmate said, "This shit was mad more than once."

At this moment, disciplinary committee held a pile of music to Oris.

"Which is mine??? This is not! This has no cover, certainly neither mine! Where is mine???"

"I just give you five minutes." Said teacher Fury.

"What are these dragon shit!!! Oh, I'm really fucking mad!!! My music has gone!!! Gone!!!!!!"

Oris cried wildly and shouted hoarsely!

"Ahahahahahaha!!!" The students laughed crazily.

"My music!!!"

"Can you find it with crying and shouting?" Said the disciplinary committee.

"I'm miserable! I'm in a hurry! I've lost my music!!!"

Oris completely came to a breakdown, just lying on the desk and crying, cared nothing about this fucking world.

At the end of class, a kitty girl wrote a note to Oris, "Your music is thrown into the urinal of the ladies room by Lancelot and his evil parties."

Heard that, Oris just laughed.

He picked it up from the ladies room, took a whole lesson, wiped carefully the bear shit and leopard urine with his own clothes, then changed a new cover.

Because loved music, love art. Because didn't care about exam grades, many parents also thought Oris was a fucking macaw big idiot.

One day after school, Oris asked the girl at the front desk what's the homework, when that girl speaking to him, happened to be seen by her mother.

Her mother pulled up daughter's collar, roared as a zombie dragon, "Fucking remember it!!! Don't play and talk any word with this bad student that has bad grades!!! Do you hear me? If you talk and play with this idiot again, I must kill you little stupid cat of Alps!!!"

Then this dragon mother said to daughter's butterfly fish deskmate, "You help to supervise my daughter, if she dare speak to that fool behind, you tell me, I'll kill her when she went home!"

From then on, the little panda girl at the front desk never dared speak any more about panda goldfish to Oris.

However, the most made Oris hardly wished to live, was his ugly hideous lemurs appearance as whale shit mixes more vegetables, hideous monkeys have more mischiefs.

"Oh fucking a glass octopus and giant grampus!!! You are not only poor!!! You are also hideous!!!"

Cynthia's icy spines sound still was like cuttlefishes pouring in ears.

"You are so horribly hideous!!! Saving pink pigs see you are scared to instantaneously explode, golds silvers coppers fly with clang all over sky!!!"

"Couldn't we just be friends?" Oris said with a timid tongue.

"My mom doesn't allow me to play with idiot! And she doesn't allow me to play with shiting ugly and fucking poor!"

Ahaha!

I fuck your mother!

Which laws do you think they are impressive and instructive?
The fucking law that everything depends on the fucking grades!!!
The fucking law that everthing depends on the fucking money!!!
The fucking law that everything depends on the fucking face!!!

Really doggone!!! Really a group of woodchucks and guinea pigs big idiots!!!

Oris would never forget Cynthia's evil and hurt all his life!!!

Really hateful!!! Really hateful!!!

But really helpless! Hopeless! Powerless!

Looked for help to the heaven but heaven didn't answer!

Looked for help to the hell but hell neither answered!

Despair!

Desperate to jump into the sun and burn like a flame meteor!

Every day woke up, even had no daisy courage to look in the mirror!

Because as soon as looking in the mirror, I must get angry! And couldn't help touching sharks to hurt myself! Couldn't help jumping into whale's mouth to kill myself!

Even I combed my hair just by cat's whisker feeling.

When I passed the shop window, I dare not looking at myself in the window.

Afraid to look directly at my elk hideous!

Afraid to face to the harsh realities of snow and ice!

Once after playing the piano in the dance room and got out, two husky girls came up from behind and readied to talk, one girl just opened her mouth, but another said,

"Oh! It's not pretty! Here we go! Go!"

Self-respect had been fatally broken!!!

Once came out of the auditorium with hugging his violin, a girl who had been listening to his playing was point at him and screaming in surprise,

"Is he playing the violin!!! It's too hideous!!! Just like cramping with cretinism!!!"

Last year at the new year's evening party, some junior girls and boys first heard Oris's playing and singing said to Oris when he just stepped off the stage,

"Really don't judge people by appearances! So ugly, but sings so nice."

Aha ha! I fuck your mother!!!

Once grade five started, a little lolita of Grade One couldn't find her class, then happened to meet Oris, she holding Oris's arm and crying, "Brother, take me to Class Two, Grade One, Okay? I can't find my class!!! Woowoowoowoo......Wawawawa......"

"You are not afraid that I would bully you just like other posers and idiots of high grades?"

"My mom said, uglies' hearts are all kind......"

"......"

Midterm examination in Grade Four, a beautiful girl who often played the violin at school singing and dancing party threw Oris the answers, but the teacher caught Lancelot. He was next to Oris. Then Lancelot's grade was dealt with 0.

"I didn't cheat!!! I didn't!!! This note is not for me!!!"

Lancelot was crying and rolling all over the ground just like a boar.

But the teacher was angry, she pointed at Oris and growled, "Could it be for him???"

At that moment, for the first time, Oris felt......To be ugly, it's nice.

As soon as went out of school, Lancelot called some posers to give Oris a good beating.

Oris didn't cry.

Just picked himself up like a cat as usual, clapped the clothes, went home alone.

At that time, others laughed at Oris's ugly, he still could fall in grandma's hugging and cried, he could hear grandma and his cat head was touching by grandma,

"Don't cry, don't cry! Oh, my angel, don't cry...My angel, you are the most handsome and beautiful in the world! The most handsome and beautiful! The people who will like you in the future must be more than the petals of the cherry blossom sea! Sure! Must! So, don't cry, angel. When see you cry, Grandma is so sad that can't breathe. So don't cry, OK...?"

Oris crying and crying but laughed suddenly.

At that time, no matter met any sad thing, as long as lying in grandma's hugging and crying, then the whole world could come back to the golden narcissus sea.

But now......

Oris laughing and laughing, but suddenly cried.

What an wretched child he was! What a poor boy he was! How innocent he was!

But he wouldn't be jealous of others' beauty for his ugly.

Because he had a great heart of art.

Treated all creatures in the world, he would be strong and brave, merciful and kind!

He believed that these sufferings and pains, just were the indispensable hell-fire trial in the art road.

He understood that all great powers are derived from diligence and sufferings.

He believed that bright and happy life would fall on him one day! As long as the dream is still bright, hope will be brilliant forever! Yes! It will!

But, Cynthia's shark shit asshole, was far beyond Oris's unicorn imagination.

Once in a snowy day, Cynthia asked Oris first, "Lend me your little swan gloves for a while, I feel colder than the little mermaid that frozen in the Arctic glacier! I'm too cold to hatch my swan eggs!"

So Oris lent the little swan gloves to Cynthia.

After a while, Cynthia saw Lancelot was playing a fan, then went up to grab the fan.

"What the fuck devil squirrel with little chestnuts are you doing?" Lancelot asked.

"I feel hotter than falling into the Iceland crater." Said Cynthia, "My swan eggs almost burst!"

"So give me back the gloves!"

As speaking, Oris immediately recaptured the little swan gloves that his grandma knitted for him.

Cynthia also loved to order Oris as a Iceland shepherd dog, play Oris as a teacup cat that eyes had different color.

"You say you like me! So prove it to me!"

"How to prove?" Oris was blinking his big cat eyes.

Then, Cynthia threw a pure blue neutral pen on the podium.

"Take it back! Don't walk! Must creep! Don't pick by hand! Must by beak! Or you don't love me really!!!"

So, in the huskies' eyes of the whole class, Oris crept from the last row, knee by knee, onto the podium.

Held up that pen with his gull beak, then knee by knee again, crept back to Cynthia, and put the pen on her desk.

"Poohahahahahahaha......"

Classmates had long been immersed in bats devil crazy laugh and couldn't extricate themselves.

Oris's chin was accidentally knocked to the corner of desk, the pain made his burning tear out from the cat eyes as meteor shower.

Thought Cynthia would smile as a rose fairy, but Oris couldn't believe......

Pa!

Cynthia put off that pen on the ground!

"Your slaver is too dirty! I don't want this pen! It's too disgusting!!!"

Kneeling on the ground, Oris mewed timidly, "So......Now you believe I really love you, right?"

"I! Don't! Believe!" Cynthia shouted as a Phlegethon husky, "Unless you give me 2,000 dollars! Or you don't love me really!!!"

"Oh......"

Oris nodded his little snow forest cat head.

He went to the cafe to play the piano again.

Two weeks later, Oris handed over 2,000 dollars to Cynthia.

"I don't want your money! 2,000 dollars is not enough for me to eat one blue cheese roast Blue Ringed Octopus!"

Cynthia threw the money on the ground, twenty new 100 dollars were flying like twenty bloody butterflies.

Cynthia gave Oris a husky look, then said savagely, "Why don't you think with your idiot Aplysia brain! My family is too rich! I lack this dragon ice shit 2,000 dollars? Take away! Buy a coffin for your mother!"

Ha ha! She doesn't love me, so anything I do all is wrong.

All my classmates around laughed to crook their corgi waists.

But Oris didn't dare to sing just one deer song.

Since I was very little, my parents loved to yell at me very much, so I'm very self-abased as starfish now. As long as someone speak loudly to me, I must be so sadly that just gonna tears, even wanted to die.

When mom and Dad were still alive, one day after class, Oris said to Cynthia, "Cynthia, I'm so upset right now."

"What's wrong with you fucking owl eggs big idiot?"

"I had a dream last night, I dreamed my dad was burned to death, he abandoned me and mom."

"Don't worry! Don't think too much, dreams are all opposite!"

"Well! Thank you!"

"Hum......It must your mom burned to death and abandoned you and your dad! Poohahahahahahaha......"

Oris stood on the corner of ice hole, laughing and laughing......

Then burst into tears!

On that day, after school, he was playing the piano crazily in the empty dismal auditorium.

The fingers were all gushing blood of butterflies and sakura in blooming.

After a few days, Oris's mom and dad really burned to death.

Because love music, because love art, because of poor, because of ugly, because of bad grades, so, so I deserve these vicious injuries!

How detestable! How pitiable!

Such helpless!

Such hopeless!

Such powerless!

"What the hell did I do wrong??? What did I do wrong!!! What did I do wrong......"

Staring up at the snowy night, Oris cried and prayed.

After beating by Lancelot and his demons, Oris didn't go home.

Just walking alone under the night sky with ice lamps blazing snow.

Desperate to kill himself!

Found a corner of the street.

Sat down hard.

Leaning against the corner, holding shoulders.

Shabby in dress! Suffering hunger and cold!

In fact, Oris's viscera all had been broken, blood flowing with fire from all sides of body.

Flower fairy's sakura snow were getting bigger and bigger.

But Oris began to spit blood, his face was white as a pure sakura tree.

Heart is paining......

Heart is paining......

Stomach is paining......

Really paining......Really paining......

Really paining......

Really paining......

Really paining......

Really paining......
Really paining......
In desperate stars and blaze tears, Oris stopped breathing.

The morning sunrise in second day, wind stopped, sakura snow was falling silently.

The sun of new world was rising, shined warmly Oris's weak deer body.

"What a poor kid!"

People lamented.

However, no one knew what really happened in that night.

That aurora snowy night, lamplight was like burning stars, sakura snow was cold and dreary.

Eyes filled with tears of fire flame stars, Oris raised his head awkwardly, supplicated to the night sky,

"Why nature gave me a poor family, and also gave me an ugly face! Why! Why does fate torture me so cruelly? I'm just born in a poor family, I'm just ugly, I just have bad grades, I just love music, just love art! What did I do wrong that nature punished me so cruelly!!!??? What the hell did I do wrong??? What did I do wrong!!! What did I do wrong......"

Wind and snow's thorns flying in his cat face, quickly condensed into ice crystals.

Never mind! Let's die!

Just like the little match girl!

Fire tears flowing, Oris sank into the dream of paradise in snow.

Just die in the snow night!

Just die!

Perhaps only in this way can I be free and happy......

Perhaps only in this way, I can fly to warm and light, I can fly higher and higher, fly to a world that no sorrow, no pain, no hunger, and no shattering of art dream......

Suddenly! A holy light burst into night sky!

Warm stars were blossoming on the dying boy, dazzling brilliance directly turned the snowfield into a gorgeous butterfly-flower sea!

Light shining all over the world!

Thousands of trees blooming sunshine and flowers!

The boy covered his eyelids with hands, then opened his cat eyes from the darkness of death, looked up at the brilliant night.

In the magnificent soft clouds and holy light, A fairy in sakura dress was coming with butterfly paces.

She gave Oris the most dreamlike and gorgeous pure smile.

The fairy shone all over the world, and her light was so gorgeous!

She had the long hair that fused by bright star river and sunshine.

Even the most beautiful woman in this world couldn't match her gorgeous smile!

Even one hundred Cynthias standing with her, they must be burned out in a flash by the fairy's flame!

The fairy stepped with bright sun and clouds, her hands held many little gorgeous flower fairies , falling slowly in front of Oris.

Her smile was so merciful and kind!

Her smile was so brilliant and beautiful!

"You......You are the god of heaven?" Oris warbled like a nightingale.

The fairy slightly opened her mouth, but singing a song,

Those kind people who love art,
you don't be sad!
Merciful Art Fairy will shield you forever!

Those persistent people who burn the life for art,
you don't despair!
The great art pioneers and art saints will shelter you forever!

Those devoted people who fully suffer the misery for art,
you don't cry!
Nature has sent me to save you!

I am the Art Fairy Florithena!
I am with you forever!
Forever! Forever! Forever!

Following the song of Art Fairy, all the clouds were singing the brilliant song! The touching melody of flower sea blossomed all over the night sky just in one flash!

Art Fair Florithena was singing, even the most beautiful song couldn't match her melody!

When Florithena closer and nearer to Oris, the song was also light and quiet as falling sakura.

"I'm Art Fairy Florithena of nature. I love music, painting, dance, poetry, literature, science, philosophy, architecture, sculpture......I love all the arts of the world! And art also includes all the areas of the world! I'm fused with the countless artists' souls in the heaven and the world. I love to be in harmony with nature. I can communicate with flowers, grasses, trees, fishes and birds. All the things in this world treat the Art Fairies as friends. We hate all evil creatures, and we help all kind creatures. My duty is to help and save those kind creatures who love art as me, and to shelter those persistent people who burn his life for art."

The voice of Florithena was more beautiful than the most brilliant piano music in the world! The melody of her voice was softer than the most touching violin music in the world!

"My child......"

Florithena knelt down grazioso, stroking Oris's cold face.

"You must be hungry......"

Oris's tears was like fire and eyes as meteors, he nodded vigorously.

Florithena waved her hands, a sakura sunshine flew over, then a cod, a windmill bread and a alpine blueberry cake roll appeared in flower sea.

"Eat! Eat these sunshine!"

Held the windmill bread by two hands, Oris was eating and eating, suddenly tears burst as fire butterflies and flying sakura, he was crying as flowers rain because of joy and gratitude, even Florithena was heartbroken when she seeing him.

Florithena spoke to Oris with sunshine words,

"Come on! Let me take you out of this suffering of the tragic world! Let me lead you to realize your art dream!"

Finished, she bloomed a dreamlike and warm smile.

Looking at the beautiful face of Florithena, Oris had already moved with fire tears! The sakura fire of appreciation was full of his chest!

"Merciful Art Fairy Florithena! Please give me the courage and strength, take me out of this miserable life! Let me realize my art dream!"

"My child! Kind child! Persistent child! You love art so much! I will give you the destiny of casting the great art! I will give you a happy family! I will give you a beautiful appearance! I will lead you out of this miserable life! But in exchange, you will pay for the equal prices and efforts!"

"What will I pay?" Oris blinking his deer eyes.

"Your kindness, your efforts, and your dedication."

"Oh......" Oris nodded his flower deer head.

Florithena said, "My child, you must strive for art with your whole life, and use your art to create beauty, create hope, create courage, create happiness for all the creatures of nature. This is the magic that necessary for the great art, it's also the necessary responsibility and belief for a great artist. So, kind child, are you willing?"

"I'm willing!!!" Oris nodded desperately, "As long as I can realize my art dream, I will pay anything for you!!!"

Florithena's smile was blossoming on the flowers' souls, "Not for me."

Oris blinked his cat eyes, "Then for who?"

"For the world! And for yourself!"

"Oh......" Oris mused.

"Even if you are suffering from the fire lava and storm, you must love all the creatures of this world, and dedicate your whole life to the happiness of all creatures! My child, will you?"

"I will!!! I will!!! I will!!!!!!"

Oris nodded reverently.

"So, come on!" Florithena spread her glary wings, "Your world will be new! In the new world, anything you get, just don't be surprised! Because they are what you deserve! Come on! My child who loves art! My kind child! Struggling child! Miserable child! Art Fairies will shield you forever! Nature will shelter you forever! Forever! Forever and forever!"

Florithena stretched out her gorgeous hands, Oris put his cat hand in Florithena's sakura sunshine hands, then slowly rose from the snow.

Blink!
The sunshine of heaven hymn shined all over the world!
The flower seas of the whole world were blooming and stretching!

**Art Fairy holds the child's hand
together fly to the warm holy light**

Chapter 6

FAIRY OF PHOENIX TREE

a brilliant butterfly sunshine dream.

There was a holy mirror lake and a narcissus sea in the forest.

Deep in the forest, among the flower sea on the lakeside, a beautiful boy was playing a lyre, a gorgeous ice blue butterfly was dancing with the melody......

"Little snow sea gull Oris! Get up from the flame rose tree! Hurry up! Mom gave you a bacon pineapple sandwich and Venice sakura milk, shall I summon hundreds of flying octopus to pull you out of bed?"

The mother's nightingale singing came from the dream, it sounded so gentle just like white swan feathers, so pleasant just like sakura fairies' song.

For many years, Oris hadn't heard mom so gentle like a swan.

Open your eyes, on the snow shining ceiling, brilliant crystal lights sparkling with magic flowing light just like Flora dancing with sakura fairies.

"Is this my own phoenix forest...?"

The gift of nature and Art Fairy Florithena is always amazing!

Once upon a time, Oris never dared to look himself in the mirror, just afraid to see his own ugliness. But today, when washing his cat face in the morning sunshine, inadvertently caught sight of himself in the mirror, Oris was stunned......

Once upon a time, the god gave him an ugly face, then also gave him a miserable family.

But now, nature and Art Fairy Florithena have given him a harmonious happy family, and a beautiful face just like narcissus fairy!

So, everything at this time is all new!

This is the brilliant gift of nature and Art Fairy Florithena, for his kindness and effort.

walk out of the room, on the huge sakura balcony, the pure white shining grand is sparkling with warm brilliant spring sunshine.

Over there, mom dresses in a pink floral dress, cooking Oris's favorite sakura milk in the kitchen. Mom's legs are intact, her hands and feet all bloom the unique elegance and fragrance of the ballerina.

In the living room, dad's suit is clean, obviously to devote himself to today's singing career. He has shaved his beard, washed his hair, and no any smell of the snow wolf old alcoholic in hell.

Yes!

Everything and everything, is so new! It's all so bright and wonderful!

"My son, today after school, mom and I will pick you up, grandma is coming to see you tonight. Grandma said she hadn't cooked for you for a long time. Today she's gonna make a good meal for you."

"Grandma...She...Is she all right?"

"Grandma has been very all right!" Mom smiling like sakura, "Grandma just missed you very much. Grandma hasn't seen her grandson for six months! My son, you are all 10 years old this year, and gonna graduate from primary school soon. Since childhood, grandma loves you more than me and your dad. Now, while grandma is still alive, give her more love, understand?"

"I see! I see! I see......"

Oris nodded his angel head with sun tears!

At this moment, he finally realized how benevolent the gift of nature and Art Fairy is! How great! How wonderful!

In the brilliant new world bestowed by Art Fairy, for Oris's art practice, Mama and Papa were never stingy with painstaking and ice dragon sapphires.

Once, after seeing the 3-year-old Oris caressing the golden sunshine melody on the piano of the deer eye forest grand theatre, at that time, although mom and dad was poor, they agreed to train Oris to be a great musician, artist!

Mom and dad didn't hesitate to take out a few hundred dragon claws sapphires they only had, "Buy buy buy! Buy the Luna blue butterflies flying all over the world all over the sky! Buy the morpho helena dancing all over the universe!"

Then bought Oris a narcissus princess snow white grand, and invited the best piano teacher. Mom and dad do everything they can to create as advanced art education as possible for Oris.

But Oris didn't use art as a tool just for hunting fame and fortune, as many eager and quick-to-profit people do.

Oris believes that his art is immature and needs more study, ascension, and exercise. Even Mozart and Beethoven in their childhood, after itinerant performance, they still needed to return home to continue their ascent.

If we only use art to pursue fame and fortune, our art will not only fail to achieve great attainments, but our talents will wither and die day after day in venomous vanity and bravado.

In the dark world before the gift of Art Fairy, Oris spent most of his time learning and improving, but he didn't spend most of his time making money, this made father eager for quick success hate most!

But in the glorious new world that given by Art Fairy, dad often tells the fairy cat little Oris, "The truly great art, is not to earn fame and fortune. The truly great art, is to create beauty, hope, courage, and happiness for all creatures of nature. And the truly great artist, he also needs to use his art to create the earthly happiness for himself, but he pays more attention to whether his art can create happiness for the world, and how much happiness he can create for the world. When we do our best to create happiness for the world, the world will naturally reciprocate our kindness and effort."

And mom often reminds fairy deer little Oris, "Tolstoy said that the true value of art is achieving human fraternal unity! Beethoven said, 'Since I was a child, my diligence and art have served who are suffering.' He said, 'Since childhood, my greatest happiness has been to be able to work for others.'"

"Umm!" Oris's flame tears shine eyes, "I remember it! Thank you, Dad! Thank you, Mom!"

Today, mom and dad never force Oris to make money with his bud art just like a little blooming sakura tree in flying swan snow.

Oris was so moved that rides a dream butterfly and flies to the flower sea of star river! Also grateful to climb to the white sakura peacock's back and fly into the Phoenix Nebula!

In the evening, grandma from the rose snow mountain to the home, when she hugging the little Oris, the white-haired grandma smiles like a fairy kitty. Grandma cooks herself, making Oris's favorite chive cod and windmill bread, and Alps blueberry cake rolls.

When Oris was eating, suddenly he cries as cherries raining.

"Silly boy! Why are you crying? Is it too hot? Isn't Grandma's cooking delicious?"

Grandma laughs more kindly than the shining angel in holy painting.

"It's delicious!!!" Oris's butterfly tears breaks out with sakura smile, he shakes his deer head desperately, "It's delicious!!! It's so delicious!!! So delicious that I just wanna melt in the blueberry jam river of candy fairy and sleep forever......I haven't eaten such the delicious food in a long long time......"

Grandma smiles, then feeds a piece of cod to Oris. With sakura tears, Oris was enjoying the most delicious, most tasty, and the most happy dinner.

He is the happiest fairy deer boy of the whole world!

In the gorgeous new world with sakura sunshine and butterfly dance, when Oris's family was so poor that just enough to eat only one egg of dicephalous ice dragon each day, grandma pulled Oris's winged fairy cat hand and stuffed a lot of sapphires from selling the snow mountain roses into Oris's green jade snail fairy pocket, then like the Queen of the ice phoenix who wore the crown with millions of aquamarines, she said as sakura with butterfly singing, "The Wistaria Queen and I are fine, don't worry, you protect yourself at this world, these aquamarines and rose jades are all for you, buy yourself some nebulae blue apples to eat, don't let the students think that we are the poor who can't afford to eat the fire dragon's eggs......"

But at the ice tree fairy table in the snowy forest, Oris clearly only saw one small ice berry jam cake just like the coral dragon fairy sleeping on the fluorescent mushroom, lonely dreaming in the sunshine of glass palace......

That day was Grandma's 70th birthday! Grandma grudged eating a piece of marble cake harder than a mango heart.

Sitting on the flame plume of snow phoenix flying to the flower-sea forest, Oris's cat sunshine tears turned into thousands of aquamarine fairies, with brilliant melodies, flew into the angel tear sea where mermaids was singing......

Later, when Grandma and the dragon tree fairy fought with the griffins of Night Queen, Grandma seriously injured by the poison claws, then also suffered from the snow cold illness in the recovery time at the moon well.

As soon as entered the door, Oris suddenly knelt next to grandma and crying like deer eye trees were falling, "I must bloom millions roses full of the swan palace In the future! I must take thousands flame scales dragon eggs full of glass palace! I don't want Grandma to suffer from the glaciers and flame rain all over the sky anymore! I must learn to control the griffin of Night Queen, and then ride to find the sunshine fairy spring of snow sakura queen that can cure this disease!!!"

As if just escaped from the Death Island of dragon-snakes with three heads, grandma said weakly like moon rabbit, "Good boy, Grandma doesn't want you to live harder than the phoenix rabbit fairies who bravely fights over the feather snake by the ice seaside, Grandma is afraid of your tiredness, Grandma is afraid of you getting hurt...... Grandma is gonna pick some iceberg roses and tulip Queen roses and make you snow stream rose creams that you haven't eaten before......"

Looking at Grandma's silhouette with withered feathers, Oris suddenly found that Grandma is old, and ill......when holding the sea grapes wall and stumbling out, she already couldn't step out any falling sakura singing just like Flora......

Afterwards, Grandma was frozen and feverish while protecting the frozen green phoenix children in the dragon demons snow and wind, everyday as hazy as the hummingbird fairy on the magic class, and in a trance, couldn't see which of the wings of ice butterfly and the white flame plume could fly over the diamond mountains of art forest. Even Oris's mom and dad, grandma all recognized as peacock butterfly and snow blue lightning phoenix.

But what's rabbit fairy amazing is that when Oris came to see Grandma by the golden bird's bed, Grandma suddenly bloomed the smile with hundreds of sea fairies riding fish at Oris.

Heard the piano melody of the prince at dolphin palace, heard the violin melody of the fairy on Lepus nebula, and the mermaid fairies' singing in Cetus, Grandma smiled like the purple flame humming-bird, "Oris's music and singing are like the golden morning sunshine in aquamarine tears of mermaids, more and more gorgeous."

Afterwards, Oris and mom came to the rose snow mountain to take care of Grandma, they made the fairy berry cake rolls full of magic rabbit palace for Grandma, and picked up the aquamarine tears in sun-fish sea full of Cygnus.

Bright night, Oris and mom slept next to grandma on the bird-star bed.

When the Lyra fairies were playing the lyres and singing for pleni-lune and sun-sea, Grandma suddenly awoke from the gorgeous dream of Cetus, through the Milky way brilliant, Grandma groped over to Oris and pulled up his star-moon quilt.

Saw Oris's mom wake up, Grandam said with the sound of irides-cent hummingbirds gathering purple wisteria nectar, "I wanna see if the child's star-moon quilt is covered. Don't let the brilliant stars on the quilt fall as sakura to the ground and catch a cold fever."

Covered the star feather quilt for Oris, Grandma came to golden

ART FAIRY

wire bed and sink in dream blessedly.

Grandma's blue sea breath with butterfly dancing and sakura falling, was more clear and dazzling in Lyra fairies' gorgeous singing.

In the dark night of star river, there was a drop of sea dawn tears flying from boy's mermaid eye.

Many years later, after the blood and tears in demon's fiery brambles, Oris finally rode the griffin of Night Queen to the sun mountain and found the ice deer fairy spring, then grandma's body just like the sakura phoenix of sunshine sea forest gradually better and better.

"Grandma, from now on, we will live happily ever after, just like the sea rabbit fairies and jade berry fairies on the sakura-pink moon tree, right?"

"Yes! It will be! With the shelter of art holy light and phoenix sun wings, we will be more and more happy! We will be!"

"Well! Grandma you are so gentle! As gentle as Swan Queen on the jacaranda sea! Grandma, I love you forever! Forever and forever!"

Oris fell into the faerie wings embrace of Grandma.

Touching Oris's moon rabbit head, Grandma smiled more kindly than the Swan Queen who had just saved a bud baby from the blood teeth of scorpion-bat dragons.

After eating the Lyra Fairy's dinner, at this moment, Oris is playing Grandma's favorite piano music for her.

Under the golden brilliant crystal chandelier, Oris is playing affectionately, singing with deep emotion, blooms the great emotions of brilliant melody to full blossom, so thrilling, and sakura sea blooming all over the sky.

Grandma listens and weeps suddenly, star tears just like flame rain. Because, that splendid singing and melody, illuminate her deep

missing, attachment, and deep love for Oris's grandfather who defended the motherland but died in battlefield......

Every year in chilly winter with sakura snow, Oris's mom and dad would laugh as parrot at grandma that she wore a velvet hat. Until a new year with holy light, Grandma whispered as falling star, "This hat, it's Oris's grandfather bought for me, it's the last velvet hat he gave me before he went to war, or he would have knitted one for me every year......"

By that time, Grandpa had been dead for twenty years.

Today, Grandma refused to take off that velvet hat every winter.

Before the young grandfather went out to battle, he put that velvet hat and a bunch of bright blue star flowers in Grandma's hand and held her tightly.

Afterwards, Grandma often had such a dream......

A knight with golden sword and gorgeous armor walked with his lover in a splendid flower sea on the side of mirror lake.

At the lakeside of clear diamond lake, his lover found a delicate beautiful star blue faerie flower, her cat eyes suddenly glowed with admiration.

"Handsome knight, would you like to pick me a small bundle, all right?"

But the brave knight fell into the diamond lake when he picked the flowers, and the heavy armor made him unable to swim or even breathe!

When sank into death, the knight threw the flowers to his lover regardless of everything, and cried out in sunshine tears, "Forever love! Please don't forget me! I love you forever!!! Forever!!!"

From then on, the knight's lover wore the blue flowers in her hair day and night to show their true eternal love......

For thousands of years, when people approached that sea of star-blue flowers, they heard the sunshine singing and whispers of the flower fairies,

Don't forget me......
True love......
Eternal love......
Don't forget me......

Actually, a long long time ago, when the Art Fairy Florithena finished giving names for all the flowers, an unnamed flower cried, "Oh! Florithena! Please don't forget me!"

Florithena smiled with holy sunshine, "So, this is your name."

When Florithena finished giving the color for all the flowers, she heard a little fairy clear cry, "Please don't forget me!"

But at this time there was only a little pure blue, Forget Me Not fairy still happily accepted this pure star river blue.

Now, every year on Grandpa's Day, Grandma would put a bunch of star river Forget Me Not in front of Grandpa's tombstone.

As the gorgeous melody on Oris's finger tips dancing with blooming sakura and butterflies, Grandma seemed to see her beloved, who was gone forever, slowly coming out of the holy light......

It's still so young with hot tears!

Still so handsome and beautiful!

Holding a bunch of starshine Forget Me Not that Grandma's favorite.

"Honey, are you back? There are a lot of things I wanna tell you, our little grandson now grow up, he's getting better at playing the piano, and more dulcet at singing......Now you are back! You are finally back! Our lives will be happier......We will be happier......"

Grandma talked to herself with shedding the sunshine tears of happiness.

Yes!

Is not the true value of art to create beauty, hope, courage and happiness for all creatures of nature?

Of course, all the creatures of nature include our closest relatives and loved ones.

One song after one song, one dream after one dream.

In Oris's faerie song and sakura melody, Grandma feels as if in full bloom of sunshine dream, one tulip after one tulip, seems to be back in the youth age of passion and shining dream......

The melody ends. The sakura falls.

"Well! So great playing! So perfect singing!"

Grandma smiling and applauding.

Grandma's holy kind smile, is full of the happiness with pure star tulips and blue butterfly Forget Me Not.

Looking at Grandma's smile, Oris smiles too.

Smiles so joyfully! Smiles so happily!

Smiles so feelingly! Smiles so gratefully!

Yes! With our most brilliant art, create happiness and beauty for Grandma, this, may be the best gratitude for Grandma.

In the miserable world before the gifts of Art Fairy, the winter with cold sakura snow in fourth grade, when Oris passed a high class musical instrument shop, he pointed at a delicate rose wood violin cried like a whale and screamed like a dolphin, but Papa didn't buy him!

"Where the hell did I get the money from selling whale shit to buy you such an expensive violin???"

But little deer Oris just crying like a sea gull, then Papa kicked him over the ground. Poor Oris got up, cried all the way back to the sunflower home.

I thought I would be comforted with sakura spring by my Mama, but when I was crying like the heron with opening mouth, my Mama just spat a big puff of fire fish into my mouth.

Oris immediately closed the little mermaid ice crying.

From then on, whenever Oris was bullied as a battered cat at school or beaten by wild boar Papa, Oris never looked for the flower warmth from his puffin Mama anymore.

He had learned to bear alone.

He had learned to endure in silence.

In the miserable old world, Papa found a blue phoenix violin in the dustbin of conservatory for Oris.

A worn violin, just like the little mermaid black and blue that survived under the giant claws of the ice dragon, and cruelly discarded by a demon cat.

But with this broken sakura violin, Oris played the most beautiful and most brilliant summer sunshine melody of the whole world.

But in the gorgeous new world of Art Fairy, first grade summer vacation, Oris went to the rose snow mountain to visit grandma, grandma is a very frugal person, after Oris went, Grandma bought Oris the first delicate rose fairy violin in his life, with all sales of iceberg roses and tulip queen roses, almost 3000 dollars.

At this moment, Oris is playing the violin with gorgeous summer sunshine Canon for Grandma.

"Oris, you must be an artist that creates happiness for the world! Grandma believe that those who hear you play the piano, hear you play the violin, and who hear you sing, will surely feel the endless happiness and beauty......"

"Yes! Thank you, Grandma! Grandma is always the best person in the world for me! Grandma, I love you! I love you forever!"

Oris lifts his snow mountain fairy little cat head, happily smiles out thousands of little sakura butterfly fairies.

In the gorgeous new world blessed by Art Fairy, Oris will never burst the violent Iceland volcano to grandma! Never!

He will never let grandma stumble to buy food alone again!

Never let grandma wash his clothes with ice cold water for him in the sakura snow winter! Own flower feather clothes, Oris will wash them with his own snow deer hands!

He will never hurt Grandma again!

He never wants to lose Grandma again!

Never! No more!

After all, Grandma is the one who loves you the most in this world. Once was! Now is! Forever will be!

On the night with moonshine, the Art Fairy turns Oris into Lyra fairy, he flies into the demon dragon nightmare of the bear kid Lancelot who bullies his grandmother.

The third-grade Lancelot stayed at his grandma's home during the summer vacation. He watched the stupid cartoon from the morning to the fucking 12:00 every day, ate lunch but picked the food, threw the food out of the fucking plate, and stole the hard-earned money from grandma planted nemesia!

As long as Grandma said, "Lancelot, you can't do this! Please listen to Grandma, okay?"

Little Lancelot immediately quarreled just like the fucking crazy husky, he felled to the ground, rolled and cried as wild boar, sprayed Grandma with whale shits, "Fuck your mother! You stupid old sulphur-bottom! Why don't you be torn into thousands of rosy sea rabbits by nautilus sirens!!!"

Oris flamed his eyes just in one flash! He picked up the wooden stool and threw it on the closet next to Bear Lancelot, then pointed to him and roared as the indignant dragon, "If you dare to bully grandma again, I will let your head bloom the nemesia! Do you believe I can tell my three-headed flower dragon to bite off your bad bear head right now! Turn you into a rosy sea lily! Then let the lava small witch in deep sea eat you with savoring every mouthful!"

After waking up from the nightmare, little Lancelot covers his chest, swearing and panting, doesn't dare to disrespect grandma any more.

"Grandma, I'm so sorry......I didn't know I was such a fiery piece of fire dragon shit before......Grandma, please forgive me this fire dragon shit, okay?"

"Silly kid! Grandma don't care you beat me and scold me. Grandma only care if you eat well or not, and you are happy or not......"

"Grandma!!!!!!"

Little Lancelot Hugs Grandma tightly, a sob blooms in his throat.

Just bursting into sakura tears.

The girl of fourth grade little Cynthia, as soon as her cookie mood broke like the lemon macaroon, she would hit her Grandma, but in the brilliant Lyra star dream, Oris threatens her, "If you dare to bully Grandma again, I'll throw you in the oven of Candy House and bake you into a witch finger biscuit, and then let the blue fiend cake little succuba chew you up just like chewing the fire sakura!!!"

"I don't believe it!" Little Cynthia has a proud and cute dragon face, "You big unicorn idiot, you can only sing and play the piano, you don't fucking dare to throw me away!"

So Oris one-handed picks up this little haughty cat, opens the door and throws her into the heavy death snow with flying devil beauty butterflies.

In the cold winter with dead butterflies at 23:00 in the night, Cynthia cries in despair and tears fall like ice sakura.

Grandma wants to open the door for her granddaughter, but suddenly stared by snow owl Oris's flame eyes, so she slowly withdraws her old deer hand.

In the devil butterflies sakura snow, little Cynthia cried despairingly as a injured kitten, but suddenly hears the gorgeous singing of Art Fairy,

Left wing is beauty
Right wing is demon
With fluttering of two wings
Light of goodness will shine all over the world

When the first morning sunshine dawns, as soon as little Cynthia wakes up, she bursts into tears in Grandma's arms and out of breath.

"Grandma! I, I dreamed that a big brother hit me last night! He twisted my arm and smashed me into flour, then threw me into the oven of Hell Candy House and baked me into witch finger cookies! And let me be eaten by blue fiend cake little succuba with savoring every mouthful! Then he threw me into the death heavy snow with devil beauty butterflies flying! Now I wake up but still with a pain, a pain in my arm! I'm so scared! Woowoowoowoowoo......"

"Let me see! Let me knead for you!"

Just see the holy light pour from Grandma's fingertips, the wounds on little Cynthia's arm also dance with sunshine and sakura.

"Is it still hurting?"

"Emmm......Suddenly it doesn't hurt. Grandma, do you have magic? It really doesn't hurt!"

"Everything will be okay." Grandma touches the little Cynthia's fairy kitty head.

But little Cynthia bursts into tears again, "Grandma, I, I know I am wrong! It used to be my fault! In the future, I'm not gonna be mad at you anymore! No more anger! Woowoowoowoowoo......"

"Don't cry, don't cry! Grandma know you have a bad temper. Grandma just forgive you! My angel, don't cry......As soon as saw you crying, Grandma would be so heartbroken that couldn't breahte, don't cry, okay?" Grandma hugs the little Cynthia into her feather embrace with the wings of Swan Queen.

"Grandma, thank you for being so kind to me. Grandma, I love you forever......" Crying and crying, little Cynthia suddenly smiles out thousands of light butterfly fairies all over the world.

She smiles so happily, so gratefully.

She smiles, so kindly.

In the glorious new world given by Art Fairy, looking at the children who become more and more kind, Oris also smiles with relief.

Heard Cynthia said with an orang laughing, in the first exam of grade 3, she and Oris were in one classroom, at that time, her shark eyes were attracted by the foolish of Oris.

"I was very impressed with you at that time, I thought you are very special, just like the only big piece of lion shit in thousands Sahara camel poops, very very different! Hahahahaha......"

Cynthia laughed more playfully than a raccoon who ate the devil prickly lizard, you just wanna grab her plush tail and throw her into Cetus.

"I just finished the paper forty minutes ahead of time, and the big rhino invigilator refused to hand in the paper in advance, then I get my head in the desk pocket, but I couldn't put it out! And hurt like a hairy deer pig that nose bitten by Akita dog, jut barking 'Ah ah', so the teacher and classmates pulled goddamn radish together, finally only broke the desk top to rescue me! Once I was foolish than a teacup pig, but after two goddamn years, is it necessary to bite on my ass just like a blood-sucking jellyfish???"

"Ahahaha! I just wonder that how you stuffed your pig head in? Ahahahahaha......"

"I really wish I have a pig head! That way I could get my head out! I just wanted to hide in the desk pocket and eat a packet of raccoon crisps and a bottle of mango yogurt."

"But you are sitting in the goddamn first row under the podium! Really children with intellectual disabilities are more happy! Do you know, smash your pig head and the desk would be rescued! Hahahaha! Oris you big pig head!!!" Cynthia always loves crying out "Pig head" to Oris downstairs after school in koi crowd.

"Pig head, pig head, big pig head!!!"

Remember the goddamn first exam day of grade 7, Oris raised his horse face and asked, "Teacher, can you hand in the paper in advance? I'm done! And checked over! I'm gonna hand in advance!!!"

"No, you can't."

So, in full view of public, Oris took out his phone and plugged up the headphones to listen to music. Really goddamn cool.

"You can't listen to music in the exam. Put it in your pocket."

"Oh."

Then Oris put his stupid husky head into the desk pocket, just in a moment, he screeched as an antarctic sea pig that roasting alive by hell fire. The students threw down their black pens, talked and laughed it one after another. And a bunch of goddamn raccoon were taking photos.

"Hahaha! You deserve your big pig head!"

"Hahaha! Cut off your head!"

"Hahaha! Hunger him for hundred days! Thin a whale shit so could come out!"

"Hahaha! There is school! We must show what we have learned! Em......In physical, expand with heat and contract with cold, just drop a Arctic glacier!"

"Hahaha! This is the end of eating in the exam!"

Even the teacher couldn't help laughing as snow owl.

Thinking back to those years, in the grade 3 at primary school of lifting girls' skirts and kicking boys' crotch, the teacher pulled up Oris that threw chalk and took a mirror almost blinded the teacher with sun reflection, let him answer questions, but he was so shyly that stuffed his head in the desk, then couldn't get head out, later the police came, but he also couldn't help anything.

The teacher called the fire alarm, they came with an electric saw and asked teacher, "Save his head or desk?"

The teacher glanced at Oris's textbook that had been painted with flying butterflies, bees and pegasus, then said, "Save the desk, after all, it's very expensive."

Of course it's just a goddamn joke. Finally, the female headteacher was strong enough that directly lifted the desk top.

Since then, Oris had been famous throughout the whole school. Later again, it's several classmates dismembered the desk so that rescued Oris.

"I always do this." Oris looks so proud, "Every school I went, I must try if desk could be put my head in."

"Ahahahaha......" Cynthia laughed out spraying sakura petals all over the sky, "So your head has been squeezed by goddamn desk thousands of times! Hahahaha! Oris you big stupid pig!!! Big pig head!!!"

As soon as look up, suddenly wonder that sakura trees is in full bloom.

The Sakura Blooming City that Oris rambles across corals and flies over the sky, it's a delicate small city in northern waterfall sakura sea. Thousands of blooming flame sakura trees are sleeping in the city.

Ice green glass streets. Jade lush mirror lake and forest. Flaming snow sakura on the hillside. The white house with colorful flowers on the beautiful stone path. And the small corner with falling sakura and gentle breeze.

Red Mountain Sakura. Spring Welcome Sakura. Wind Bell Sakura. Light Leaf Sakura. Sky Mountain Sakura. Snow Falling Sakura. Waterfall Sakura.

The flower flame are overflowing out of mountain. The blooming sakura are like snow. Every year from March to April in the clear clouds with pure sunshine, inadvertently raise your head, just warmly bath with sakura bright, suddenly Flora's wind whispers with petals all over the sky.

When the wind is quiet and tree is sleeping, the star petals rain all over the world, softly fall on the shoulder of boy that overturned from bicycle, fall on the sakura waterfall hair of girl that chasing a cat, fall on the furry claw of Scottish Fold teasing a Spitz.

Fall in the pure shallow waves of daisy sea.

Fall in the ray with smiling tears of Iceberg Queen and Tulip Queen.

Fall in deep crevices of every thorn.

Fall in gorgeous whirlpool of every flowering spring.

Fall on every bright dancing step of sunshine creek.

Drifting profusely and disorderly, fall in the whole world that full of splendor, and the flutter quietly.

In the world that blooming sakura sea with gentle breeze, blue sky and pure sunshine, there are many brilliant boys and girls just like gorgeous tulip sakura growing.

Oris early heard Cynthia's notoriety of night queen under the dark tulips just like Thor punctures your ears. As if she strangled ten thousand sakura rabbits on the podium, no one in Sakura Middle School doesn't know, and no one doesn't fear.

Obviously she isn't a smooth girl. But Cynthia has a ice face with full blooming paradise lilies.

Big enchanting eyes are like flame tulips. Tender face are like icelanter and jade dew in sunset glow. A hummingbird nose. A delicate small mouth that lips blooming sakura wave. And the slender figure is just like glittering crystal-clear Venus Morpho.

Her appearance is so gorgeous that many boys who ate too many fluorescent squids fell in love with her at first sight and suddenly plopped themselves heavily down on the ground.

Because, even the African lion that blinded by purple sun cactus, is far less violent than Cynthia.

In grade 4, one day after school, stupid raccoon boy Lancelot was washing his face with sea pig dung, sweeping the floor with fluttering wastepaper all over the classroom, so monitor bear Cynthia forced him into the corner, she picked up the broom and hit the boy on the head, as soon as the boy cried, Cynthia just stuffed his little parrot mouth with a chalk duster!

Another time after school, Cynthia were fighting with Lancelot as a bear and tiger, it's said that grabbing a new textbook.

"Stolen my new goddamn textbook and exchange??? Your textbook has been folded into whale shit! Why don't you use it yourself!!! Take it away and wipe your goddamn porcupine ass!!!"

Cynthia, the incarnation of bear fusing with rhinoceros, just scratched, kicked, pulled, pushed, pinched, thumped and slapped at that week deer Lancelot! Little Lancelot was no match for her, finally had to drop the new textbook, just cried and escaped as mouse hugging a cat.

In primary school, girls are much more aggressive than boys. Just as the Arctic snow gazelle runs into the end of rime forest and collides head-on with a demon lion, boys in the class are very afraid of girls, girls often gang to assault the tremble boys that in the little deer and gazelles.

At that time, in Cynthia's class, there's just one little princess rabbit girl who loved carefully playing her hair as fairy cat teases the fire-breathing fish, except her, all of girls assaulted boys!

Among them, it's Cynthia hit the most goddamn bloodily! It's the sort of slap, fist, kick, holding a chair, and the bloody assaulting with spanking ass and butting as springbok.

Cynthia really loves assaulting others! Especially loves beating her little gazelle deskmate boy Lancelot who's frightened as a deer by stream.

When asked Cynthia why, she just cried with pouring innocent flame tears from her cat eyes, "I don't know why! I just love hitting Lancelot! Everyday I couldn't help gonna hit him! If I don't hit him, I just feel like my eyeballs are rolled away by rhinoceros dung beetle! I feel goddamn sick!!!"

However, as long as could sit with such a girl like Cynthia who's so beautiful and dazzling that shocks Alps into avalanche, all the boys of class are willing to be kicked around like dung balls by the Princess of Snow Thunderbird Cynthia.

The autumn with red maple trees of fifth grade, one day in the morning, Cynthia is running over here with smiling as purple vine fairy and windbell fower fairy in spring pixies wind.

"Lend me your math homework to copy for a aquamarine-face puffin! All right!?"

Her mood is timid as a misbehaving cute kitty, timid but lovely. That pair of Venice cat eyes staring at Oris, are flowing the dazzling moon spring water shine with adoration just as butterfly adoring narcissus heart.

Although got the glorious gift of Art Fairy, Oris's math scores still doesn't have any changes just as little bees with big buttocks and big heads flying here and there bumping buttocks and heads each other.

Most of all, nature and Art Fairy will never shine the bear children with bloody tusks who loves pursuing profit, loves exam, and insanely robbing score.

Great nature and Art Fairy, only favor the the narcissus cat children who love creating happiness for the world.

In fact, the math homework of last night are just some calculation problems as poison dragonflies pulled off the wings, really simpler than the purple blood of dark dragonflies adding some honey, just chew up with savoring every mouthful and check the answers.

But Cynthia brings her chair and sits beside Oris, so close to his arms, as close as two sun-wings of a flame-tailed oriole fairy.

Then she's writing one line by one line, one letter by one letter, one word by one word for a very very long time, even longer than the phoenix fairy hatching ten sun-eggs.

As if afraid of writing too quickly so that her notebook would be torn with little fire of venomous dragon elves, and the pure blue pen would prick the butterfly pixies' wings.

Cynthia also helps Oris correct some golden squirrel little mistakes.

Until more and more classmates walking in the classroom as koi, so Cynthia has to reluctantly return the exercise book to Oris, and then very slowly moving away as a clingy kitty.

But suddenly! Cynthia comes back and takes her pure blue pen with aquamarine crown that she deliberately left on Oris's desk, then she smiles at Oris just like a charming fairy cat.

Finally, Cynthia is walking away with jumping steps and soft claws......

Chapter 7

All Beings Are Equal In Art

*O*ne night with moonshine, a tulip-sakura fairy flies into Oris's Lyra dream. Her little sakura fairy helps her tell Oris everything.

My name is Artemis, when I was born, I was just as deaf as if my ears had been set up a home by the peach blossom jellyfish and moonshine jellyfish. I could only hear a little faint melody of mermaid singing. My mom and dad thought I was a little deaf glacier mermaid, so, just a few days after I was born, I was dumped on the back of a narwhal in ice sea by Mom and Dad. I have forgotten Mom and Dad's appearance, maybe they look like the sirens with sharp ears.

A few months after I was born, my grandpa died while riding a blue whale, so in this snow ice world, only Grandma is the goddess of warmth and sunshine who loves me the most. Every day, Grandma made the conch jam cookies for lunch and the serenade blue ocean cakes for dinner. Grandma didn't have any blue bubble coral culture, and she never forced me to do questions and exams, but when I said I like music, when I said I wanted to learn to play the violin, Grandma made a promise to me, "My angel, I'm sure I'll save money to buy you the delicate narcissus fairy violin and the brilliant sunshine sakura music score, as long as you are happy, it doesn't matter how much work I pay."

But Grandma's body was more fragile than the tulip sakura tree on the top of Alps, and the Arctic snow gull whose wings and feathers melted and bled in the Icelandic volcano, she could only be a wave cleaner on the sea street and pick up some star conch bottles for money.

Last winter, when Grandma picked up a bottle on the roadside, she was scolded that tears all over the face by a haughty passer-by whose heart gushed spiders and venomous snakes, if it wasn't for a little kind-hearted deer fairy boy's help, I couldn't image what kind of bloody Christmas elk that Grandma would be whom bitten by that evil-minded snow wolf.

Over these years, I have always been grateful to my Grandma.

But one day in the school auditorium, while rehearsing New Year's Day's evening ensemble, a proud cat girl in our class who could play the piano thought that the melody I accompanied her was a little gorgeous that covered her fairy cat light, so halfway through the performance, she suddenly hit the piano hard and stood up, just one demon cat claw, she slapped the brilliant sakura music score my grandma bought me to the stage floor, and then, in front of hundreds of people in the auditorium, as if her cat tail was bitten by a little baby corgi, she yelled at me bitterly and ferociously just like a leopard.

"A stupid duck in Cherry Valley still longs to fly in the sky just like the snow swan of mirror lake! A stupid aplysia deaf fantasies to play the violin just like Beethoven! What a fucking fairy tale! Did your head be shat by Christmas tree sea worms and sakura anemones? Why don't you learn some other stupid duck art? Why don't you do the questions and exams just like everyone else? You are wasting everyone's flamboyant conch time! Do you understand? You really princess anemone big idiot!!!"

Everyone laughed like the viper fishes and flame shrimps.

Only I cried like a clown butterfly fish.

When the audiences dispersed, I was hiding alone on the sun-coral stage of auditorium, just crying loudly, despairingly.

No one came to comfort me.

Even if someone comforted me, I could hardly hear it.

At that time, how helpless I was! How desperate I was! How miserable I was! At that moment, how powerless I was!

How hopeless I was!

After school, I ran out of school crying, fell several times on the road, came home and had a big row with Grandma.

"Why am I so different from others! Why am I so different! Why! Why! Grandma you tell me why! What did I do wrong, so that God punishes me so cruelly??? Beethoven was deaf but he could still play the piano and violin, he could still devote his whole life for music, for art, and couldn't I??? Why does everyone look down on me! Why is everyone laughing at me! Why!!!"

"But why do we have to be like others?"

But no matter how much Grandma comforted me with flowers and feathers, she still was bitterly wept by m fury and grief.

"I have done my best, there's nothing more I can do...... Woowoowoo......"

Since childhood, I have never seen my Grandma cry so heartbreakingly, so heartbreakingly for me......But while crying Grandma was still making my favorite seashell cookies and ocean cakes for me.

Later, Grandma suffered a heart attack, lay in the hospital for a few days, and then, she died while riding a whale.

Once, when Grandma was awake, she told me to gonna the ward, then took my kitten hand, said with difficulty to me, "Grandma is out of money now, can't buy you music, can't cook the seashell cookie and ocean cake for you. Everything in the future will be on your own...... There's nothing more Grandma can do for you......"

My tears flew down just in one instant, the flame tears burned my fairy heart.

The last time I went to see Grandma, she clasped my fairy kitten hands, as if the fairy rabbit warrior who had lost her children in the star rain on a volcano, she gazed to me and said in despair, "Sit with Grandma for a moment. This time, Grandma really couldn't get out of the Demon Owl Palace......"

My heart hurt so much! Really hurt! Really hurt so much!

After Grandma died, every day, every day, I was regretting rowing with Grandma, really regretted, regretted so much......

I couldn't remember clearly how much humiliation and suffering Grandma suffered for me and my art, but Grandma always remembered that my favorite food was seashell jam cookie and nocturne blue sea cake.

I really regret not being nice to Grandma!

Really regret so much!

Now, I play the violin very hard every day, but Grandma could no longer hear...... I'm thinking everyday, Grandma, could you live for more years, let your granddaughter repay you well, Grandma, could you resurrect and let your granddaughter play the most brilliant violin melody for you......

Suddenly, the tulip sakura fairy Artemis hears the gorgeous singing of Art Fairy, "I can realize your dream, but in exchange, you have to pay the equivalent price and effort."

"What should I pay?" Artemis blinks her deer eyes.

Art Fairy goes on to say, "Child, you must strive for art all your life, and use your art to create beauty, hope, create courage and happiness for all the creatures of nature. It's also the responsibility of a great artist. Kind child, are you willing?"

"I'm willing!" Looking at the gorgeous pure sky, Artemis bawls with sunshine tears, "I'm willing! I'm willing!! I'm willing!!!"

Art Fairy smiles softly.

Just in one instant, there are thousands of dazzling holy lights flying out of Art Fairy's brilliant soft feathers.

Artemis's grandmother comes slowly out of the holy light. She is smiling at her granddaughter, just smiling......

Smiling so kindly, smiling so beautifully!

Artemis rushes up and hugs her grandma, just cries loudly!

"Grandma!!! I don't wanna lose you anymore!!! Grandma!!! I'll always be with you!!!"

"Grandma won't leave you again! Not anymore! My dear, my little lovely angel, don't cry, let's go home, Grandma make your favorite seashell cookies and ocean cakes."

Grandma also tightly hugs her little sakura fairy granddaughter.

By this time, the Art Fairy has taken Oris's hand and flown into the cloud with holy sunshine, Oris looks back and says to Artemis, "The people who loves us are still in this world, so cherish them! Give them more beauty, more hope and courage, give them more love, more warmth and more happiness!"

"Yes! I will!" Artemis nods her fairy head.

Looking at the Art Fairy taking Oris's hand and flying higher and farther, Artemis and her grandmother tightly hugging each other, smiling out the dazzling sunshine tears.

Before Art Fairy took Oris to fly away, he told Artemis with nightingale singing, a long long time ago, Artemis's grandmother once said to him, "My clever poor little granddaughter often tell me with sign language, if she learned the violin, she must play the most luxuriant melody for me. I am looking forward to one day, I will alive to hear my granddaughter with her violin melody......"

At this moment, on the pure narcissus violin in Artemis's hand, brilliant sakura melody is shining with thousands of moon goddess butterflies and light fairy butterflies.

The melody is flying with the splendid hymn of Art Fairy......

"Don't be sad, don't despair, don't cry! In front of art, all beings are equal! Art is alive! Music has a soul! Close your eyes, feel it with your heart. As long as you are willing to pay your kindness, your effort, your dedication, so no matter how difficult it is, nothing can stop your pursuit of art! No matter how big the cost it is, nothing can stop you from realizing your dream! As long as you are kind, hard-working, as long as you can create beauty and happiness for the world, nature will return your endless beauty and happiness!"

So, Artemis plays the violin more affectionately.

Looking at the little granddaughter, you see, the smiling that blooming on Grandma's face, how happy and beautiful it is!

From then on, every time Grandma makes seashell jam cookies and serenade ocean cakes, the tulip sakura fairy Artemis will help Grandma cut the chocolate lava bread and mango cream cake rolls, make warm golden artist tulip milk tea for Grandma, knead holy deer shoulder for Grandma, massage the legs for Grandma.

Every time Grandma is gonna mop the jasmine madrepore floor, Artemis will help Grandma hold the huge dragon bone conch mop of princess anemone.

But Artemis's height is less than grandma's shoulder, even walks wobbly, dragging a huge dragon conch mop, just like a small rose aplysia holding a snow gull's claws that dancing in the clear sky, swings excitedly, but fells in a huge wave and face is pasted by a starfish.

Grandma hears granddaughter's heartbreaking mermaid crying, as a frightened but brave deer fairy, she runs over here just in one flash, picks up Artemis right, check to see if she is hurt, and then put her on the soft big sea moon jellyfish bed, coaxes her exhausted granddaughter into deep sleep with warm sunshine words, then turns and picks up anemone mop to clear the sun coral floor.

In the glorious new world given by Art Fairy, Artemis's ears are getting to hear more flower sea melodies, she also plays the violin more and more gorgeous just like the blooming sakura in glorious sunshine.

Thus, little tulip sakura fairy Artemis continues to love her music, Grandma also lives healthily and happily day after day, year after year.

In the glorious new world given by Art Fairy, they are carefree, happy and beautiful. They are strong and brave, merciful and kind.

Artemis no longer feels inferior for her birth defect, and no longer be discouraged by the ridicule of others! Because Artemis forever remembers the glary revelation of Art Fairy.

In front of art, all beings are equal!
Every artist has the right to use his own effort and art
to create happiness of this world for himself.
Everyone has the right to use his effort to
create happiness of this world for himself.
The great artist and great people,
they would use their own efforts to create happiness for this world.
So they deserve the happiness of this world.
We must let every kind people who creates happiness for the world
and fights for dream
rightly deserve the happiness of this world!

Afterwards, in the golden melody with morning sunshine of gorgeous sakura sea, the tulip sakura fairy Artemis says to Grandma with the golden waves of tear sea, "Every other child could call her mother 'Mama', but I have never seen my mother. Grandma, I want...... I wanna call you just one 'Mama', secretly, okay......?"

Grandma nods her swan goddess head, with the flowing sunshine tears, she clasps the little tulip sakura fairy to her heaven feather bosom.

"Mama! Mama!! Mama!!!"

Mama......

Once upon a time, in the dark miserable old star world with aurora, just for the filthy ruby of snake and scorpion, just for the stupid wild boar examination score, mom and dad didn't hesitate to push the little Oris into the star sea of suicide.

At that time, mom and dad were vicious to Oris into the bottom of volcano in Arctic deep sea.

When mom's legs weren't crippled like frozen mermaid, there was one time, the 6-year-old little Oris's examination scores fell as octopus demon into the bottom of death sea, mom ferociously wrung Oris's fairy rabbit ear and said viciously, "If next time you do exams so badly again, I'll wring your long ear and throw you into the Icelandic volcano just like throwing a dark devil rabbit, and then pick up another little good snow rabbit back!"

After a moment of silence, Oris raised his flower sunshine rabbit head and said stubbornly, "That little good snow rabbit you pick up back does exams badly too! Is also his princess rabbit mother thrown out!"

"Ho ho......gonna close the sunflower door."

Hearing Mama said so, Oris's legs just shivered into the wings of Arctic sun bird. Closes the door and just turned around......

"Ah!!!!!!"

Oris's little rabbit head was beat hard by Mama with a iceberg rose violin. But Oris thought, as a strong flower sunshine rabbit came from the snow fairy mountain, he should resist the snow tears of sakura creek.

"Aha! You don't cry, do you? I guess I didn't beat hard enough, so you haven't learned your lesson yet, right?"

So Mama beat more brutally just like a vulture, Oris naturally cried out the sakura tears of snow creek.

"Still crying! Look, I'm gonna beat you stupid little bunny to death!"

"Ah! Woowoowoowoo......Ah!!! Woowoowoowoowoo......"

After beating, Mama asked, "Do you know what's your fault?"

"I don't know......" Oris babbled as parrot.

"You don't even know what's your fault???"

Papapapapapapa!!!

His mother slapped him over a dozen flame cactus.

"Do you know what's your wrong?"

"I got it......" Oris nodded his fairy rabbit head.

"You do know but still make mistakes?"

Papapapapapapa!!!

"Do you know what's your wrong?"

"......"

"No talk? Your wings are so tough now, right???!!!"

Papapapapapapa!!!

The flame cactus exploded too loudly on Oris's face, he could not hear clearly what the Siberia serpent Mama was farting.

In the summer vacation of grade four, Oris went to see grandma in Rose snow mountain, before he left, Mama smiled like a dark lizard, "I wanna keep an alpine Husky in the home, and when you come back and it doesn't know you, he'll shout at you, doesn't let you enter the door of sunflower, ahahahaha hahahahahha..."

Oris was scared to think whether to bring a Norway forest cat back to protect himself. Of course, when he came back, there's no Home Destroyer Husky and stuff.

Many times, when the family ate together, Mama had a red wine stewed in the duck breast, she bit it, but thought it was not tasty, then she threw it into the Oris's bowl and said, "Don't waste it! If you dare not eat, I'll smash your head with the violin and break the blood!!!"

Haha......

Once, Papa asked Oris to give the fairy water of the star cluster to Mama, he wanted put the cup into Mama's hand but accidentally sprinkled the water fairies on his mother's Snake Griffin arm.

"Mom!!! I dare not do it next time!!! Please don't smash my head with violin!!! Please!!!!!!"

Papa said, "There are too few water fairies, pour more."

Then silly Oris poured the remaining half cup of star cluster fairy water on the Mama's Snake Griffin wing. After the reaction, Oris realized that he misunderstood Papa's meaning and hurriedly hid himself under the purple vine piano.

"Come here, I promise I won't beat you into an ice crystal panda." Mama said.

Oris hesitated several small flames raccoons, then only one parrot step by one parrot step cowardly to move over.

"Did you think I didn't dare to beat you!!!???"

Mama directly smacked one ice demon cactus on Oris's face.

"I never thought you dared not hit me...!" Oris covered the face, cried like cat and sobbed like rabbit.

"You, gonna take the daffodil violin yourself!"

Mom is cruel, and want me to offer the tools that hit me.

"Go, shut the sunflower door."

Turn off the shining sunflower door and turn back...

Ah!!!

Ah!!!!!!

Ah!!!!!!!!!

After finished hitting, Mama rubbed the medicine to his head and neck with heartbroken face, asked like a meek serpent, "Mink rabbit silly boy, why didn't you run???"

Where the fuck could I run???

The first time Oris played a concert because he was reluctant to play the rubbish works he hated, which led to his father losing money just like sucking his blood.

After the ending, Papa was laughed at in public: "Is this your son Beethoven's reborn panda rabbit? Ha ha ha ha ha!!! I'm almost laughing into a singing donkey!!!"

When got home, Papa grabbed Oris's hair and hit on the wall! Hit on the piano! Blow it on the keys! Then, Papa slapped Oris a dozen flame cactus!

Oris's ears were slapped that seemed to fly into one million dark forest tiger wasps.

When dad got tired, Oris rose up from the ground, He just wanted to say, "Papa, did you eat blue whale lunch?" To ease the atmosphere, but with a trembling mouth, he said, "Dad, haven't you eaten fairy lunch???"

"What the fuck do you say!? Roll the fuck over here!!!"

Realized something was gonna fuck again, Oris hurried to hide in the room and shut the door of moon sunflower firmly.

"Open the door! You open the door! " Dad beat the door of flowers tears and with frenzy. "Just open the door! I promise I won't beat you into a skull parrot tulips!!!"

After a while, Oris quietly opened a gap in the door, but Papa just "popping" kick the door open.

"You promise not to hit me!!! You promised!!!"

"I just promise not to kill you Caribbean volcano rabbit!!!"

A flame cactus flew here, and suddenly everything just went to dark......

Woke up and touched the rabbit face, It's still warm and burning, like just bitten by Hellfire Raccoon.

Ha ha!

In the miserable world with ice rock and roaring flame, Papa and Mama's dragon teeth were poisonous that put Oris fall into whale demons' mouth.

But now, in the glorious new world bestowed by the Art Fairy, Papa and Mama have become very new!

They no longer force Oris to wither his young bud art in the aurora glacier just to make money!

They never push Oris to get the exam scores just like a boar hit trees!

They no longer beat the young soft cat narcissus little Oris!

Mama and Papa, have become very very merciful and kind!

Once Papa's orchestra rehearsed the chorus, the volcano stage suddenly collapsed! Papa broke all over the body and lay on the cloud bed for a whole season with flame sakura. He couldn't move, but suddenly woke up in a falling sakura evening.

Papa's mouth was always rustling like hummingbird, Mama approached his ear and said, "Don't be anxious, you have me swan fairy beside you!"

"Our son might go home now......" Papa was as weak as a Paradise bird running out of Iceland lava, "Could you go home and make the fairy lunch...... Our little angel said he wanted to eat egg yolk juice lamb chops and lemon seafood rolls. When I came home, I bought lamb chops, squid and lobster, and put them in the fridge......"

On the day Papa's accident, before went to school, Oris said to Papa,"I wanna eat egg yolk juice lamb chops and lemon seafood rolls."

Papa remembered.

In the coma of sakura snow sunshine dream, in the glorious and beautiful world, Papa remembers forever!

"Rest assured! All what our son wants to eat, I'll do it for him! If I can't do it, I try to learn to do it!!!"

Holding Papa's hands, Mama's sunshine tears were dancing in the eyes.

When Oris was 5 years old, Papa and Mama took all their savings and exhausted the power of summer sakura, bought a narcissus triangle snow piano for Oris, invited the most conscientious and the most beautiful piano teacher for Oris. But the life of family was strapped to the crater of Iceland, and bitter cold to the Arctic glacier.

Remembered a winter, the heavy snow with dead butterflies drowned Mama's purple vine knees. That day, Oris practiced the piano so excessively that got a had a high fever, In order to get Oris a doctor, Mama was carrying him on the back, one deer step by one deer step, walking from home to the children's hospital five kilometers away. The second nurse took Oris, Mama just heavily fell down on the ground.

On New Year's Eve, there was no money at home, Mama did not ask anybody for money. She sent Oris to his aunt's house, then went back to the humble and ruined sunflower home.

On New Year's Eve, Mama and Papa just ate Siberia lily bulbs and Iceland lava bread sticks.

At first, I thought it was something made my mother send me to aunt's house to celebrate the new year, because my aunt's family was in good condition, and brothers and sisters played with me.

Now, when I grow up, Mama told me: "Every time I send you to aunt's home, it's because I there's nothing to eat at home. I'm afraid to starve to you."

At this moment, it is difficult to sleep at night. I feel very warm and happy when I hear Mama's breathing with sleeping.

Mom and Dad, with your companion, I am so happy, really happy.

I love you!

Love you forever!

Forever and forever!

In grade four, Oris went to the final of Sunflower International Piano Competition alone, mom and dad both have music and dance performances, they couldn't accompany Oris, so he ate out at noon and delivers awards in the afternoon.

But competition terrain only had a tulip forest away from home, so Oris jumped back just like a deer. Because didn't tell mom and dad, when Oris entered the door, mom and dad were startled to jump as snow antelopes!

Oris looked at the table and said, "How could you only eat lavender roast corns and devil potato chips?"

Dad said, "You didn't say you would come back, we haven't had time to prepare......"

Mom smiled with glistening waves and said, "If you don't eat at home, we'll just eat some swan fairy food......"

Oris sat down, ate and ate, then cried with falling sakura and mirror lake, cried out the flower sea and petals flying with wind.

Later, because mom and dad worked hard day after day as cedar, the conditions of Oris's family are gradually flourishing with thousands of jacaranda trees, they also bought a Provence white rose harp for Oris, hope that Oris can comprehend by analogy on the snow mountain way of music and art, learn widely from others' strong, make fusion and innovation, like the diligent bee fairy, melt thousands flowers and make them into one mel your own.

Oris wanted to put the harp in the sitting room, but mom and dad wanted to put it in their Phalaenopsis bedroom, they had been arguing all the time. Finally, mom and dad had to compromise.

Many years has past, one day, mom told Oris, "Actually, once I wanted to put the harp in our bedroom, just because I want you practice in our room, so you could accompany us more......"

At that moment, Oris could not help crying out sakura tears while playing the harp. He immediately moved the rose wood harp to mom and dad's room. Ever since then, Oris plays the most beautiful flower sea melody for mom and dad every day.

The happy smile of my mom and dad, is my greatest and best sakura sunshine encouragement.

Remembered when Oris was very small and small than the silver fox rabbit, one day he was sick, dad fed him medicine, but Oris was choked, so mom scolded dad:"Look at you old stupid arctic bear. Why are you so careless? Choke our little Oris into the little snow rabbit that couldn't gulp Pearl jellyfish. Quickly! Roll out like ten thousand hamsters!"

Dad quietly rolled out the snow sakura room.

Later, Oris looked for dad, and saw him crying in the living room just like a little panda hare who broke the narcissus fairy's moon crown.

When Oris was 3 years old, his little mermaid sakura hand were burned by the boiling voodoo that made with submarine magma by children-eating Siren, It's more painful than the snow fairy unicorn that steps into Iceland's magma. But miraculously, Oris's little mermaid hand did not break and bloom the scorching sun scar in rose buds.

This section of sea apple memories, Oris has alrealy lost as stars rain on the cat coral' gem tail, when he grew up, is mom and dad who told him as silent feathers on the deer creek.

Now, in the glorious new world with spring sun and dews, butter-flies and orioles, once dad made the sea horn sakura lunch of red deer hall for Oris, but accidentally hurt by the cat eye fire of sun coral pan, Oris was so frightened that hurried to find the Jasmine Fairy Spring to wipe dad's wounds.

Looked at the little Oris Prince of Lyra Star, who was carefully poured the sun-lustre fairy spring, Suddenly dad bloomed more heart-breaking than seeing his snow rabbit child butten by the volcanic thun-derbird's poison claws.

"So that how badly hurt it is burned by the cat eye flames, I don't really know once how you suffered and got through it with Narcissus Princess......"

In a flash, Oris's sea sunshine gem tears fell to the gorgeous clouds, and in a twinkling of one second, just flying with flowers rain all over the sky!

Papa, as long as ypu really love me, then no matter how big the dragon flame fire scars can not burn up the sakura spring and flower sea in my heart!

Em! Papa I love you forever!

When I was 5 years old, dad liked to ask me to go with him to Art Forest and buy scales of three heads flower dragon, on the way, dad always gave his little finger for me.

When met the shop selling purple pearl cherries and white jade cherries, I asked dad directly, and dad also liked to buy them for me.

Now I have grown up, once dad asked me to go with him to buy flaming tulips and sea mangoes, I walked behind, but saw dad's little finger still protruded, just as I was holding him when I was a child.

Really can't help the tear of Oriole Fairy......

Mom and dad in the new gorgeous world, have become more and more benevolent and kind!

Once upon a time, in the miserable world before the gift given by Art Fairy, sometimes after school, Oris didn't wanna gonna aunt's home to eat dinner with bearing rebuking just like blue dragonfly in the nepenthes, so he went back home and cooked his own cherry fairy dinner.

When making Sea Fairy cake, the eggs were burnt in the oven and hard to pick off. When making mango heart tarts, just opened the oven but eggs exploded all over the cat face. When making a raspberry creamy roll, but choked by cream into an ice fire drangon face flower.

Sometomes in the school beaten by the husky classmates who loved whirling buttocks and farting fire, so when Oris came back home simply didn't wanna make fairy dinner.

No any condensed milk mood to cook!

No any sea honey mood for eating!

But now, all sorrow and suffering have been purified by the light of Art Fairy!

In the glorious new world bestowed by Art Fairy, Mom and Dad's love for Oris is as luxuriant as Waterfall Sakura trees all over the city, as blooming as the flower sea all over the sky!

Everyday before school, Oris would tell Mom what kind of vanilla steak he wanna eat for dinner, what kind of fried lavender oysters, what cream onion roll prawns, what shrimp papaya lime salad, want scallion cookies or not, want pineapple pie or not, want what kind of angel mousse juice, what kind of wine snow pear cherry juice, and then after school step through the home door just can eat delicious sakura sunshine fairy dinner!

Everyday mom would make lobster spaghetti and mango cake that Oris's favorite.

"I'm learning Provenve fozen yoghurt today." Mom is confident like Flower God, "When you come home from school, you can just eat it into your small moon orioble mouth."

Oris is just deeply moved into the meteors of Cygnus!

When I was 7 years old, I was seriously wounded by sharp claws in a fierce battle with the flame eyes scorpion lion who loved eating souls of children. The lizard poison witch doctor said the fox and wolf words, "Within three days, Oris will die in the Moon God's flower arms with princess sea anemone."

At that time, my family was so poor that even could not afford to eat rainbow lily of the valley on Spring Flowing tree, relatives and friends all advised my mom and dad not to spend any more precious bloody demon palace rubies in the claws of griffins, it's better gather the branches of snow dragon trees and respberrirs of Arctic cedars, get ready to cremate me at the top of Flaming Parrot Mountain.

But my mother still wove a pair of bright flame wing with gorgeous pure star for me, as she swept, but helped me connect the rose scars of butterfly sphenoid.

"Are the wings fit? Does the wound still hurt?"

I nodded my kitty head, but in a twinkling I wobbled the Lyra Fairy head. Saw Mom flowing the star sea tears of Fairy Queen, I couldn't help crying out thousands of little flaming butterfly fairies any more.

A few days ago, Mom had a high fever, and Dad wasn't at home, so I fed mom sakura lake fairy spring.

I can't forget that when I approached mom, she covered her mouth and nose, whispered with a spirit of sakura bud, "Hurry to walk away! Don't infect you with the small dark moon poison sunflower evil elves!"

However, the sakura sunshine of memory rayed in my eyes......

When we are very young, when we had a high fever, we lay in the swam arms of Mom, listening to her soft feathers and flowering words......

"My little angel, Mom will forever be with you."

Mom as a Ballet Fairy, daily rehearsals are harder than the Swan Fairy fighting snow mountain ice dragon and lava fire dragon.

At this moment, looking at mom's beautiful back with cooking, Oris sees very clear that the scale wounds of tired all the day with bloody feathers then finally go back home but still need to cook for dinner.

Think of myself sitting at the piano just like a snow nightingale prince foolishly waiting for sakura dinner after school everyday, Oris is really more ashamed than the snow rabbit soldiers who hides in ice cave to escape the fire dragon! Really more heartbreaking than seeing the Lyra Goddess in order to save all living creatures so die with ice dragons and fire dragons!

The butterfly heart is so painful that broke into the sakura petals all over the sky!

Then hugs the daffodil mom behind.

"Mama! I love you! Forever love you!"

Just like ten angel narcissus blooming on the lips, Mama smiles out ten little tulip fairies, "My angel, mom love you, too! You are forever mom's Narcissus Prince!"

Oris's heart is full of bright spring, blue cat eyes just overflow happy sunshine tears.

Later, when the Art Fairy leads Oris to search for suffering of the world, Oris saw so many miserable and tragic sunmmer sakura children!

Said a snow gull fairy in the heart of Aegean......

Today, I painted a Pegasus Unicorn on the gorgeous contract of harp warbler fairy, when my porcupine father from black forest saw it, he just directly raised the flaming cactus and "Pa pa pa pa pa pa pa" slapped me several fiery dragon fruits, then he screamed just like his porcupine cub was stolen by Siberian snow wolves,

"Why the fuck don't learn other people's kids? You don't do the test well, just doing these dog fangs rubbish all the day and every day which can't add points of test and can't make money! If you paint more even one, I must kill you little squirrel from Harp Fairy Forest!"

Then my gorgeous contract given by harp warbler fairy and my Pegasus Unicorn all were torn into sun-angel tulips with sakura flame and blue star fire all over the sky.

But when my kindness and effort moved nature, the whole world flamed to very new look!

Now, when I paint snow sakura white peacock with lily fairies, my Snow Heron Dad and Orange-headed Golden Weaving Mom never abuse me Alaska Husky anymore.

Then no longer tear my Sakura Fairy art works into falling snow and flying sakura.

Not only that, but they bought me a lot of brushes, pigments, palettes, canvas and colored pencils, they also bought me the biography and notes of Da Vinci as thick and exquisite as sunflower parrots.

They hired me the most conscienrious painting teachers, sent me to the most free, the most humane brilliant art palace.

Mom and Dad also gave me the encouraging and support that I was longing but unreachable.

A sky full of sakura waterfall encouraging and sakura tree supports.

Dad said, "When mom and dad make a snowy mountain full of pinecone chestnut money, we will take you to the snow mountain with morning sunshine and mirror lake in flower sea to find the most gorgeous scenery."

Mom said, "When your painting skills are getting better just like Sakura Jade Purple Vines flying with butterflies all over the sky, you can also paint fantastic exquisite original paintings, and creat the extremely perfect animation and film."

Dad said, "When you read many beautiful and moving stories, you can also dedicate a sakura sunshine paintings book perfectly fused with true, goodness, beauty, and then use it to heal every wounded heart of the world."

Mom said, "When you have a kind heart, good heart, when your painting skills are increasingly refined, you will be able to paint many great, world-shaking perfect paintings! Mom and Dad will believe in you forever!"

Mom and Dad said, "My angel, you must remember that a great artist, his first ideal, is to strive to create beauty, hope, courage and happiness for the world, and he must get the happiness of this world he deserves."

Mom and Dad said, "Baby, we will forever support you!"

I have long been tearful with glowing heart full of flaming sakura and flower sea.

Mom and Dad, thank you!

I love you forever!

Forever and forever!

Said the Oriole Fairy of Moonshine Forest......

Once upon the time, I made a small stars river basket with Hummingbird fairy, and made dozens of White Parrot Tulip anadems, but my Spun-golden Gibbon father hit me hard with the Aegean strawberry tree, and threw my little basket and parrot anadems into the flames of hell.

With my own tulip cat eyes, I watched that the Fairy Anadems braided by me and Hummingbirds were in the fire with crying, whining......The heart of me and Hummingbird Fairy were burning with sakura blood.

Suddenly, countless little sun-parrots rushed out of the flames, flying around me, spinning, singing, lamenting, whispering, spiriting souls, and finally disappeared in the gorgeous Fairy Nebula.

I will never forget that starry night with silver river, I was crying more heartbroken than the Swan Fairy Mother who lost her children in the crater, more heartbroken than the Snow Warbler Mother who watched her babies being burned alive by the the glacier fire dragon.

But when my kindness and effort moved nature, the whole world flamed on a new look!

Now, Mom and Dad never burn my beloved Flower Sea fairies.

Mom and Dad never stop me from gonna tulip sea to look for Love fairies, Moon Butterfly fairies and Light fairies. Mom and Dad never stop me from raising a lot of bright tulips at home.

White Parrot tulips. Golden Artist tulips.

Christmas Dream tulips. Caroling tulips.

Twilight tulips. Golden Talent tulips. Ballet Fairy tulips.

Angel tulips. Love Song tulips. Dream Ship tulips.

Beautiful Queen Sakura Tears tulips. Gorgeous Sunshine tulips. Ruby Parrot tulips. Sapphire Parrot tulips.

Mom and Dad never stop me from keeping a lot of Flower Fairy parrots at home.

White Tulip parrots. Sunflower Phoenix parrots. Blue Eyes Sunflower parrot. Ice Blue Shinning Moon parrots. Blue Sunshine Sea parrots. Golden Sun parrots.

King parrot. Queen parrots. Princess parrots.

Beautiful Singing Jadeite parrots.

Scarlet Sucking Honey parrots. Rainbow Sucking Honey parrots. Chattering Sucking Honey parrots.

Daisy parrots. Snow Blue Lightning parrots. Glacier Phoenix parrots.

The Tulip Fairies and Parrot Fairies are all back! They all come back!

We are together weave the most beautiful brilliant flower baskets and tulip anadems, we together look up the clear sky, sing the most beautiful songs, we together whirl with dancing!

I'm really so happy! I'm so happy!

But oneday, the flower fairies held the faraway sakura snow singing in their hands, flew to my little bud ear.

Heard a boy said, "I really wish I could have enough fairy food to eat everyday......"

Heard a girl said, "I really wish my sakura fairy Mom could have new clothes......"

Heard a boy said, " I really want a little brilliant brush......"

Heard a girl said, "I really wanna have a small butterfly orchid painting book......"

Heard a boy said, "I really wanna have a narcissus violin......"

Heard a girl said, "I really want a jacaranda desk......"

Heard a boy said, "I wish I could afford a dreamland movie ticket......"

I can't help bursting into loud sobbing!

Tears turn into the Meteor Flame fairies chopping ice dragons and fire dragons, the fairies move forward with splendid courage, charge forward with flying feather!

Sunshine tears dancing as butterflies and flying as sakura, the gorgeous light falling as flowers rain all over the sky!

So, I sold the beautiful tulips to thousands of kind-hearted people and merciful people, then give the money to miserable children, help them live better, have money to eat, have money to see a doctor, and then freely realize their brilliant dreams.

Later, the flower fairies held the singing of summer sakura to my Crystal Rose Butterfly ears.

Heard that boy said, "As long as eat full everyday and not starving, then I will be as happy as a little snow deer walking through the blue cedar forest and silver cedar forest and then running into the daisy sea."

Heard that girl said, "My Mom finally has a new canary flower dress! Now no one else will look down upon her just because she is a humble sea star poor cleaner! I'm so glad! I'm so happy!"

Heard that boy said, "I saw a cancer girl, she used a little tender brush to beg her mother who abandoned her to stay. In the painting, the girl and her mother big hand in little hand, stroll in the gorgeous flower sea under snow mountain, sakura sunshine smile just blooming on the mother and girl's Love God faces......I swear, I will paint harder than Da Vinci, Rafeal, Michelangelo, and then teach her to paint the most beautiful and holiest scenery of the world, bring her glowing brilliant courage and power of the Immortal Phoenix Star."

Heard that girl said, "I must use my snowy mountain story and flower sea painting book to warm every cold bud heart, heal every wounded sakura sunshine soul. I will forever be with a dedicated heart, burn my own life, illuminate the whole world!"

Heard that boy said, "I must use my narcissus violin and sun art to save those homeless children! I'm gonna take them out of violence and war! Out of hunger and poverty!"

Heard that girl said, "I must use mighty literary power to save the fragile souls of people! Save our great civilization!"

Heard that boy said, "I must use the film to record the world's truth, goodness, beauty! I hope people love this world! I want all those who suffer fully forever have courage to face life, forever have courage to dedicate, and ultimately change the world!"

Many years have passed, and they all have fulfilled their glorious promises.

The world with snow, ice and flower sea coexisting, has become more brilliant and beautiful.

Chapter 8

Moon Spring and Atonement

*T*he Sun Oriole fairy of ice blue mirror lake said......

When I was 9 years old, I got 99 vanity in the test, then my evil lizard Mom picked up the math book that snakes and scorpions creeping on and hard slapped my kitty head and little bear face.

She was slapping while screaming with spurting fire, "Why you didn't get 100 vanity? why don't you study harder? I really wanna slap you to death! You sapphire arctic fox!!!"

One night I was so tired into fire rose spider of writing spider nest homework, so I watched animation just for a little while, but my mom came back and found me watching TV, she suddenly became a big monster bat fish, then immediately picked up dozens of electric eels and beat me that burst into tears.

"I wash dishes in restaurant as hard as Alps flying snow gazelle frantically bitten and chased by African lions, but you are like a Siberian little loris that so depraved!!! Just know watching TV with Norwegian potto all the day!!!"

Pa! Pa!! Pa!!!

Lava cactus and fire dragon ball cactus coming on the horizon, the hellfire stream buried the aurora and snow night just in one instant!

"Don't do your homework well??? Can't get in the first three of grade??? Are you worthy of my upbringing??? Over these years, I've fed you a handful of sulphur-bottom shit and a bowl of jellyfish urine everyday that brought you up, but you only repay me with the mermaid tears of Coral Castle!!!??? Do you believe I'm gonna take the rose loster of fluorescent coast right now and smash the TV into stars rain and sakura petals!!! Do you fucking believe it!!! I really wanna slap you to death!!! You arctic blue star fox!!!"

I was crying more heartbroken than the Flower Lyra Tree fairies under fire rain with flying petals, more despairingly than the Phoenix Tree fairies burning in the hellfire sea!

I don't know what ever I did wrong about the fire mermaid sea grapes.

From my childhood, in my mom's skeleton whale evil eyes, the demon shark homework with tearing blood by fangs and the test vanity with monster bat fishes abscuring sun and sky, are forever more important than the sakura sea happiness of me.

In the second year of junior high school, my final comment was "top of the list", but my father just like frosty evil skeleton dragon that erupting ice, he said in a glacial voice, "But it's not the best fucking number one!"

When I was in high school, I accidentally missed the number one in test, so my three-headed snake father picked up a cactus pencil-box and hard slammed it on my fairy cat face, he rode a venomous lion-fish with telsons, and roared crazily with evil spirit flame, "You really are a big whaling thunderbird fool, Your handwriting is as ugly as the blue flame dragon skeleton!"

In fact, my classmates and teachers all said that my handwriting is as beautiful as Flying Feathers Snow Deer.

But these are my lemon shark parents.

Even though my grades were so good that ten thousands skeleton chihuahuas were flying out, my mom would not praise me for even just one Forest Fairy little biscuit. She just showed a fire demon face with disdain and spraying fire with crocodilian eyes, "Look at that slimy worm kid who took the number one, and then look at you this ugly stupid big rabbit ear fairy!!!"

So over time, I had the little flaming octopus resistance with rhinoceroses' horns and little flying elephant with sharp ivories to test.

Later, my grades were like ice dragonflies in the mouth of blue flaming parrots of mushroom cloud castle, just disappeared in clouds, didn't leave even one bone.

Because my poison worms test vanity were corpses everywhere, so in my parents' skull blood demon eyes, whatever I did, all just like wearing the fulgurite fire boots with dancing, everything of me is just big big big mistake.

But I couldn't hate my mom and dad just like lion succubae.

On Mother's Day, I lied to my mother that I wouldn't go home to eat blue bean fairy lunch at noon, but actually I went to Summer Sunshine Lake to buy fairy flowers.

At the Phantom Irene Butterfly Door of home, I was holding the unicorn flowers and phoenix feather orchids, put the sea sakura letter that I prepared for three fairy night with shining moon on the sun blossoms, dreaming to see mother's deer eyes with blooming bright and smiling.

However, the fact just like the devil chihuahua jumped out of my ice hole little expectations, mom didn't seem to be as happy dolphin as I imagined, even not bloom just one smiling owl that escapes from avalanche.

"Maybe when she saw my sea sakura letter, she would be as touched and happy as the flaming feather eggs hatch......" I tried to comfort my Glacier Rose Heart.

The next week, when I returned to the Phantom Irene Butterfly Home, I found a crumpled dead butterflies paper under the sofa, then I picked up it and saw with my rabbit eyes......

Isn't my carefully prepared sea sakura letter?

I feel more aggrieved than the Parrot Princess imprisoned in the succuba flower cage!

All the sincere golden orioles sunshine words, all the tree owls family love that can't be expressed face to face, were written in this mermaid fairy letter.

I thought my mother would keep this mermaid letter as carefully as golden oriole protecting her sun eggs, but it turned out that she didn't care just like the moon fell in snow stream, so crushing my Ocean Fairy cake heart.

Even not enough seven days, that big bunch of unicorn flowers and phoenix feather orchids were thrown into the magma ice cave of Parrot Carcass Mountain.

I thought my mom would do every raspberry thing possible to keep the flowers into Butterfly Fairy Wings!

Really felt hurt by the ice thorns of Fire Dragon Nut Demon King!

"I saw all the flowers withered into stardust fairies, so I threw them away just like chewing the cat claw cookies! Don't waste dragon claw sapphires on these turtle eggs in the future, or I'll mince you little mermaid with cat eyes and rabbit ears!!!"

Since then, I had been utterly desperate for my siren mother just like flaming star rain smashing into glaciers.

Since childhood, my Coral Devil Mom had not one day without fangs cursing, me and Sea Lizard Fish dad were scolded in turn. Any nasty telsons and thorns could be pricked into your ears and eyes when mom swore.

"Slap you to death just with one tail, you little starfish trash!!!"

"Just know eating all the day!!! Even the little fairy rabbit fish's tear is better than you!!!"

"What a shame! My Dog Mother Fish' face is thrown all by you!!!"

"So stupid! I really wanna chop you to death with an axe fish!!!"

"Go away, go away!!! Don't stand in front of me just like a piece of sunfish shit!!! I'm so miserable to see you that as if my eye balls are rolled away by the King of Dung Beetle!!!"

"I'd rather not have you!!! Giving birth to a big lava sea pig or ghost dragon seahorse is ten thousands times better than giving birth to you!!!"

These shark words with venomous thorns, poke at my soft sea rabbit heart every day.

When I was seriously ill with black rose devils, my mom just left me alone, later I was almost coughing out the blood grape banshees, with swearing all the way, mom finally took me to the Black Palace to see a doctor, tiger ear doctor said that the cold medicine is 11 dragon paw blood rubies, mom thought it was too expensive, so she began to burn a baboon face to the tiger tail doctor, "Eleven dragon paw blood rubies!!! I can cure my cat-butterfly daughter when I go home! I will never let the Black Demon Cave hospital of Tiger Demon Forest cheat me one blood dragon ruby!!! Even just a small one!!!!!!"

Just in one flash, the whale smile on the doctor's face withered and fell, then disappeared without shadow.

Later, I was under the protection with fairy light rain of White Phoenix and Lyra Forest so that I could be strong to get through the sea of black rose thorns.

Mom would also abuse me like flaming dragon in the public place where the mermaids fly and snow gulls sing on the fairy sunshine sea, snuck to look at my ice fox tail bag, peep at my little Star Rain Flaming Rabbit privacy, when met my samoye classmates, she would mock the other little corgi classmates, when at parents meeting, she would also burst a hag clash with my classmate's black succuba mother, and so that made me isolated in the wind with flowers raining of silver bell trees, and then I was bullied as raspberry-loriot by classmates on the blueberry trees.

"Mama, could you be kind to me shining blue warbler with just a little cat tongue milk cooky? Could you give me a little small cherry respect on the cat claw marshmallows?"

But my mom didn't think she had any trampling and cruelty under the Nightmare Flaming Horse's hoofs, "Can you fucking stop screaming with wild fangs like a bat-chihuahua? Respect you fucking Milk Emperor Roasted Dragon eggs!!! Without me, you are just as worthless as ice dragon's shattered egg shell!!! Understand??? Who the fuck gave you the courage to talk to your mother like that!!! King of husky!!!???"

Mom was as sick as the gazelle that had escaped from death in the mouth of Blood Eye Griffin, so every time burst out a quarrel with me just like fighting with gazelle horns, it is all ending up with my head bleeding, burning scars and hiding on the sakura tree in grievance, the lantern fish kinfolks with fangs in deep sea also didn't recognize whale's black and shark's white, they only would gnaw my burning bleeding scars with my mom.

I had been holding back the flaming dragon's blood tears and didn't tell mom, every time the conflicting with gazelle horns, not only your heart broken like Devil Cake, my little Cat Cake Heart also would be so wronged that just wanted to be pierced through instantly by Thorn Dragon's silver flaming tusks!

Mom and dad's icy sarcasms and fiery jeers, made me not know how soon could it take me to involuntarily walk into Shining Moom Forest and touch the dragon to suicide.

At New Year's Eve concert, I was emotionally singing with mermaid fairies on the Crystal Phoenix Palace.

But mom just said in front of the crowd, "You are singing like hell! It's really like be choked to death by the shits of parrot-mouth fishes!!!"

The students were all laughing that their mouths spewing out thousands of whales.

Therefore, up to now, I dare not sing resoundingly with Lyra on the gorgeous blue sea with flying mermaids and dancing jellyfishes, even though my mermaid friends said that my singing was more beautiful than the lyre playing of dawn fairies, I still dare not sing resoundingly with the waterfall sakura of faery forest.

Later I painted, painted the little Sea Rabbit Fairy on the Flying Pegasus Unicorn, but mom said with the disdainful lemon-sharks face and distasteful flaming dragon eyes, "It's so fucking ugly! So fucking ugly that I'm about to spew out ten thousands butterfly-dogs who love eating mango demon cakes! What can you do with painting??? Can you catch the bloody dragon claws rubies with them???"

So, all these years since I was as small as Alpine fox-dog and now as big as Madagascar's blue-eye lemur, I've been looking forward to the faraway shining sea and sunshine, but also dreading all the flaming sirens and demon dragons.

I'm so timid that even the sunflower parrots flying out with feathers from phoenix trees would scare me into sea-aquamarine tears falling all over the Flying Rabbits Forest.

I'm afraid to talk with people about little raccoons, little pandas and little honey bears, because every time I yearned for glory and affirmation, all I get just is black rose negation that full of boundless thorns flower sea.

It should have been a beautiful childhood and adolescence just like gorgeous sakura trees in sunshine to everyone, but to me, is just a nightmare of bloody demon-dragons with Night Queen Griffins' carcasses all over the snow mountain.

I still remember that just like branding on my bones, at the end of primary school, the day of parents' meeting was a cloudy day with bloody butterflies, but because my test vanity were not as good as evil spirit black dragonflies flying all over the sky, so after the meeting went back to Phantom Irene Butterfly Home, mom were abusing me with dragon tusks all the way.

Then when walking up the stairs of Demon Dragon Palace, between the second and third floors, mom was scolding but suddenly turned around, clenched her teeth and said the icy sharp words that I would never forget and be cured by sakura in my whole life......

"You are the biggest stain with scale scars of my whole mermaid life!!!!!!"

From then on, the sharp bone-piercing inferiority and burning sensitivity tightly entangled me just like a young ice dragon and a young fire dragon with thorny thunderbolt tails.

Once before the exam, I lost sleep until 3 o'clock in the morning, then had just sunk into Milky Way Star Dream for a little while, at 4:30, my mom swore and shouted like a frenzied three-headed snake-wolf to wake me up, the reason was merely, "I'm afraid you'll be late! What if miss the test! Get the fuck up!!!"

So I no longer had even just one ghost flaming rabbit sleepiness.

That day I still had severe stomachache so that couldn't straighten up my snow rabbit fairy waist, but mom didn't care at all, opened mouth and closed and opened again in the so early morning just for bloody shark examination, just for thorn vanity, just for the ice-spewing fire-bursting stupid famous university.

"Look at other people's pitaya children, then look at you little Sea Moon Jellyfish sneaky homunculus!!! Treat the exam so carelessly, how to get into a famous university in the future? Really a big idiot Aegean bear!!!"

My aquamarine tear fairies were just flying and dancing in the golden sunshine and snow cloud all over the sky, "Please don't scold me, please don't scold me......Okay......? Please......Woowoowoowoowoo...... Really please!!!"

But mom still continued to scold just like a glacier giant wolf with bloody tusks.

"I have never seen someone like you so stupid honey-stealing little raccoon, the retarded fox frozen thousands years by Snow Succuba is better than you! With an Alpine iceberg to break your head open, it will definitely capture the spirits of all desert dung beetles so hungry that not picky and choosy!!!"

Scold me every day.

Scold me every day.

Scold me every day.

Every day! Every day! Every! Every! Every day!

Any Snow Demons and Icy Thorns could be spewed out!

"Why don't you gonna die? Why aren't you gonna die!!! Really You really useless!!! You are really a great waste of ghost whale shit!!!"

"Wild boar brain! Sea pig brain! What a really porcupine brain with venomous thorns all over the head!!!"

"Just know eating the Blue Bean Fairy meal!!!"

"Disgrace!!!"

"Even a devil rabbit of Black Rose Forest is better than you!!! Three-headed hell raccoon is ten thousand times better than you!!!"

"So Such simple question you can't answer! What a starfish crap you are!!! What a sea pig brain in your head!!!"

"Can you stop humiliating me!? You don't feel humiliated with mermaid face, but I am so ashamed of you!!!"

I have never understood why I have made so many sakura sea anemones mistakes, why I couldn't do any little sunfish things rightly.

Whatever I do any flying feathers of mermaid thing, every day, I still live in the frenzied trampling and venomous fiery scolding under the flaming hoofs of demon horses.

Until one day, I had grown up with the Alpine snow fox-dog and then I knew, what mom and dad really loved crazily like frenzied wolves with venomous tusks, just were......

The exam and vanity of demon thorns.

The grade and rank of shark tusks with blood tearing.

The famous school and university of ice-snow bursting.

The profit and money in demon dragon's claws.

All they love crazily like frenzied wolves with venomous tusks, just are these dark dirty iceberg fire dragon eggs.

They think that as long as having the thorn vanity is equal to having the dragon eggs and success, they think that getting in a famous university is equal to having the ability to earn a lot of dragon claw rubies money.

Their eyes are just full of demon little vanity and fire dragon big rubies.

"Is this stuff good for exam?"

"Can you get a bonus on the exam with this?"

"Can you sell them for money?"

"Can you make money with them?"

For so many years, no matter what I say any phoenix butterfly feather dreams, no matter what I do any flaming mermaid things, only these four words are heard the most.

So one day, I asked my lion-scorpion dad and snow-demon mom, "Am I important or is the vanity and money with flying wasps more important?"

Mom and dad said dismissively with blood-pecking faces, "Of course it's the blood ruby vanity and money in the eyes of whale-tearing thunderbirds! If you can't get vanity and money, then why did we have you stupid parrot egg?"

Late at night, I cut my cat-wrist with the golden Lyra string, then found by my parents and they sent me to the coral hospital.

The wound was not as deep as the mouth of blue whale, the emergency doctor handled it in time, so I didn't die happily in whale singing.

Like a winged flying feathers gazelle with breaking wings rolling down the Alpine snow cliff, I was too weak to open my glacier blue deer eyes, but the huge big demon parents were still chattering like sucking blood, "Why didn't you slit your wrist more deep? You don't have any ice dragon eggs ability about studying in school and exam, but about the abilities of autotomy, suicide, acting pitiful and stuff, you are way more clever than Madagascar's tree-flying lemur!!!"

I cried in despair with falling stars, "Did you ever think what if I really died in the fire rain whale mouth?"

crocodile tusk dad said without even a little hesitation, "Then we'll have another flaming shark egg, have a more excellent tusk devil fish! Or we'll adopt a bat dragon egg! Anyway, other people's little mermaids all are more obedient than you!!!"

At this time, the white angel with incarnation of sea fairy said, "Do you know, what I've always remembered is, last year, in the emergency room, an eight-year-old sakura rabbit boy leapt from the windowsill on the eighth floor of his home, when he was sent here, he's already dead, and his parents even didn't know why. Sometimes I meet the parents like you, I don't wanna criticize and blame, I just wanna sit down calmly and chop you into jellyfish donuts!!! We struggle every day between heaven and hell to save lives from demon, but you don't even care about the safety and health of your own children, all you have in minds is dirty fire dragon shit vanity and ice dragon shit money!!!"

But mom and dad still said with the disdainful crocodile faces,

"The children who can't get the high vanity in exam, who can't get in the famous university, and who can't make a lot of money, all are fucking damned to die!!!"

White angel and her incarnation sea fairy both were silent.

She turned and asked me with heartache, "Kid, for the shark egg parents like them, it's worth jumping into the whale's mouth to suicide? Is it worth?"

I cried, "I have never felt what the parents' sakura sunshine love it is, so it's no any scale scars nostalgia to me for cutting plumage and jumping into whale's mouth......"

There are four species of flaming woodpeckers in the world.

One is that they can't fly up to the Golden Rain Rose Tree growing on the top of Phoenix Mountain, and their offsprings also don't know how to spread wings and fly.

One is that they can fly up to the top of Sea Moon Fairy Tree, and their offsprings also can fly up to the top of Star Rain Fairy Tree.

One is that they can't fly up to the Moon Aquamarine Palace, but their offsprings can fly up to the Galaxy Stars Tree.

And one the most abominable is that they can't fly, then lay the Snow Mountain Swan eggs, but hard break their brilliant swan wings, and force them with poison claws, "You must fly up to the top of Bat Thorn Dragon Tree and grab the fire dragon ruby eggs back to me!!! Or I'll peck you crystal rabbit-ears ugly duckling to death!!!"

What the more nauseous that make you puke out an Alps of ice dragon shit and fire dragon shit it is, the so-called "fly up" in their eyes only means two kinds of rotten dragon carcasses......

Vanity and money!

Later, without any even just one little bit of hesitation, I jumped into the Stars River Mirror Lake of Fairyland Forest.

I don't know whether Moon Sea fairies saved me to the shore of flower sea and sent me to the hospital. I just heard that my whole body was convulsing like hummingbird, my skin was full of Night Queen dark tulips, and my mouth kept blowing pink mermaid bubbles, my heartbeat was once frozen by Alps snow succuba.

After more than two hours of spider crab rescue, my bubble breath finally stabilized. But if didn't let Shining Moon jellyfishes treat me further, my life still had the risk of being torn up by ghost sharks into millions of Sea Butterfly little angels.

But my Blue Ring Octopus devil father and my Styx Jellyfish demon mother just said, "We are not treating her, we'll take her back to the Demon Dragon Palace!"

Dad said, "We work in a sorceress bakery just for ten days, we only can get two thousand dragon paw rubies each month, we have no money to treat our child, let us take her back, we treat her with starfish flowers and dragon blood trees."

White angel said, "Taking her back to the Demon Dragon Palace, there will be a very little hope of cure. How about waiting until tomorrow to observe the kid's condition, and don't make the Azrael Decision so early, please!"

But Dad said, "If we have dragon paw rubies, we could treat her, but we don't have money, then we are not treating her."

White angel said, "Please leave the kid in our Moon Goddess Hospital, give us just one day! If then her poisonous sea anemone still hasn't be cured, you could take the kid back to the Thorns Demon Dragon Palace."

So, Dad finally agreed with big hesitation.

But the next morning, Dad come again to find the white angel, and still was gonna take me back with full of ghost sea serpents and devil jellyfishes.

The dolphin hospital director said to my dad, "Please leave the sea rabbit kid to treat, we will pay for her rubies medical fee, we can guarantee that the Moon Goddess Hospital will not ask for money to you!"

Then, with big anxiety, Dad finally left the moon jellyfish ward.

At shining moon night, the Art Fairy brought my parents to the future.

At that time, I was already dead.

But Mom and Dad just forever lived in the flames of hell. They were running helplessly, crying and shouting, kneeling on the fire land with deplorably blubbering.

In a flash, they fell from the eyes-burning flames into bottomless ice abyss with piercing glaciers, then they were falling from the bitter wind of ice abyss into the flying magma fire of Hell Demon Dragon, afterwards, they fell again on the tusks of Frozen Dragon in Snow Ice Owls Bone Mountain.

So cycling and never stop.

They are longing for lives but never gain, they are longing for deaths but also never gain.

When they finally burst into sunshine tears of remorse, the gorgeous singing with flower sea of Art Fairy was blooming in the bright clouds......

Your evil is rewarded with evil, only love can save you!
You are sinful, only love can make atonement for you!

The next day when taken off the respirator, saw mermaid Dad, I reached my arms to hug him. Don't know why, suddenly feel that everything can be forgiven. However, Dad is shedding sakura sunshine aquamarine tears at my sickbed.

Suddenly, Dad hugs me tightly and crying very loudly, just repeating in his mouth, "I'm sorry! So sorry! So sorry! Sor sorry! Dad is so sorry to you! Dad is so sorry to you! Dad is really so sorry to you......"

When return to the Flower Goddess Palace, as soon as entering the door, mom just kneels at my feet.

She keeps banging the dolomite floor with her forehead.

Dad is also kneeling on the floor with silence of mirror lake.

Mom is crying loudly and slapping herself, "Once we were so bad! Do you know, the Art Fairy let us see a lot of beautiful families! They are so harmonious! They are so happy! But why we ruined and all died! Why!!!???"

"Do you know why? Because all you have in mind is vanity and money!" My sakura tears have been flying all over the sunshine sky, "Because as long as you are in bad mood, you must scold me and hit me! Because there is nothing in your octopus brains but vanity and money! Nothing!!! Nothing!!!!!!"

"Please don't blame me, please! Mom already know the fault!!! Mom already know the fault!!!"

"Once I begged you to stop scolding me but you never stopped, now do you know what the feeling it is???"

"Shall I die now......? I'm kneeling at your feet until death, okay......?"

As speaking, mom begins to desperately bang the moon stone floor with her forehead, "Please forgive me! No one ever told us what is right and what is wrong, therefore we brought so much harm to you! It is all our fault! We are so stupid! Please forgive me! I beg you! I beg you! Please! Please!!!"

Dong! Dong! Dong!

Dong dong dong dong dong!

"Could you get up first?"

"I won't get up unless you forgive me!!! If you don't forgive me, I won't get up forever!!!"

Mom is crying still.

"I forgive you, I forgive you, I won't blame you anymore! Mama, I forgive you!!!"

I cry, too.

Hugging my mom, I'm crying loudly with Mom.

But raise my head, just seeing the gorgeous golden rain of holy light......

In a flash, I return to the bright sakura snow childhood.......

The Art Fairy starts my whole life all over again! Those moments of pain have disappeared with sakura fairies all over the sky without any trace! Everything of everything, is a new beginning!

In the new world with blooming and gorgeous sunshine, I see these words in my mom's diary of Purple Vine Queen......

"I will never seek many dragon claw rubies and blood eye succuba crowns, as long as I have such a blue oriole fairy daughter, then I will be as contented as white plumage owl overlooking an avalanche. I don't expect her to get high vanity in the future, or what kind of thorn university she will get in, and whatever how much money she will make in working. I just want her to be safe and happy with phoenix fairies all the life, I just wanna try my best for giving her the best warmth and happiness with sakura and sunshine all over the sky......"

My sakura fairy tears have been flying with butterfly sea and dancing with sunshine pixies all over the sky!

In the bright and tender new world, one day I have a terrible stomachache, just lying in bed and crying with rain of cherries, mom just clasping my kitty hand and said, "Do you know, I really wish I this swan fairy could take the place of your pain......"

I bloom the narcissus smile, but mom just turns around and cries.

Looking at mom's back with tender plumage, I suddenly feel so warm and so happy!

The little evil spirits of Dark Moon Poison Sunflower in my body, also disappear with butterfly fairies in the bright singing of mermaids.......

Dad has giraffe leg disease, one day Dad accidentally falls down the stairs on meteorite steps, then with my swan mom's hard supporting, dad finally stands up again. From falling to standing up, dad used whole ten thousand meteors' light.

Knowing that Dad's deer legs are not good, so every time climbing the meteor stairs, I always stand in front of Dad and give him my little deer angel shoulder to hold.

In fact, what I envy most, is watching other parents' little raccoon kids riding on their dads' necks and running around, but my dad told me clearly, "I'm really so sorry, Dad don't be able to do it......"

Then one day, I break my knee carelessly and crying with meteor rain at home, dad painfully looks at me and says, "Dad let you ride on the neck, my dear, don't cry, okay......?"

Hearing dad say that, I suddenly laugh that aquamarine tears all miraculously transform into thousands of sakura fairies riding on the Rose Crystal butterflies and flying to Cetus Nebula!

So, at home, Mom helps me ride on Dad's neck, then Dad walks from this Ruby Coral Palace to that Aquamarine Coral Palace.

Although it's only a few short parrot steps, I'm really happier than the Parrot Princess putting on Phoenix Flower Plumage, and the blood scar pain on my knee has long disappeared in boundless fragrant sakura rain.

When I return to the land of sakura fairy, Dad says to me with an apologetic face, "Actually, Dad's greatest regret in life, is couldn't make you as happy as other children. When you were a baby, I heard you crying and saying that you envied other children who could ride on their fathers' necks, Dad was very sad, even just such a simple little cherry request, Dad still couldn't do it...... Daughter, Dad is really so sorry to you......"

Hearing that, I drop my head and hold back the cherry fairy tears, pretend to relax and say, "It's all right! It's just a little cherry thing on Snow Angel mousse dew, Papa, don't worry about it!"

Actually, at that moment, my mermaid sunshine tears have already transformed into millions of aquamarine butterflies reelingly dancing with flying sakura!

Every sakura snow winter, before gonna school, mom would personally put the little swan gloves on my hands.

But this year I say, "I put on by myself, I'm already not a little baby of Alps Fairy Cat!"

Mom is holding my kitty hands and says, "Even you grow up as big as flying-plumage deer, but in front of Mom, you are still a fairy cat lively kid who needs to be cared and loved."

At this moment, my fairy tears in cat eyes are flowing out once again with stars rain......

One day in summer, I accidentally fall into the moon well of Star River.

Mom runs to the well and jumps in without any thinking.

The moon spring in the well has buried me completely, then Mom quickly lifts me up high with her arms.

Fortunately, soon we are rescued by passers. Except choking with a little moonshine spring pixies, I'm still all right.

When come out from the hospital of Moon Goddess Palace, I smile at Mom, but Mom just hugs me and crying loudly.

Later I live at school for some days, Dad suddenly calls.

I ask sleepily as sea-moon jellyfish, "Dad, what are you doing about cat claws cotton candy cookies?"

Dad says, "Oh, there are no any cat tongue little cookies......"

"Dad, what ever are you doing about tiger skin parrot cake rolls???"

I'm more nervous than the tiger skin parrot that escaping from the Dark Forest owl's venomous claws, afraid of some avalanche terrible thing has happened at home, otherwise Dad should know this time I still would fly in the dream of Sea Butterfly with Moonshine in Aquamarine Jellyfish Coral Palace.

Dad says apologetically, "Nothing......Just missing you, so give you a call, now you go back to sleep......"

"Oh, so, I'm gonna sleep. I just dreamed that the firefly pixies singing for me! He he! Bye."

Soon the message flies in, "Daughter, I just dreamed that you fell into moon well again! I was so afraid that even wanted to jump into the depth of moon spring to see if you were in there......"

"Papa, I'm all right, don't be worried about any little narcissus pixies......"

Sinking into the gorgeous dream of mirror lake, my fairy tears in deer eyes are still so warm and brilliant......

Later, Mom calls and says sadly as falling sakura petals, "You are not in the Blue Parrot Tulips Home, I could just blankly stare at your photos and say some little shell cookies......Your dad often went to your crystal butterflies room and sometimes called out your little golden oriole fairy name......"

In the gorgeous new world with blooming Dream Boat tulips and Love Song tulips, Mom never scolded me for wasting any flamboyant shells money, and never praised any other people's children were better than me in front of others.

When winter vacation is over that going back to school, mom insisting on sending me to Grapes Palace School.

Got on the bus, mom gives me all the dragon claw rubies money she had on body, just leaves dozens of little flamboyant shells for herself.

When she got out of the bus, she again takes out the flamboyant shells money of rest and stuffs them into my little pocket of rabbit-ears fairy, just leaves two sea star parrot conches to take the bus.

I say I don't need so much flamboyant shells money, but Mom makes a "Shush" sign and ordering, "Just take them! Mom have many dragon claw rubies money!!! Don't worry!!!"

Then my shining tears of cherry fairy are flying and surging out with gorgeous wings of swan......

On Mother's Day, Mom suddenly disappeared with the owl plumage on Souls Tree. Then I find a letter of Rose Fairy on the desk.

"Don't gonna the Spirit Tree of Fairy Valley to look for me. I'm ill. White plumage has broken. I don't wanna drag you and your dad just like a blind snow owl in volcano!"

Fortunately! Dad rushed out of the Tulips Home Door and running so madly that fell on several cactuses of Golden Bird Nebula, and almost hit by the car into ten thousands of phoenix crystal eggs, and then finally found Mom. Get to the hospital and after a checking, then find that Mom just got a common little evil spirits infection of sea anemone.

I'm hugging Mom and crying, "Whatever old, ill or death, we should be together forever, side by side to break through the poisonous vines and ice peaks, hand in hand to look for sakura trees with treading snow mountain, we should together cherish this hard-won happiness in flower sea, okay......?"

Mom nods in tears, constantly wiping the sea butterfly tears of mermaid, fiercely nodding the sea fairy head......

Actually, Mom's illness is not as serious as Night Queen Griffin's claw piercing little snow deer's fairy heart, now Mom has been getting better and better.

Maybe Mom just don't wanna bring me any more scale scars......

Mama, I really had forgiven you!

I will never blame you!
Mama, I love you forever!
I love you forever! Forever and forever!

When I was in kindergarten and primary school, for earning more money, Mom and Dad went far away and left me alone in the Sea Grapes Palace to live in school.

Throughout my childhood, all in my succuba nightmares was Mom and Dad's back figures disappearing in the Fog Forest, almost every morning I was waking up with snowstorm tears from sapphire dream.

Today, Mom and Dad are coming to pick me back to the Tulips Home.

I lowering my head, ask with sakura tears in stars rain, "Then I just had learned walking parrot step and stumbled that chasing after you, until even fell down, but you were still so cruel that even didn't turn around your blue whale heads! Were you really willing to abandon me alone!!!??? Woo woo woo......"

"My dear, please don't hate Mom......If we turned our blue whale heads, then we wouldn't be able to leave......For so many years, Mom and Dad have been so sorry to you......Please forgive us, please......"

Mom is choking with sobs, then kneels down at my feet.

I quickly hold Mom to get her up, "Mama, I forgive you! I forgive you!! I forgive you!!!" Just hugging her tightly, can't speak out even one little word of golden oriole fairy......

One day in third grade, I'm suddenly twined by ten thousand dark eel vine little evils tightly, have a fever for two weeks and don't feel any better.

Mom is taking me to run around all the red coral hospitals, but unable to find out out the cause. Mom thinks maybe I can't live for a few meteors rain of Swan Nebula. I don't know how many aquamarine tears of mermaid Mom had wept for me.

Every time seeing the white dolphin doctor, Mom's first words always are, "As long as you can cure my fairy cat daughter, I must kneel for you to thank you! Whatever how much dragon claw rubies money I'm all willing to pay!!! Even if I have to pay my life of swan fairy, I will not have any hesitation!!! As long as my daughter could be healthy...... Please!!!!!!!"

Later, on a bright morning of summer with sunshine and sakura rain, those ten thousand little evil spirits of dark eel vine suddenly disappear into the holy light of Flower Goddess, and then, I never catch a cold or fever anymore.

I believe, this is the glorious power of love.

Mom, thank you for your love to me as flower sea.

Before snowy New Year's Eve, Mom dresses me in gorgeous starry plumage of Phoenix Nebula, little flying boots of deer fairy, narcissus princess anadem, the flaming rose scarf meticulously woven by aquamarine parrot fairies, and, a pair of bright beautiful white swan wings. But Mom hardly ever bought any new clothes of Moonshine Goddess for herself.

Mom also gives me all the delicious mango flowing heart cake, and she just eats the lava bread stick just hard like the heart of mango.

When gonna the supermarket, Mom suddenly says she wants to drink some Provence sakura frozen yogurt, then get to the refrigerated counter, Mom picks up a bottle of sakura yogurt and looks for a little while, but quickly puts it down.

Just hear her whispering as parrot fairy, "Why is it more expensive than rose candy of starry sky in the world of snow and ice......"

But that bottle of sakura yogurt is engraved only two dragon paw sapphires......

"Why is it more expensive than rose candy of starry sky in the world of snow and ice......" Mom's snow reindeer hand has reached out again but quickly draws back.

However, as long as buying the Provence sakura frozen yogurt for me, Mom has never hesitated so many Cetus meteors.

In fact, after a long time, I secretly see that every time after paying my ice dragon eggs tuition, Mom and Dad had to eat the demon potato chips for a whole month.

Mom says, "I want you to eat more delicious jasmine blueberry cake rolls, and wear more beautiful plumages of swan narcissus fairy. I don't want your husky classmates to look down on you, I don't want your chihuahua classmates to laugh about we are paupers in the Golden Loriot Fairy Mountain......"

Then my aquamarine tears are turning into thousands of oriole fairies and flying all over the bright sapphire sky!

When I was very young that smaller than fox face lily, Mom and Dad didn't have moon spring time to take care of me, so they handed me to Grandpa and Grandma lived in Pine Cone Maple House, they took me into the Candy House of Rabbit Faeries Forest.

Every four weeks, Dad would come back to see me just one time, I spent the whole weekend clinging around him just as a narcissus vine fairy, so the separating was sadder than tearing and melting my phoenix wings.

Every time Dad was leaving, I was crying and shouting just like clinging a lava cliff with falling fire rocks and thousands of rolling ice dragon eggs, "Woowoowoowoowoo......Papa, don't leave......Please don't go! Please don't leave me alone!!!"

Dad said to me, "Be good, dear, just waiting for Dad at home, Dad is gonna buy some snow cherries of Spirit Tree for you."

Then he just was walking toward the Faeries Forest, faster and faster, farther and farther......

I always knew, Dad would hide behind the Spirit Tree secretly watching me wiping rose cherry tears.

And so was he.

Now I have grown up as big as Icelandic owl, now I have known more than sunflower parrot, I have known it all. But at that time, I didn't know any chocolate snowball little cookies.

Once, I really missed Dad so badly, so as soon as meeting Dad, I was just crying out the sakura with cherries rain, "Papa, why did you every time gonna buy snow cherries of Spirit Tree for so long......? I really missed you badly......"

Papa hugs me tightly, whimpering as tulip parrot, "Sorry, Papa is so sorry to you......My dear, Papa will never leave you again......"

When I'm living in school, Dad has a accident, his body is hit out hundreds of phoenix crystal eggs. Mom has been concealing it from me for a couple of weeks, until I finally discover it with my mermaid aquamarine eyes.

Riding the succuba's unicorn and flying home, Mom says, "After your Papa patted by mermaid tail to wake up, he kept telling me don't let you come back, don't let you worry., you can gonna the Sapphire Coral Hospital and see him through peach blossom jellyfish glass, otherwise, if Papa sees you and cry, his wounds will be as painful as spider-monkeys crawling all over the body."

Then I creep to the ward door, it doesn't close, I see the white angel is infusing Papa with spring of Moon Goddess, Papa is staring benevolently at the white angel for a long time, long long time later, Papa says the words that melting my heart into thousands of aquamarine fairy petals......

"Do you know, once my little daughter said she wanted to be a white angel, I'm imaging my daughter will take care of the patients in the future as carefully as you do......"

With purple vine tears in sunshine, I'm blooming the glorious smiling with dancing butterflies and flying orioles in tulip sea......

Another New year's Eve with butterfly snow, I come back from the distant snow mountain college to Glorious Tulips Home, in Lilliput Kitchen, I'm helping Mom wash emerald lettuces, then Mom is cutting the flame blue apple and says, "There was a time when relatives and friends were having honey fairy dinner, your Papa was also there. Everyone knew you went to the Moon Goddess Magic College of Parrot Snow Mountain, they said you are better than volcano owl fairy, then your Papa was laughing so happily and proudly that spurting tulips petals all over the Ice Castle. Then parrot fish aunt asked your Papa, 'Do you miss your fairy cat daughter?' Your Papa laughed that his eyes just turned into sun birds flying out the Mermaid Sunshine Sea, 'No! No! Not at all! She's not here, you don't know how easy I am with my hummingbird heart!' Then your Papa disappeared before eating Bee Fairy food. Guess what Alps grape cookies your Papa did? He unexpectedly ran to the glacier parterre of downstairs garden and sat there silently like a bear in snow mountain, just wiping his ice crystal tears uncontrollably flowing out of his bear eyes! Ah ha ha ha ha ha ha......"

I just stand by the sink, washing turquoise lettuces with head down, while washing, my tears of Parrot Princess are flying with dancing, even couldn't speak out any little promontory windbell flowers......

The next snow morning at six o'clock, Mom has made the Provence mango fire dragon roll and get me up to eat, but I'm so sleepy that my fairy cat eyes are pasted by sunshine dream fairies, I just say I don't wanna eat any ice dragon eggs and fire dragon eggs.

After a little windbell flower falling in flower sea, I finally open my ice aquamarine kitty eyes. Just seeing Mom coming to my bed with holding the steaming mango fire dragon rol and two little ice dragon egg tarts. When I was a baby, my favorite faerie dessert just was ice dragon egg tart.

"Mama, what are you doing about chocolate bean cookies......"

"Our little angel seldom comes back to Tulips Home, so Mom hold them to you!" Mom says with parrot smiling all over the face.

I don't say anything, just take them here and eating them all with my cat mouth. I don't care how hot the mango fire dragon is, and how icy the ice dragon egg tart is.

Just aquamarine tears from cat eyes have been flowing, just a little ashamed that couldn't help crying out the promontory windbell melody.

Remember that the last PE class in fourth grade of primary school, in the race, I stumbled and fell just like little corgi biting poisonous roses, then my ankle hurting as ten thousand Aegean bees had wormed and crashed in.

I was lamely walking home alone, I was so afraid of mom would scold me into leg-broken little corgi, so I didn't dare to see if the fire wound was as deep as demon dragon's magma cave.

As soon as I stepped in the door of Tulips Home, I pretended that there was nothing about hatching dragon eggs happened, but Mom's peculiar owl sun eyes still noticed my honey-sucking hummingbird little mood.

It felt like stealing waterfall sakura honey and caught by sakura fairies, I was so scared that just kept flapping the purple vine wings! Just quickly hid back to clove tree room and looked at the wound.

If didn't look, chihuahua didn't know it. If looked, corgi just startled!

The rose fairy blood had run out of white plumage pants!

I was so scared into snow mountain little freezing bunny!

Carefully uncovering the pants......The wound was as big as an iceberg rose bud! As deep as a snow blue lightning parrot egg!

Hugging a fox-dog pixie! Brooding and thinking! Thinking and brooding!

Finally I decided to tell my owl mom!

Tottering out of the room, I was shivering my flower fairy legs, before I spoke, Mom just said, "What's the matter? Did you fall into the poison rose sea?"

I gently nodded my Phoenix Forest cat head, the wound hurt as ten thousand Aegean bees worming and crashing in......

I showed Mom the fire wound, even owl Mom was also frightened to startle, the wound had been as bloody as withering hummingbird-sakura and dying falling-sun roses!

Mom said, "Oh, no! You have to be stitched by bee fairies!"

Suddenly my crystal windbell heart just "Pa pa la la" breaking as ruining Sky Ice Castle all over the floor!

Stitching!

Every girl said that stitched by bee fairies was more painful than fairy cat big eyes pecked by fire-mouth woodpeckers!

Ah ah ah ah ah ah ah!!!!!!

Mom put down the cherry pineapple pie in her hands that done half, then took me to the Baby Tears Hospital nearby.

Along the way, she kept comforting me with soft swan feathers, "Don't be afraid! It won't hurt out thousands of pink flying little elephant-octopuses!"

Then Mom told me a joke, "One day, a group of tadpoles were swimming back and forth looking for their mom, then they saw a frog on lotus leaf and shouted excitedly, 'Mama! Mama! We finally found you!' But the frog mom just asked, 'Have you finished your homework?

How many dragon claw sapphires do you think you can earn in the future?' As soon as little tadpoles heard that, they turned their heads one after another and said, 'Let's go, she's not our good mom!'"

Then Mom was laughing as sunflower parrot.

But I still was so nervous that the hummingbird-aquamarine feathers shaking off a flower sea! I was clinging tightly to beautiful queen-tulip mom, longing for her to give me the brilliance and power of snow mountain and flower sea.

Got in the Baby Tears Hospital, I was clasping Mom's rose queen hand, and Mom was clasping my narcissus princess hand, too. Suddenly, I found Mom's hand a little rough, but still soft like swan wings and warm as little rabbit fairy.

Mom was around cheering me up all the time.

Anesthetized by bee needle, my wound gradually lost consciousness, I didn't feel any pain when the bee fairy was stitching me. Although after a while, my iceberg snow deer leg was hurting more than before, but my heart was totally incomparably soft and warm just like little flying rabbit.

Because Mom's swan fairy hands had never unclasped.

Every other day, the fire wound needed to be washed with the spring of moon well, so Mom took me to the Baby Tears Hospital. When tearing off the white rose gauze, some bee fairy needles stung me, then Mom was uncovering the white rose gauze very cautiously just as healing the wings of Love Goddess shining butterfly, Mom also asked me with sakura melody from time to time, "Does it hurt? Does it hurt?"

My heart was in full bloom of the sun-tulips all over the icebergs, but also rippling a stream of snow-lemon heartache.

Because when Mom was lowering her head and applying the spring of moon well for me, I saw in her gorgeous and glorious sakura goddess long hair, a few white hairs were shining like star river......

They were not as bright as the meteors of Andromeda nebula, but it did deeply prick my fairy kitty eyes and rabbit fairy heart......

For so many years with whale-meteors, Mom was working hard day and night as owl fairy just for happiness, but she never asked for any repay from Soul Tree. But those star river hairs were singing with flower melody and fairy songs to me, singing Mom's hard working with wounds of blood feathers, singing Mom's sacrifice with sakura snow, and singing the dazzlingly blooming mother love as flower sea with sunshine all over the iceberg in Mom's heart of swan......

The poisonous wasps final at the end of fourth grade, I did so bad that Dark Demon Palace was collapsing and Devil Dragon Basilica was falling, I was walking dejectedly on the way home with blood rain and dark rose thorns, my legs were trembling as if the little snow rabbit surrounded by hundreds of huge glacier wolves, I was thinking that, "Now I'm fucking dying with my goddamn fire dragon diamond eggs! Will Mom pick up the huge electric eel and whip me into a broken-leg husky......???"

But when I got back to the Golden Talent Tulips Home, what astonished my rabbit eyes was Mom not only didn't scold me with dragon fangs, but also said to me as the Art Fairy with blooming flower sea......

Don't care about the demon thorns exam and stupid husky vanity, there is nothing in the world more stupid than exam and vanity. From earliest time to the present day, I have never seen any worthy and great entomb so much time and energy into rote, doing problem of exam.

In fact, reading, practicing, thinking, cultivating talent and absorbing knowledge are the most important and worth investing

time and energy.

Whatever any age, what the most we need forever is talent and knowledge, forever not exam and vanity.

The time of childhood and youth is limited, we can't waste even just a slightest bit of time.

Nowadays, we are not short of opportunities and stages, so the most time of our childhood and youth, must be used to cultivate talent and absorb knowledge, rather than rote, doing problem of exam.

The reason why no great is born, it is we neglect the process of forming the great soul.

If we love some fields, we can gonna see the greats in these fields from ancient to present, their biographies, their works, their every word and every deed, what they read and did every year and every day, see if they spent so much time into rote, doing problem of exam.

Once we know them, we should take the essence, discard the dross, and keep pace with the time, combine with our own situation, make hard effort, learn widely from other people's strong point, make integration and innovation. I believe you can find the right way for your own.

What I'm saying is not to tell you what are the specific methods of cultivating talent in all fields, but want you to seek by yourself, because teaching a man how to fish is better than giving him many fishes.

But in general, the way to cultivate talent in all fields is,

Reading　Practicing　Thinking

The increase of reading, practicing and thinking, is equal to the improvement of talent.

Just there are many different proportions and contents in different fields. So this requires you to search in the lives of greats in all ages.

Nowadays, the books are so numerous like sakura sea, the information of internet age is so well developed as galaxy river, I believe you will find your own way.

Hearing Mom saying this, in a flash, my heart was warm as blooming thousands of Golden Artist tulips in summer sunshine, so I quietly make up my blue giant star mind of Lyra nebula......

"I must be excellent in what I love! I must In return for Mom's understanding and devotion, in return for Art Fairy and great nature's brilliant gift to me!"

Dad also loves me so selflessly as flowers rain.

In the fifth grade, I have to go back to Angel Tulips Home alone every day after school, one day near to after school, I don't know if the sky fairy is sad or angry, she darkens her fairy face, just in one flash, a blue parrot lightning is tearing the quiet sunny sky and clear clouds, then the thunder pixies are singing awfully with lightning all over the sky!

"Wow!", raindrops have become the Lyra ice crystal strings, very heavy rain is pouring down tempestuously as if the moon well fountainhead has collapsed, my pink angel hummingbird heart is so scared that almost flying out of my sakura fairy mouth!

Looking out the window of Crystal Palace, I'm thinking that, "It's pouring down so heavy Lyra pixies rain, how could I get back to Angel Tulips Home......"

After school, the rain is still raging than iceberg demon meteors, my classmates all have been successively picked up by their moms and dads, only me is left alone standing at the demon dragon ice cave mouth of school, I'm really so cold and scared......

Suddenly, there's a familiar sound of footsteps flying from faerie ice rain, so I raise my cat head and look up......

Oh! It's Dad! It's my Dad!

The polar bear Dad is drenched through by faerie ice rain, his kind bear face is as red as sunset-jade purple vine, and lips keep shivering as little ruby hummingbirds.

But Dad doesn't care about these little pandas and little raccoons fighting for rolling pine cones and chestnuts.

He comes up and and says anxiously as a giant goose loses her baby, "My little swan angel, waiting for so long, right? Dad is really so sorry, Dad is too late......"

While speaking, Dad puts the faerie plumage on me, suddenly, I feel warm as if falling into the hugging of giant swan!

Then I'm blinking my fairy aquamarine eyes and ask, "Dad, are you cold?"

Dad just smiles like polar bear king and says, "I'm not cold at all, as long as our fairy cat angel isn't cold, then I won't be cold at all!"

At once, my mermaid heart just becomes dazzling and glowing as being embraced by Andromeda meteor fairies, the flaming aquamarine tears are slowly flowing from my flower goddess eyes just like falling sakura in shining stream of Mirror Lake Forest......

Mom and Dad's love of sakura and sunshine deeply moves me!

Family love is selfless, is precious. No one can measure it in terms of virulent wasp vanity and dragon claw money.

Therefore, I must struggle hard, cultivate talent, absorb knowledge, in the future, I must be an little art fairy to create happiness for the world, to repay the Art Fairy and great nature's glorious gift for me.

Mom calls and asks, "Has Dad picked up you kitty-eyes little fairy? So, what phoenix fairy food do you wanna eat?"

Actually, every time before going back to Angel Tulips Home, I would tell Mom in advance what rose fairy food I wanna eat.

This time, I still take the phone and tell Mom, "I want Hungarian seafood soup, I want little squid fried lettuce, and cream spinach fried lobster, fire dragon fruit spaghetti, Napoleon beef pizza......"

But Mom is laughing as snow mountain owl, "You can just eat some pink dolphin fire dragon eggs! Ha ha ha ha ha ha ha......"

"Ha ha ha ha ha ha ha!!!!!!" Dad and me are laughing loudly in the Lyra stars rain. "Your mom is as cute as rose tree squirrel!" Says Dad with snow owl smile.

But as soon as I push open the door of Angel Tulips Home, I find all the tulip fairy foods I want are all on the golden rose tree table, and Mom still is busy in the kitchen just like bee fairy......

At once I shed one hundred aquamarine tears......

After fairy dinner, Dad goes out for something, in home, just me reading the Fairy Revelation and Mama washing narcissus crystal plates in the kitchen.

Reading and reading, thinking and thinking, then I'm so confused into Ice Fog Forest by the fairy sunshine words in Fairy Revelation just as holding the snow owl's feathers shaky and unsteady in Ice Valley, gonna ask moon fairy Mom, But Mom also can't understand any rose crystal little butterflies, so I have to ask the sun oriole little fairy tomorrow.

Then at moonlit night with frozen halo, through the sunflower door, I see Mama's room shining the sunfish light, so I'm creeping up to the door, then gently push open a jellyfish gap and seeing......

Mom is reading a book, then I watch with rabbit eyes again......

Oh! Isn't it my Fairy Revelation......?

Seeing this, I have understood all the sea moons and mermaid's singing......

Because the clothes I wear are less than narcissus petals, suddenly I sneeze and found out by Mom, I think Mom must criticize me for still not sleeping so late, but Mom doesn't blame me with any bee pixies.

She's just blinking her aquamarine cat eyes and apologetically saying to me, "Mom is so sorry, couldn't help you understand this Fairy Revelation......"

I'm just shaking my head vigorously, and blooming a sunshine smile of narcissus heart to Mom......

Once Papa said to me, "You are my heart of sea rabbit, only you are as happy as little flying rabbit in Cloud Palace, then I could be happy, too......"

When Papa comes back at moonlit night, he makes the blueberry cherry juice, but I just see only one cup, so I'm blinking my fairy cat eyes and ask, "Where are yours and Mom's?"

Papa says, "We are just two old snow rabbits, we don't need to drink it. But you are still smaller than rabbit-ear cat fairy, so you should drink more juice, today I haven't seen you eat fruits, and you eat too little vegetables."

Papa! You are forever the person who loves me the most and sacrifices for me the most!

Papa I love you forever! Forever and forever!

Later, every time I eat delicious orange cherry egg tarts, I always give Papa to eat, but Papa is always saying every time, "I don't like eating this squirrel pixie little egg tart, it's not delicious at all!"

At first, I feel Papa really makes my cherry fairy heart so cold, I just like sharing the happiness of flower sea with Papa.

Until our condition is getting better and better, then I give Papa the orange cherry little egg tarts, Papa is finally willing to eat.

"So delicious." Papa says while chewing.

Perhaps he has forgotten how much he dislike eating orange cherry little egg tart once he said.

Only then I finally understood it......

In the distant past with flying snow and falling ice, Papa just wanted me to eat more cherry fairy food......He just wanted me to eat more and better......

I remember when I was very young that smaller than the cat fairy of Mirror Lake Forest, I was pointing to a big cute plush cat in shop window and said, "Daddy, I want it......"

Papa was touching my fairy kitty head and said, "Daddy has no dragon claw rubies money, could......could we stop wanting it......?"

So, I nodded hard my cat-eye fairy head and said, "Umm! I will wait until Daddy has the mermaid aquamarine tears to buy it!"

Papa hugged me up and left, but from time to time he still looked back at that big cute cat fairy.

After a few steps, I said to Papa, "Papa, don't cry, okay......? When we have many ice dragon egg sapphires in the future, then you buy a lot of big plush cat fairies for me, okay......? Don't be crying, just be good......"

I was helping Papa wipe his aquamarine tears while weeping.

Later, because of Mom and Dad's cedar effort, our condition have become as good as blooming purple vines in Aquamarine Palace of Parrot Mountain.

Today, whenever I see my favorite cute big cat fairy and sakura little fairy, Papa must buy them for me. Whatever faerie clothes, goddess hairpins, princess dolls, flower fairy brushes, golden angel tulips, or the Revelation of Art Fairy......

As long as it's what I want, as long as Papa and Mama's deer fairy shoulders can afford, they must do everything and the best with their full strength to support me and encourage me!

Of course, I never ask Papa and Mama to pay too much blood feathers for me. I love Papa and Mama. I don't want them to be more exhausted than the snow mountain fairy deer escaping from fire dragon's virulent claws.

I love Papa! I love Mama!

Because of the glorious gift given by great nature and Art Fairy, now, I have always been in the warm sakura praise of parents and kinsfolk. I'm not self-based just like in iceberg cave, I'm very confident just as tulip sea.

The people around me all recognize me, affirm me, but I also know myself very well, so I will never be arrogant and conceited.

In the gorgeous new world with art brilliance illuminating every corner of the faerie land, I'm growing up in the praise of sakura snow all over the sky, so I'm always as happy as Love Goddess butterflies flying with dancing all over the trees of soul.

I really wanna thank my father and mother, they love me, praise me, they no longer turn the black rose vanity and dark dragon ruby money into succuba thorns in fire dragon and ice dragon's claws, then bind me tightly.

Mom says, "As long as you are happy, any dragon claw sapphires Mom is willing to pay! Any mermaid aquamarine tears Mom is willing to sacrifice!"

So now, I have been struggling hard and living happily every day.

Struggling hard to cultivate talent and absorb knowledge.

Striving to create happiness for the whole world, striving to create happiness for Mom and Dad who love me deeply, striving to return all the kind and merciful people who love me.

Today, I still remember clearly like sakura in sunshine, in my childhood, Papa always like putting me on his shoulder when took out to play, at that time, I really felt Papa's shoulder was so wide.

So I was just sitting on Papa's shoulder, grabbing Papa's hair, and growing up slowly......

Today, I still remember brightly like dazzling sakura trees in summer, long long time ago, for buying me a new swan plumage for my first violin performance, Papa and Mama were eating the lava demon potato chips for a whole month.

At that time, school distributed cherry fairy pies every afternoon, I begrudged to eat, I wanted to give Papa and Mama to eat, but Papa and Mama had left for working in the Rose Garden of Snow Mountain.

So I saved the cherry fairy pies on my narcissus fairy tree, then saving and saving, waiting and waiting......Until a sunny morning with sakura snow, Papa and Mama finally returned to the Golden Art Tulips Home!

I was personally holding the cherry fairy pies in my cupped hands for Papa and Mama to eat.

But Papa and Mama just said, "You eat, we don't like eating this kind of fruit fairy pie."

I suddenly burst into Mermaid Sea butterfly tears just in one twinkling!!! Then shoving the fairy pies into Papa and Mama's lacerated but soft Flower Goddess hands!!!

Until today, I still can see clearly the pure shine that Papa and Mama weeping sun-sakura tears while eating......

Still can see.

Forever can see!

Papa and Mama! Really thank you! I love you forever!

Forever and forever!!!!!!!!!

Chapter 9

Holy Pure Wings of Art Fairy

*I*n the gorgeous new world with art brilliance illuminating every corner of the fairy land, although Oris is growing up in praise of blooming sakura trees, but Papa always reminds Oris of the humility.

"All these honors, they are just a small achievement at this stage. Your art, is yet far from the true greatness. You must forever remember that, the road of art, forever is a never-ending journey with iceberg, snow mountain, sunshine and limitless flower sea."

"Umm! I will never be complacent and arrogant! I will keep striving! Keep climbing the iceberg and snow mountain! Keep seeking the limitless flower sea of art! Art is forever limitless!"

Papa is smiling with relief, stroking Oris's narcissus prince head, then Papa encourages him with sakura in sunshine, "There is still a long way to seek in the future, Papa and Mama will send you into the best art forest of the world's top for learning and practicing art! Of course, you also must struggle harder yourself! Papa and Mama will forever support you! We must do everything we can to support you and your art!"

"Papa, Now may I play the tune what I want?"

"Of course! Just play what you like and what you think it's true beautiful art."

"Umm!!!" Oris is nodding vigorously! Flying butterfly tears just like flaming sakura rain!

He's crying again!

Crying so moved! Crying so grateful!

When Oris was very very little, every time Mama saw Oris's plump cat hands were playing on the piano, jumping as rabbit fairies, dancing as blue love goddess butterflies, and often singing gorgeous melody while playing, at that moment, Mama would applaud beside, and then dance with melody.

In this kind of time in flower sea, Oris was always such happy as a phoenix parrot singing and laughing so melodiously.

No matter whether he played and sang well or not, Mom always praised him and encourage him with gorgeous mermaid singing, let him deeply feel Mom's warm, bright and fragrant mother love in tulip sea.

Actually, no matter how excellently Oris plays the piano, violin and harp, he still is a narcissus kitty who's longing to be loved.

One day, Mom sees Oris's soft cat little finger has a wound, so asks anxiously, "Oh dear! Why is your finger like a Aegean ruby gull???"

Oris speaks haltingly as nightingale whispering, "I was inadvertently cut by the rose violin string yesterday......"

Mom asks, "How come I couldn't hear you cry?"

Oris says, "I thought you weren't home......"

Mom suddenly can't help welling the Swan Fairy aquamarine tears......

In the new world of art light, living in this sunflower family though not rich, Oris doesn't look up the luxurious life of wealthy.

He is proud of his parents, because he has a lot of golden sunflowers that can't be bought by dragon claw sapphires.

When Oris was a cat fairy baby, he already had feathered the blue butterfly wings of sensitive art, and always liked sleeping in Mom's arms.

Every time, Mom saw Oris curled asleep, then put him on the cradle of Moon Goddess, but who knew that as soon as Oris was parted away from Mom's fairy swan arms, he just burst into tears loudly, so Mom had to coax and hug him again, until very late at night, she finally could drop the wings and sleep at ease.

Every morning Oris would drink a glass of sakura milk, eat a fire egg of Aquamarine Phoenix, noon and evening, is also the delicious meal in sumptuous Tulip Fairy Palace, dazzling gemstones all over the view, the crystal cups and plates are all singing cheerfully.

Every time Oris can see Papa and Mama so busy in Lilliputian Kitchen that turn into big bee pixies, so Oris is always eating fairy meal very seriously, for living up to Papa and Mama's sweat and love.

Before sleeping, Mama often tells Oris many myths of snow mountain , fairy tales of Mirror Lake Forest, and narcissus legends in flower sea, so Oris is fantasizing all the day that he becomes moonshine night little fairy and sakura little pixie, although now those myths, fairy tales and legends have flown hands in hands with moonshine night fairies and sakura pixies to Mirror Lake Forest, but the golden sunshine in that flower sea, today is still clear and pure.

When I was seven, Papa and Mama had been busy in working as bee angels, they were always on the move as cherry blossoms and leaves in rain and wind.

After school, I often stayed alone in our Sunflower Home, just playing the narcissus princess piano, while waiting alone.

However, every time I heard the promontory windbell singing, I felt that was the most beautiful melody in the whole world! It's my Papa and Mama coming back! I jumped up as a paradise rabbit fairy, very excitedly opened the door of Aquamarine Sunflower, jumped up to hug Mama tightly, then hug Papa tightly, and then hug them two tightly just as windbell purple vine!

As long as tightly hugging Papa and Mama, I suddenly felt the loneliness before just was flying away with sakura snow pixies!

As long as Papa and Mama are in my side, then I can possess all the fairy joy and flower sea happiness!

Life is always so warm and fragrant.

Today after school, Oris and Mama are standing in front of the Phoenix Tree Flower Castle watching fairy tulips, then Mama stands face to face with Oris for a moment, after a little sakura fairy falling into Mirror Lake, Mama suddenly bends down and kisses Oris's eyebrow.

Oris's heart suddenly jumps like rabbit fairy, then they are as if nothing has happened. Oris turns around to disguise, but the sea sunshine aquamarine tears in narcissus cat eyes have been shining brightly......

When Oris turns back, Mama just crouches and hugging him.

In a twinkling, thousands of Love Goddess butterflies are flying with dancing in the art brilliance shining every corner of the whole world!

They are smiling and laughing, dancing and whirling, then with the fairies of Sea Goddess together melodiously singing the mermaid song......

They are forever so kind and merciful!

They are forever so happy and beautiful!

How about Papa and Mama themselves?

In the gorgeous beautiful new world shined by holy pure light of art, they are forever so merciful and kind.

Mama was also beautiful when she was very young, many people adored her as much as white daisy petals adoring golden flower heart, but Mama was determined to marry Oris's Papa who was poor desperately but devoting to dazzling art dream.

At that time, they were so poor that couldn't afford to eat sea dragon's sapphire eggs. Once Papa came home and brought a jar of sakura milk to Mama, Mama just took a sip with her little cherry-cat mouth, then smiling as oriole and said, "I've never drunk this before, it's really so delicious."

Then put the sakura milk into Papa's hand, "Let's drink together! You take one sip, then I take one sip, ha ha ha ha ha ha......"

They were both laughing happily.

Whenever Papa's career was at its worst like lotuses in rainstorm, Mama still never thought of giving up with falling sakura in snow mountain and withering to death with the golden roses of Sun Goddess Iceberg.

When Oris was two years old, Papa was overworked by singing, and also his throat fell ill, at one performance, the stage suddenly collapsed, Papa broke his legs and lying on the bed, lost the ability to earn dragon claw sapphires.

And misfortune never comes singly, because of overworking, Papa also got the cancer with blood feathers and entangled by demon thorns.

But Mama never gave up in meteors rain! She was just working desperately day and night, singly running here and there performing to make ice dragon sapphires.

Mama used her pure wings of swan goddess, alone supporting the collapsed ruins of our whole Flower Goddess Palace. She took Oris's Papa to see doctor all over the country, spent a lot of dragon claw blood rubies, owed a lot of Night Queen Dark Griffin's evil debts.

The pink dolphin doctor said to Oris's Mama, "Don't see doctors for your husband anymore! Is just wasting dragon claw sapphires!"

But Mama said, "I know it's wasting meteors time wasting dragon claw sapphires, but I have sold all the rosewood furniture that I can sell, and I have borrowed all the succuba dark larks that I can borrow, the dragon claw sapphires I owe, I almost couldn't pay off even with my whole swan fairy life, but I still don't wanna give up in meteor storm!!! I still can't give up in nebula river!!!"

Then one day, Mama was hugging four-year-old Oris and said, "My little angel, when your Papa is gone, let's gonna the blood rose sea at the gate of Dark Ice Dragon Palace for begging succuba food......"

Four-year-old Oris was blinking his big cat eyes and said bemusedly as in snow night, "Mama, I'm so scared of the thorn banshee in blood rose sea, and I don't know how to beg for succuba food, so what could I do......"

Oris's words made everyone in the ward suddenly cry with sakura rain.

Papa's condition was getting worse and worse like magma bursting, he said inarticulately to Oris and Mama, "I have wasted our ice dragon claw sapphires too many, so please give me a beating......"

Oris was crying, "No matter how many sapphires we have spent and will, as long as for you, Papa, Mama and me forever are willing to pay!!! How could we beat you! Papa!!!"

Papa said weakly as wings melting, "If you don't beat me, well, I'm giving you a smile......"

So Papa was smiling out sakura petals with all the soul strength of flower goddess. Papa was so thin like tulip stalk in pixies rainstorm, but at this moment, he was smiling so kindly and beautifully......

Many years have been past, Papa says to Oris, "At that hard time, I really wanted to jump into whale mouth and kill myself, I really didn't wanna destroy the happiness of you and your mom with my disease! But when I was staring at you, I felt you and your swan fairy Mama look so much alike, just as a nebula butterfly flower and a aquamarine goddess butterfly, so I really wanna live strong, and bring you up to adulthood day by day, year by year......"

Papa is saying with clear clouds and refreshing breeze as butterfly alighting on heart of sakura, but I have heard their love story of golden rose sea in snow mountain......

Those years later, in the glorious hymns of Art Fairy and nature, Papa's throat, legs and cancer all were miraculously cured! He can sing passionately with swan fairies on stage again!

In the flower sea warmth of holy pure art light, Oris with Papa and Mama all have been pouring out the sunshine streams of grateful sakura tears......

Once Mama was a little singer and little actress at school, whenever she 's speaking was always like standing on the stage of Crystal Palace, always cheerful, always like flying puffin and dancing flowers.

Mom says, "Long long time ago, I had fallen in love with music, music can always inspire me with shine of sakura tree, and always gives me the joy of Mirror Lake. My mom also was very supportive of me, just as I support you."

"What about your mom? I mean, what about my grandma? How come I've never seen her?"

"Because when I was a very little swan fairy, she had already died in a battle with bloody feathers that fighting against Night Queen griffins."

At that time, I just was eight years old, just smaller than Moonshine Nightingale in the poison claw of Snow Mountain Blood Griffin.

My heart of sea rabbit suddenly jumps up like rabbit fairy being chased by snow wolf demons, I suddenly feel the thorns fear all over the purple vine sky rushing up from the Dark Rose Sea......

"So when I'm eight, would you ride a narwhal and leave me me forever?"

"Never!" Mama engraves on Oris's Fairy Contract and says with golden sunshine melody, "My fairy cat little angel! Mama will forever be with you!"

When Mama was in primary school, she was the art fairy of school, singing solo with child's voice, leading singing with girl's voice, leading ballet dancing with thousands of flowers, nothing she couldn't do. And Mom often played the flower fairy and angel of Soul Tree on the stage of Crystal Palace.

Mama was a nightingale singer, her family was poor, so wood dog classmates looked down on her, although they still wanted her to contribute her art for school of Husky Kingdom.

The hostility of wood dog classmates hurt her deeply, but she was not as shy and weak as the emerald lake magpie with bloody wings, not at all.

"I had my own art dream of pure sunshine."

"Mama, what kind of art dream of pure sunshine?" Oris is blinking his cat eyes.

"Dreaming of joining the Ballet Troupe of Swan Meteor Palace, dreaming of becoming a nightingale singer on the Sunflower Castle, when I was standing on the stage of Flower Goddess Palace, I didn't care what others thought of me, I just did care about my audiences. On the crystal stage of Flower Goddess Palace, I'm forever invincible!"

Mama always can feel the flower sea story hiding in music, but also can make the brilliance of flower sea bloom more dazzlingly.

She can transform herself into thousands of different flower fairies and swan angels of Soul Tree. She can forget herself flashily, and completely immerse in a shining stage dream, or a melodious singing of nightingale.

On the stage of Crystal Palace, Mom felt the freedom with cloud and sunshine of pegasus unicorn, she was eager to be a ballet fairy as flying and dancing Swan Goddess.

The army often employed ballerinas and singers to perform for knights returning with blood feathers from battlefield. At that time, defending the country was the most glorious, and performing for the knights was also the highest honor to ballet fairy.

Mama believe she could be chosen, and the emerald oriole teachers also highly recommended her. The fox-dog classmates also said Mom was excellent and unsurpassed, whether the nightingale singing or swan dancing. But eventually Mama still lost into the ice abyss, so Mama knelt on Rose Iceberg crying all the snow night.

But at that time, she met the white bear god Papa, Papa gave Mama a whole snow mountain full of blooming fantastically sakura encouragements! Because of Papa, Mama rebloomed the flower sea self-confidence of her own ballet fairy's road.

However, in the tragic old world, after Mama's legs were broken by the metal spotlight falling from stage dome, for curing Mama, Papa spent all the dragon claw savings of family, and owed the three-headed huge snake's odious demon debts of a whole Dark Rose Forest.

At first, Papa still loved Mama so much and almost never gave up. But neither the sun nor human heart of the old world can stare directly.

Gradually, finally, after all, anyway, Papa still......

Gave up the swan fairy Mama by magma hell.

Every day came back home, as soon as saw the mermaid Mama lying in bed, Papa just didn't help cursing furiously, couldn't help pulling Mama's long hair of Sea Goddess from the bed to floor then beating and kicking!

Papa was hating Mama. Hating her couldn't use her dance and art to earn the dragon blood rubies for him as before.

Mama was hating Papa, too. Hating him that his love for her had so easily been destroyed by disaster and poverty in succuba owls war.

Remember one day in the fourth grade of primary school, Papa still had not returned to Dark Sunflower Home at 2:00 in the morning, so Oris asked Mama, "Mama! Mama! Is Papa gonna have an affair?"

"Silly kid! What are you bullshitting about?" Mama was laughing, "Your Papa......Maybe in an accident! Ah ha ha ha ha ha ha!!!!!!"

The execrative hate and sneer that engraving bones and burning heart were emerging as whale on Mama's face. At that moment, in Oris's forest little cat heart, just full of miserable ice, he just was shaking as escaping from a big group of snow wolves.

Remember one day in fifth grade, Papa and Mama were fighting with chamois horns. Mama was desperate as flaming stars rain, she sobbed to Papa, "If one day I die in the mouth of Succuba Owl, you are still young, so find another little swan fairy!"

But Papa laughed bitterly, "I have found one! Now just waiting for the Succuba Owl to peck you to death with savouring every mouthful! Ah ha ha ha ha ha ha ha......" The bloodcurdling crazy laugh was reverberating in the icy dilapidated maple house.

But Mama was stunned.

Stunned for a long time. Then, she rotated hard the wheelchair, and locked herself in the aquamarine ice cave. Ten seconds later, Papa rushed into the room! Oris also rushed followed.

Eight floor!

The fluttering curtain was hissing as frightened cat......

The icy wind was flying down as dark demon's blood feathers......

When souls were still suffering from the shock, but they suddenly found Mama just lying in bed and sinking into the star moon dream of Mirror Lake.

Mama was not gonna die! No injuring herself! No cutting wrist! No jumping! Mama's mermaid aquamarine eyes were just burning with fire rain and flaming tears. Mama was just falling into the mirror lake and flower sea of shining dream.

Seeing Mama's calm breathing, Oris's snow rabbit heart finally had settled down, then he and Papa sighed with relief at the same time.

Actually, in that miserable old world, chopping each other or together dying in the mouths of millions of dark succuba owls, it's their best relief.

But now, in the gorgeous new world, with brightly blooming flower sea of art, the swan legs of Mama are soft and healthy, flawless and perfect!

Papa and Mama almost never quarreled with sunflower parrot mouths, and never fought with chamois horns. They never tortured each other, also never hated each other.

They are living together happily so much, they help each other in the time of poverty, they are forever together staying on the same boat of trouble, they are forever deeply loving each other.

Forever and forever!

Since got married, they have hardly ever quarreled as tulip parrots or fought as chamois. Even if there was a little quarreling with sunflower parrot mouths, still were mainly Mom's pettishly charming manner of cat pixie and Dad's counterpunch spoiled manner of snow mountain forest cat.

The dirty works, fatigues, heavy works and light works at home, such as washing plumage, cleaning rosewood table, sweeping sapphire crystal floor, almost all of them Papa has taken in hands, Mama just is mainly responsible for cooking the pixie food and dancing with swan fairies.

Today, Papa' singing career is bright as golden tulip sea, dazzling as the wings of Sun Goddess, and Oris's family life has never been as happy as today with sakura trees in sunshine.

When the family goes to supermarket, Oris is sitting in the shopping cart and says he wants to eat the Little Bear Cookie House, but Mama is pulling Papa's deer arm and saying she wants to eat rainbow fairy jelly.

Papa bows his head and says, "Son, be good, Mama is still very little, we all take care of Mama, first to buy for Mama, okay?"

The family "Ha ha ha ha" laughing loudly, just sweet as cherry jam.

Later, when passing by Mama's former school, Papa points to a Swan Palace and says to Oris, "This was your Mama's Ballet School, I was always waiting for her at that aquamarine gate!"

Mama is laughing as deer fairy, "That gate was called Moon Gate! Umm......Right! Moon Gate! Ah ha ha ha ha ha ha......"

Mama and Papa are both laughing while staring at each other.

In the beautiful new world blessed by great nature and Art Fairy, Papa and Mama just had a few quarrels.

One day, when Oris came home from school, Papa looked as if the Parrot King who had accidentally rolled off the fairy owl eggs at snow cliff, extremely irritable, so he replied defiantly to Mama with some phoenix parrot mouths, then Mama directly cried as a jealous cat seeing her owner touching another pretty cat, just screaming as a crazy mermaid!

"You have disliked the fairy food I cook, right!? You don't love me anymore! Right or not!? Is there a enchanting moon fairy prettier than me in your chorus!? Have I recently grown so fat that into moon mango rabbit so you dislike me!!!???"

"No......I just......"

"What's her name??? Is she in better shape than me??? You quickly talk!!! You shark egg big wretch!!!!!!"

"All right all right all right!!! Your bosoms are bigger than the fairy cat in Golden Rose Queen's arms!!! I have lost to you!!!"

Pu chi! Mama burst into laughing!

Then sitting on Papa's legs and crying as mermaid with sea goddess tears, Papa was wiping out the aquamarine tears for Mama while comforting her with morning sunshine.

Papa said with smiling, "After all these years, had I ever said the fairy food you cooked was not delicious? Even if there's no jam, no cheese, and the Blueberry Tree bread stick without bacon, but as long as made by you, it must be the most delicious fairy food in the whole world! Actually, as long as it it yours, I must like it......"

Hearing what Papa was saying, Mama was turning her head gently.

All of a sudden, Mama kissed Papa!

Mermaid eyes were rippling sakura sea tears with sunshine pixies. Then they are reconciled as before, the happiness and beauty are still there.

Another time Papa and Mama were quarreling, so fiercely that about to collide insanely with chamois horns, Papa said indignantly, "This Sunflower Home I really can't stand it any longer even just one more second!!!!!!"

Just about to slam the door out.

But Mama's cat eyes suddenly became soft like swan pixie, as if knowing that Papa was going out to drink the moon spring with dog friends an cat buddies, then just said as nightingale with soft wings, "Well, don't drink too much fairy moon spring, and come home early......"

Papa was inwardly struggling for a long flower-falling time, finally didn't step out of the Flower Goddess Fairy Door.

Later when they made peace, Papa said to Oris, "At that time, your swan Mama was really so tender......"

Afterwards, again a orioles quarreling, then Mama ran away in anger from home. During the time, Papa was trying all kinds of calls and messages consoling and apologizing, but the sun oriole little fairy Mama just brushed him off impatiently.

However, Oris called Mama and just said one sentence, Mama immediately stepped into Moon Sunflower Door. Then Papa kept asking Oris, "What the budgerigar little cookies did you ever say so useful???"

Oris was so self-satisfied just as flash Narcissus Prince and said, "Admit it, Papa, you have been out of favor! I just told Mama I was starving into iceberg sea pixie."

When Mama was cooking the fairy food, Papa hugged her from behind and said, "The scenery you do up your hair and cut the vegetable carefully, as if shining the whole kitchen with flowing tender light of Phoenix Nebula......"

Mama smiled and beat him, then just reconciled.

While eating primrose fairy meal together, Mama suddenly stared at Papa and smiling with aquamarine hummingbirds, Papa was a little overwhelmed.

After five seconds, Mama reached out her hand and wiped off the coral lily on Papa's mouth, then put it into her own waterfall-sakura cat mouth.

Later, Mama ate a petal of Provence rose, but suddenly didn't wanna eat, so just opening her mermaid mouth, biting that rose petal with teeth to Papa, then Papa was just kissing it into his tulip-cat mouth.

Today in the evening, the family is watching TV and chatting together, Mama says, "Just as a little flying bear escaping from the avalanche burial, I always have a backache, and my whole body is hurting! Because rehearsing too long, I feel my ankles are hurting so much just like the springbok legs fiercely bitten by little Pine Cone griffins!"

Oris says, "Mama, maybe you are out of ice dragon eggshells, you should eat more snow mountain owl eggs and drink more sakura snow milk."

Form the beginning to end, Papa has been silent with mirror lake just as flaming sunflower pixie.

But the next day, Papa just is moving back three boxes of ice dragon little eggshells, two boxes of snow mountain owl pink eggs, and a box of white sakura snow milk.

The flower goddess Mama just be touched that crying out mermaid aquamarines all over the sunshine sky!

Papa's chorus often rehearses late into night, harder than the egg-pushing little cat-dragon of Sun-Parrot Mountain.

On Sunday morning, Oris wakes up but finds that Papa still hasn't come back, and Mama has just made a pot of cherry mango porridge, then Oris walks over and sees the pot of porridge is too much.

"So much porridge, we can't finish it, the rest will be enough for blue-snow little parrots who has just learned singing fairy hymn to eat for three years."

Mama says, "It's not letting you eat it all, there's still your Papa."

Oris says, "He also couldn't finish even he comes back."

But Mama says, "I just make more, so your Papa can eat some before working at night, then won't be hungry. And it's so cold at night, eating some will make your Papa warm, he can also take it to his chorus."

At that moment, I suddenly heard the golden rose sea melody of Papa and Mama's love......

But one day, the stage suddenly collapses when Papa is rehearsing, more than thirty members of chorus fall off the stage into magma hell.

Before the second collapsing coming, in order to push away the friends, Papa's legs are hit into raspberry bread stick by spotlights, there are multiple fractures all over his body, and also hurt his moon dolphin brain.

At the time, Papa's throat still has serious noxious actinia little evil spirits, any sapphire apple and little amethyst jelly that couldn't do, he just can be paralyzed as a seagull with broken wings in the purple vine bed of Narcissus Goddess Palace.

After the operation, Pap's eyes are dull that eyeballs turn hard as if they are being hugged by koalas, right hand is wildly scratching and grabbing as a flame-leg rabbit rolling down the snow cliff, but the left hand is motionless as a dark emerald princess woodpecker frozen by snow succuba, couldn't hear any iceberg owls' crying.

His speaking is also so slurred as throat has been stuffed by the moon-jellyfish elves of Dark Sea, even listening seven or eight times we still couldn't clearly hear any little ice jacaranda-tree cranberry on snow mountain, and the voice is so lighter and quieter than the night roses blooming with ice buds and crystal petals falling in stream.

Mama says to Oris, "In the time of thousands of waterfall-sakura trees falling in mirror lake, Papa has already recovered better than the nestling of Phoenix Tree, and in the future, he will be better and better day by day! Yes! He will!"

"Umm!" Oris is vigorously nodding his flame-rabbit head.

It still need the time of hundreds sakura trees' blooming as phoenix fairies and falling like snow for complete recovery.

Now, Papa needs to bathe the fire exercise, from every tree with phoenix spirit songs to every tulip bud with shining feathers and spreading wings, all he has to practice little by little in stars rain.

Papa's every quiet phoenix word, Mama always bends down her Swan Queen waist, then listens the butterfly melody very close to Papa's mouth with her rabbit fairy ear.

"Speak louder, and speak clearly with one phalaenopsis by one phalaenopsis......"

Then Mama repeats very rose crystal little butterfly Papa wants to speak, until he hard nods to affirm.

Papa wants to talk with Oris, then Oris listens closely, but he can't understand any ice-blue little butterfly of Love Goddess Papa's talking about.

But Mama hears a pure white butterfly of Sun Goddess. She turns her head and softly says with sakura smiling, "Papa said, my dear, let's make an effort to bloom for the shining dream of art!"

I have tried all my strength to hold down the mermaid tear fairies, but finally they are still flying out with brilliant aquamarine fairies, totally out of narcissus hands. I couldn't speak out even just one moonshine tulip, just keep wiping the sunshine tears of Mermaid Goddess.

Mama is training Papa strictly as flaming woodpecker, encouraging him gently as gorgeous Lyra bird, taking care of him never wearily just like colorful sunflower parrot, and never laxly just like the sapphire skylark meticulously protecting her babies with sparkling eyes on the tulip fairies tree.

One morning with sakura snow and bright sunshine, Papa is clamoring to return the Aquamarine Sunflower Home, so the swan Mama is carrying him as a wounded narwhal back from the Moon Jellyfish

Palace Hospital.

This time Papa is able to sit steadily himself, and Oris and Mama are trying to help Papa stand up, even mount the marble steps of Nebula Palace.

But after all, Papa is still unsteady on his feet just like the pullus of nightingale, not to mention walking with stretching wings.

But he's so anxious as the Rainstorm Puffin falling into magma, can't speak out a little iceberg rose but crabbily wants to puff a tree of rose pixie word, can't walk half a parrot step steadily, but crabbily gonna run through the Owl Pixies Valley.

Mama often becomes the Sun Wing Oriolus Queen and yells at Papa, "Rushing to grab the eggs of honey-stealing bird and help her brood???"

In a twinkling, she suddenly feels heart ache and says with shining aquamarine tears of mermaid goddess with soft swan wings, "One little whale flowers by one little, all right......?"

While eating the Aristaeus Cat fairy food, Papa is sitting next to Oris. A fter eating the last Magic Fairy Forest cake house, Papa looks like rising abruptly out of the ground just as Faerie Deer Souls Tree.

Mama immediately shouts with oriole voice, "What are you doing about puffin eggs???"

At once she is running with deer steps over to hold Papa. But Papa is insisting on standing alone into a tall unicorn tree.

Mama says seriously as a snow owl, "Now you still have to practice sitting on the back of green tree-horned deer, not yet to the time of standing alone under the phoenix tree bursting into flame-lily sea, just one little jacaranda flower by one little ,all right......?"

But Papa can't hear any blueberry cupcake, still trying to get up, then with a sudden effort, Papa just has got up like the Butterfly Rabbit Souls Tree in golden rose fairies' brilliant singing.

Mama just shakes like deer but still holding Papa, then start yelling like angry fairy cat, "I really don't wanna take care of you big stupid snow bear in Ice Tree Forest anymore! You think you can ride a whale in deep ice sea! Right? You think you can crack-up an aquamarine iceberg, don't you!!!???"

But Papa is just leaning on Mama's angel swan shoulder and in silence with tender feathers.

Oris's mirror lake rabbit ears have heard, Papa is weeping.

So Oris buries his head in Fairy Candy House and dare not stare at them, just afraid to weep out the sea melody of windbell flowers and purple vines.

After the silence of blooming a sun-sakura flower, Mama suddenly says softly as nebula oriole, "You have been great as the rabbit-ear parrot breaking through volcanoes and icebergs. But don't be so anxious about it, a spring after a winter, a flowering day after a snowy day, everything is getting better and better, we should doing it one lily pixie by one lily pixie, I believe we will get to the day with blooming sakura sea! Don't be fidgety as the bee pixie on deer eye lily, don't be anxious as the hummingbird fairy on crystal butterfly flower, all right? My dear......?"

Mama has been like swan goddess touching Papa's iceberg deer back with tender ice feather pixies.

After a while, Mama says, "Go sit down on the daffodil sofa, all right?"

Papa nods his flying deer head. Then Mama is holding Papa and moving toward the Jacaranda Room one phoenix-parrot step by one phoenix-parrot step.

Umm. Don't be weeping. Staring at their flower god and goddess back figures, just don't be weeping......

Gradually, Papa can take care of himself. One day eating the fairy meal, Mama has made the cream rose Christmas tree cake, then Oris takes a sapphire-parrot spoon to eat with his big cat mouth.

However, Papa just takes a Sea Rabbit Queen spoon, gently as rabbit digs out a cream rose and feeds to Mama's cherry fairy little mouth. Mama is staring at Papa, then opens her cherry mouth, with mermaid tear fairies, together swallows that cream pink rose.

There's a rose tree restaurant in the Sunflower Castle, couples can have a photo taken after meal, there's a tree of rose vines covered with hundreds photos.

One day after school, Oris is playing the piano in the rose tree restaurant, during the break, he is looking for whether there's someone he knows on the rose vines, then he finds that Papa and Mama were biting a same straw and drinking a same cup of angel cherry dew in a pink photo......

So, on the pure white narcissus fairy grand piano, with streaming the aquamarine tears of mermaid fairy, Oris is crystally playing a tune Merry Go Round of Joe Hisaishi.

Flower fairies and sunshine fairies are flying with dancing all over the sunny sky! The flower sea by mirror lake are blooming with stretching all over the golden world!

Gradually, Papa can also speak out the snow deer fairy words.

After eating the grape fairy dinner then going out for a walk, Papa just picks up Mama and whirling for five jasmine yogurt doughnuts.

The next day, Papa has made a big table of Phoenix Forest meal, and longing the praising to Mama. "All right all right all right! Our Arctic flying deer is the best of this world!" But the praising is not enough, but also wants Mama to kiss him with her sakura red lips, so

Mama just kisses Papa.

Every time Mama is angry as a flaming cat with Papa, then Papa is just sticking to Mama as a Norwegian forest angel cat.

"Little nightingale forest princess~"

"Little rose pixie~"

"Little swan fairy~"

Until coaxing Mama into laughing as parrot fairy in flower sea and swan goddess on Golden Rose Castle, then Mama gently hits Papa with butterfly tulip.

Yesterday, Mama saw a news that a narcissus little pixie had a cancer of dark sunflower, but to save dragon claw sapphires for her family, she fled with wings from the hospital, resolutely gave up the treatment.

Before sleeping at night, Mama asks Papa in bed, "If I have a cancer of dark sunflower, would you treat me......?"

Papa has almost sunk into the sun-fish dream of mirror lake, but suddenly jumps up as flaming koi, "Don't talk such stupid candy house of squirrel pixie cookies tale!!! Even lose all of my fortune, I must treat you with my everything!!! And you are my everything!!!"

Mama is blinking her moon cat aquamarine eyes, "What if you get it?"

"Then I won't treat."

"Why?"

Papa says, "Just leave you a little swan fairy alone gonna volcano and glacier for demon dragon sapphires, you don't know how much my heart will ache!"

So, in the bright moon night, Mama is rippling aquamarine tears while sinking into mermaid sunshine dream......

Long long time ago, Papa and Mama still were young as rose lintwhites, one day they were sitting on the bus, quarreling as parrots and colliding each other with chamois horns just for watching the Delphinus movie first or eating cherry mousse cake first, at last Mama cried out as angry crying fawn, "Why don't you roll with golden bear-monkey onto Sri Lanka mango tree!!! What a whale-eating jellyfish demon big idiot!!!!!!"

Papa immediately got out of the bus and turn around to leave. Mama also was angrily striding as flying deer in the apposite direction without saying one word. Streaming the cherry pixie tears of deer eyes while striding. Striding almost for three hundred flaming windbell trees.

Actually, springbok Papa was already following Mama for a long time, trotting along while apologizing with candy fairies.

"My dear I'm so sorry all is my fault I really should have jumped into husky castle and been split by ten thousand huskies!!! Please!!!"

When Papa was silent, Mama still worriedly looked back, found that Papa were still quietly following, so Mama fiercely stared him with rabbit eyes, "Humph!!!!!!" then turned around and walked on.

Seeing had almost walked to the sakura heart giant tree of Mama's home, Papa thought he was done with forest dogs and fire dragon eggs, she must be in love goddess anger for a whole faerie night!

But, standing on the candy crystal steps, Mama suddenly turned around and opened her fairy arms......

"Hugging......"

Papa immediately went up and hugged her.

Tightly hugging her.

Just heard Mama leaning in his arms laughing as parrot while saying as butterfly, "I'm still in swan fairy anger! Hee hee......"

In a twinkling, the aquamarine rabbit hearts of mermaids were just melting in the sea sunshine of sakura tears......

As soon as Papa returned to his chorus, he became busy again like Hummingbird King. One day, Papa had made an appointment with

Mama to play out together, but the chorus suddenly had temporary performance and no time to explain in detail.

Mama was waiting for Papa for two hours at the appointed place. When Papa met Mama, he was afraid so much that she must be angry, but Mama was just blooming the pure white smiling on sunshine dew of narcissus and saying, "Big idiot in Flower-Dragons Forest, quickly coax me......" Seeing Papa was nervous like sakura rabbit, Mama tiptoed and hugged him.

Today Papa says to Oris, "At that time, your Mama was really dazzling and pure as holy Flower Goddess! Every pure white narcissus and tulip all over the body was shining with flower fairy's tenderness on swan feathers......"

Cured by the light of art and own effort, Papa has recovered, but his throat is totally exhausted because rehearses too long, the burning sensation is like ten thousand sun elves rushing into the mouth of glacier owl one after another. Now Papa is resting at home, even speaking he must be softly.

At this moment, Oris is reading the score of Joe Hisaishi, a little tired, so he's gonna play the piano at balcony for relaxing. Out of the door, just seeing Mama sitting on the soft tulip carpet, her head is resting on the sunflower sofa, staring at Papa with tilting head. Papa is gently stroking Mama's fairy cat head, they are whispering some happy things.

"When our little Oris grows up, let's gonna his concert together, shall we?"

"Okay! When he finishes, we'll hand him a big bunch of brilliant golden faerie tulips!"

They are immersing in the flower sea of sweet love, from time to time rippling a few mermaid sakura laughter so beautiful as nebula windbells.

Suddenly, Oris's meteor tears are bursting and flying with sunshine of sea, then turning into thousands of butterfly pixies all over the sky!

He's crying.

Crying so feelingly just as sakura rain!
Crying so happily just as tulip sea!

"Art Fairy, thank you! Thank you for everything you gave me!"

"Don't thank me. You deserve this. You should thank yourself. Thank for your kindness, thank for your effort, thank for your persistence, thank for your dedication, thank for your sacrifice."

"Umm! I understand!" Oris is vigorously nodding his fairy cat head.

Then little fairies of sun-sakura on Narcissus Princess piano are dancing trippingly again with shining melody as butterflies, brilliantly singing with mermaids for the Goddess of Sea......

A beautiful flower fairy tale is blooming in the mermaid singing......

On the Tulip Fairyland, there is a beautiful pure girl, she particularly likes pure white things, from the snow mountain dress to every furniture in her house, all are pure white as narcissus.

She often prays to Art Fairy for making her marry a lover as pure as her.

In a cold night with sakura snow, someone is knocking on the white rose door, the girl opens the door and sees a dazzling fairy in flower sea dress and with flower rain wings, she says to girl, "I know there is a pure boy in this world who can match you, so I'm coming to tell you."

Then, the fairy gently picks a pure white bud from her flower feathers and says to girl, "This is a pure heart only existing in the Faerie Forest by Mirror Lake, you just plant it in a vase of star river, sprinkle some fairy water every day, and on the eighth day it will germinate, the branches and leaves will also flourish slowly, but above all, you must keep your soul and body pure every day, and kiss it once a day."

Before girl opens her mouth, the fairy has disappeared in the dark night with sakura snow.

The girl plants the seed very carefully, then sprinkles with fairy water and kisses it every day just as she was told.

The pure fairy buds are breeding from winter, until near the sunny summer it blooms. The buds breeding longer, the fragrance enduring longer. And the leaves of fairy flowers, are also keeping green for thousands of years in wind, frost, rain and snowstorm.

Then in the clouds and sunshine of midsummer, the girl finally sees it blooming the pure white elegant flowers! The seemingly casual blooming, has also been undergoing a long-lasting effort and persistence.

Another half a year has passed, one night in bright moonshine, the fairy suddenly appears, the girl is happily telling the pure fragrant flower and the experience of this year.

The fairy says, "Your are really a holy pure girl, you will have the most pure boy falling in love with you forever." Then the flower feathers of fairy's wings are falling, in a twinkling becomes a pure dazzling beautiful boy.

From then on, they are living together happily ever after.

They are singing with flower wings!

They are blooming with flower seas!

They are forever kind and merciful!

They are forever happy and beautiful!

Forever! Forever!

Forever and forever!

.

Lightning Source UK Ltd.
Milton Keynes UK
UKHW042336280219
338227UK00001B/136/P